BORN FOR YOU

The Viscount's Vow

By

S. K. Snyder

Copyrights © 2024 Sharon Snyder
All Rights Reserved

Contents

DEDICATION	i
CHAPTER 1	1
CHAPTER 2	5
CHAPTER 3	17
CHAPTER 4	37
CHAPTER 5	57
CHAPTER 6	63
CHAPTER 7	70
CHAPTER 8	80
CHAPTER 9	90
CHAPTER 10	105
CHAPTER 11	121
CHAPTER 12	127
CHAPTER 13	142
CHAPTER 14	158
CHAPTER 15	167
CHAPTER 16	185
CHAPTER 17	199
CHAPTER 18	206
CHAPTER 19	218
CHAPTER 20	230
CHAPTER 21	248
CHAPTER 22	260
CHAPTER 23	279
EPILOGUE	309

DEDICATION

To my faithful cats, A.J., Buster Brown, Antoni, Collin, Frederick, Giles and Henry, whose personalities are displayed throughout my fictitious nobility, as they inspired me daily.

To Hall of Fame and World Champion, English bay gelding, William Grant (Scotch). The gentle giant, who inspired Spartan. My time spent with this prodigious, kind, and loving hunter jumper made it easy to bring Spartan to life.

Last, but most assuredly not least, my husband, Jack. Who picked me up when I wanted to quit and never allowed me to stop believing in myself and my writing. He is my real-life rake and loving and devoted nobleman.

CHAPTER 1

LATE SUMMER 1807

Get off me, you brute!" "No!"

Olivia struggled beneath the weight of the young man. She tossed her head from side to side, the dying grass and newly fallen leaves gathering in the locks of her flaxen blonde curls.

The young man only stiffened as he pinned her tighter to the ground.

She felt the pebbles from the walking path pierce through the muslin sleeves covering her arms. Olivia closed her eyes, holding back the tears forming in them. A shadow crept over her. She peered up at the second young man.

He stood still, fists at his waist, with an angry countenance. She resumed her thrashes without a release from her captor. "Get him off of me, now!"

"Do something, Andovir!" the youth, who appeared caught in the middle, appealed to his friend.

"Not yet!" Andovir stood firmly, glaring down at the restrained young girl. "Not until she promises to go home."

"I won't!" Olivia declared in complete defiance. Tears trickled from the outer edges of her lids.

"Put your weight on her, Sheffield," Andovir retorted.

"I'll hurt her," Sheffield looked up in concern.

"No, you won't! She's as tough as a brock and devilish as a wild cat, with an irritating squeaky little voice."

"Jack!" Olivia pleaded, trying to hide a sob.

Jack noticed the tears and relented. "Fine, fine, let her up."

He backed away, giving his friend room to release the pint-size kraken.

Hesitantly and with fervour, James Sheffield, coerced into apprehending and detaining the young hoyden, leapt from her. He had seen her unleash her fury on his best friend. He was taking no chances, uncertain how he had come to be the unfortunate soul ensnarling her. Still, he respected her resilience, stalwartness, and the deserved forthcoming comeuppance.

"How dare you pin me to the ground James Sheffield? You call yourself a gentleman, treating a lady as such."

Olivia jumped to her feet, straightening her skirt with the annoyance, indignation, and sarcasm that only a girl of ten years could summon.

"And you," Olivia viciously swung around, turning her wrath on her nemesis. She raised her arm with unladylike behaviour and poked a finger into his chest, "are no gentleman!"

Pressing his chest into her tiny finger retorted, "and you are no lady!" Jack barked. "Once, I would like to leave the house with my friends without you tagging along."

Jack backed away, raked his hands through his hair, and glared at her small frame. His fists again on his hips, "I will not tell you again, go back to the house. I mean it, you are not welcome this time. Do you understand me?" He bellowed and raised his arm, pointing toward the main house. "Now go!"

Olivia's bottom lip quivered as tears began to form again.

She stood there in silence, staring in consternation.

Olivia crossed her arms and bit her lower lip, attempting to stop the flow of tears. She felt them breaking across her lower lids and turned her back to the evil boys. Never would she let these two see her cry. She stomped up the hill without another word, wondering when they had become so spiteful. Jack had never been so vile until he went away to school.

The boys grinned as they watched her departure and heard her mutterings. The words clearly not those spoken by a young lady of consequence.

James Sheffield brushed the dirt from his breeches and shirt sleeves wiping off his boots. "Your sister is something else." Shaking his head, not certain if out of respect or contempt.

"Firstly, she ain't my sister. Secondly, she's tough as nails. And..." Jack paused, "...and God help my blasphemous soul, I am the cause of it." He picked up the fishing poles and bucket of worms scattered alongside the narrow pathway leading to the lake.

"What do you mean she is not your sister?" James stuttered, thunderstruck. "I thought..." Disconcerted, he didn't know exactly what he thought.

This was not James Sheffield's first visit to Birkshire House. He and Jack Norrys had been friends for nearly five years. They met their first year at Eaton and instantly became fast friends. They spent many holidays together at Birkshire House with Jack's family and at Belmont Castle with James' family, The Duke, and Duchess of Ratcliff, sealing a lasting friendship. Olivia had always been at Birkshire, and James assumed she was Jack's sister. Jack treated her with the same disdain as a typical loving brother, and Olivia epitomised the younger sister, always underfoot, irritating, and relentless.

There was one rather disturbing difference with the tiny Olivia; at ten years old, she could catch and gut a fish quicker than he, shoot a pistol with deadly accuracy, ride a horse astride, jump a six-foot hedge and ride neck to nothing back to the stables.

After five years, Sheffield learned she wasn't his sister. Moreover, by Andovir's own admission, he had created this little wretch.

"Who is she? And what in God's name possessed you to teach her to shoot a gun like that? You bloody well know one day; she is going to shoot us both!" James looked at his friend, astonished.

"It is a long story," Jack said as he handed a pole to his friend.

They continued their trudge to the lake. Two companions, caught somewhere between boys and men. "If the fish ain't biting, I will tell you about it."

CHAPTER 2

MARCH 1815

Olivia leaned against the built-in seat staring out the large window in the green saloon overlooking the west lawn. She placed a hand on the glass to study the darkening clouds. The pane, cold and moist, she quickly withdrew her fingers to the warmth and security of the room. Tucking both legs underneath, she sat on the cushioned bench, pulling the multiple ruffles of her skirt around her.

Her morning ride on Spartan, her beloved thoroughbred, was threatened by the ominous weather. An accomplished rider, she learned to ride before walking. Olivia's father had been a breeder of fine hunters, and she was happiest on the back of one of his prime bits of blood.

A male figure strolled into the drawing room, sat on a small sofa, crossed one top boot over his knee and relaxed into the corner, letting his arm drape over the back. He focused on the young female at the window. He hadn't intended to make a quiet entrance, but his entry had gone unnoticed by the mesmerised miss. In his insouciant, devil-may-care posture, he broke the silence.

"What has captured your attention?" His tone was complacent and nonchalant, an incessant grin on his unshaven face.

"Only the clouds," she said dryly, still staring at them, "I want to ride…"

She jumped from the bench, whirled, froze in place, and stared at the foreign figure.

The lean, muscular, young man bore dark chestnut locks mixed with strands streaked by the sun; the piercing violet-blue eyes held her transfixed. He was casually dressed in tan breeches, a white muslin shirt, waistcoat, but no topcoat. The superior quality top boots of Hoby were polished to a bright shine.

Scrutinising the figure, he appeared older than she remembered, with tiny lines around the eyes. However, when he smiled, there was no mistake; the perfectly even lips framing the straight white ivories that never ceased to melt her heart. It was indeed Viscount Andovir.

"Jack!" She squealed. She dashed toward the viscount ignoring the sleeping yellow tabby curled up on the rug between her and her destination. An unwittingly placed satin slipper found the tail of the unsuspecting cat. The rotund and portly Frederick sprang straight up, unleashing a blood-curdling shriek, its down and awn hairs expanding in every direction as if struck by lightning. When the feline finally touched down, there were several futile attempts for traction before escaping through the open doorway.

In the unfolding confusion, Olivia lost her balance, tumbling headfirst toward the mahogany table in front of the small sofa.

Jack instinctively raised both hands to catch the young girl or at the very least, soften what was sure to be Olivia's collision with the wooden table. Swiftly swinging his boot to the ground, at the same instance pushing the table aside, he neglected to notice Olivia flinging her arms towards him. In the chaos, his boot found multiple layers of ruffled satin and lace, just as the five-foot, seven-stone, airborne, minx crashed into him, pushing his parked foot from under him as they tumbled to the floor, one atop the other.

Jack managed to catch Olivia with one hand while softening the impact. When both had stilled, he slammed his head to the ground and let his arms drop to the floral carpet, questioning his innate act of chivalry.

Olivia had landed squarely on top of him, her face buried in his dishevelled muslin shirt. He raised his head and peered down at the motionless lump of blonde hair.

"Still a bit clumsy, I see," he said, gasping for breath.

Jack propped up on his elbows, attempting to right himself, finding heaps of satin and taffeta ruffles sprawled over his lower extremities and the flaxen blonde still buried in his chest. She lifted her head, seemingly unaware of the impropriety of the trapped male beneath her.

"You are home," she said, gasping for breath.

He reeked of sarcasm as he acknowledged her.

"Yes, you little hoyden, I assume you are happy to see me."

With the unwanted cargo planted in his midsection, he was out of breath but not oblivious to the improper scene.

"When did you arrive? You were not expected for at least a fortnight."

His dignity desecrated, and only partially recovered from the fiasco; he momentarily disregarded the situation to consider the question. He was unsure he wanted to divulge his late-night arrival in his disadvantaged position. Certainly, the little spitfire would find the strength to wallop him for not waking her. So, he erred on the side of caution and ignored the question.

"Was I not?"

She rose into a seated position, paying little heed to her location, overwhelmed by Jack's early arrival. "Do not be silly. You sent a letter," she snorted.

"Aww, so I did!" He teased.

Jack was beginning to wonder if she intended to take up residency atop him. Olivia was chattering, asking one question after another but not pausing long enough for a reply.

He, however, was becoming increasingly aware of their inappropriate position. Without question, she was no longer ten years old, and he had no desire to explain the delicacies of the unsuitable arrangement.

His two and twenty-year-old brain, however, was taking notice of the voluptuous curves where boyish angles had been only two years before. He choked at the sudden sensation overwhelming him. He had to get off this rug immediately without startling the half-woman half-child, innocent chatterbox still casually lounging on him.

Peering into her light blue eyes, still gleaming with delight, he raised his eyebrows and slowly lowered them to his midsection, trusting hers would follow. They did. The naïve eyes followed down his thick neck, broad chest, and tapered waist. Observing tangled flounces of feminine material draped where tan breeches should have been, Olivia screeched.

"Oh! Oh, no, oh, how did…? I am sitting on…on top…"

Flustered and struggling to find her feet, which continually landed on immovable rows of crushed taffeta, Olivia found herself tangled in the spider web of multi-layered flounces. The twisted wreckage was sprawled under, over and around her. She struggled to free the captive legs, but the more she did, the worse things became. She pulled at the skirt, perplexed at the failed attempts; she grabbed the muslin material of Jack's shirt, nearly hoicking it from his breeches.

Clearly unable to assist, Jack closed his eyes in disbelief at the exhibition, slamming his head back to the floor. But the mischievous rake overruled his better judgement and, with head in hands, raised his eyebrows to scrutinise her endeavours. The amusement of her pursuits coupled with his own inappropriate sensations had him enjoying the performance.

Olivia finally located her wayward feet and attempted to remove herself; but, in her haste, placed a small satin slipper firmly into Jack's inner thigh.

With a howl, he snatched the offensive footwear and tossed the slipper, along with its occupant to the settee in one quick motion and slammed his head back to the floor.

"Good God!" He closed his eyes as his fleeting moment of pleasure quickly bolted.

Olivia safely on the divan, hands covering her face in embarrassment, parted two fingers, peaking down at him.

"I am off," she announced totally humiliated! Huge sighs and exhalations sprung from the sofa. She fidgeted with her skirt, attempting to dismiss the irregular presence of the man beneath her and the mayhem of the past few minutes.

After the fear of losing his manhood and the inability to produce an heir passed, Jack stared up at her. Seeing the silent and mortified soul on the sofa, he could do nothing but burst into laughter. He pulled into a seated position, bent one knee, rested his elbow, and confronted his attacker. With pink cheeks, she refused to look at him. But remembering past outrageous and ridiculous situations they had found themselves in as children, she could not hold back the giggles surfacing, and they both erupted in uncontrollable mirth.

Still giggling, she attempted an apology, "I do beg your pardon, I forget myself. After all the instruction in graces, manners, etiquette, and dance, you would think…" she giggled again, taking a breath. "The absurdity of it, I was pronounced – accomplished!"

They both burst into laughter again.

"I do not understand," she took a long breath when she finally stopped giggling.

Jack, with his arm propped on his knee, attempting to control his own laughter, lifted an eyebrow… "The cat."

Her eyes widened. "Oh, Frederick! I forgot, but I did not see him," she laughed.

"Obviously! The pitiful thing was terrified! I am certain he will survive." he laughed again. "Hair straight out, frightened to death."

"Oh, no!" She snickered. "Was he? Irregardless, I am sorry for pouncing on you," she chortled one last time.

Jack could not hold back another laugh at Olivia's unintended pun.

"Let us agree to leave future pouncing to Frederick," he gave her a sly grin. "It is doubtful I will forget this welcome."

He saw her cheeks turn a deeper pink. Raising himself to a standing position, he wandered to the liquor cabinet. Inspecting the carafes, he quickly located the dark, amber-coloured liquid. Aww, brandy, he thought, as he raised the vessel of spirits and conceded he deserved a drink after the preceding events; not that he needed a reason to take brandy this early, it had become a regular habit these days.

As he poured, he felt compelled to glance at Olivia. He watched her pull at her ruffles. The frills hid the curves of her hips and the long shape of her legs, which he was certain had developed as well. However, the tightly fitted bodice could not hide the developments which occurred in his absence.

Eyes fixed on the shapely figure, Jack raised the glass to his lips. Like a pointer hound unable to draw his gaze from his prey, he nearly missed his mouth. Olivia, unaware of his gape, was concerning herself with her dress, smoothing wrinkles and straightening the soft muslin; she slowly moved her hands down each side.

Jack was transfixed at the care she gave her frock and was having clothing issues of his own, the fall of his breeches becoming a bit snug. He watched her nescient nature move one hand to her chest, making three light brushes across her breasts. The brandy had barely left the edge of the glass and passed his lips. He suddenly choked on the liquid spewing it across the room.

Olivia watched as he dropped the glass to the buffet and grabbed his throat. His windpipe demanded air after the amber fluid sent fire down the vessel, clearly not meant for spirits.

"Are you all right?" He heard her ask as she rose from the sofa.

Alarmed, he sensed her approach and threw up his palm, bringing her to an abrupt halt. With a ragged breath he managed to mutter, "I am fine." His thoughts mingled with gaining breath or saving his dignity behind the Louis XIV mahogany liquor cabinet.

Olivia was standing, arms akimbo, staring at him in helpless concern. Red-faced and still gasping for air, he assured her it was nothing. For God's sake, this was Olivia. Another quick look and even from a side glance, he knew the young woman standing in the middle of the room was no longer the irritating, childish hoyden, but good God, she was like a sister.

Jack poured a small glass of soda water. His windpipe and throat had finally reached a truce, but he took the glass with him in case of a break in the ceasefire.

"What has happened since I have been away?" Taking a deep breath, he made his way to a chair across the room.

"Very little changes here. Why?"

"You seem…" he paused, guarding his words, "well - a bit more… sensible."

"Just so." She replied defiantly. "I have been persuaded into a great many things," then lamented, "I had tutors in all things…appropriate. Aunt Annabelle, finally taking notice of me, was displeased. She was not in agreement with my form of felicities and abruptly put an end to them. Except for riding, although she has no notion of my way of it, which I am certain she would not approve of. But I oblige her in other forms of correction, and since she does not ride, she leaves it to me. But all these lessons seem quite ridiculous and unnecessary. Spartan has no appreciation of it."

Jack raised an eyebrow, "you keep the company of more than Spartan, I dare say?"

"Not really." Olivia flipped a ruffle on her skirt, then laid it back, "The local vicar's daughter, Miss Jamison, I see on occasion, but she is terribly busy assisting her father with visitations and caring for those in need. He is a widow, you know, and Lizzie is the eldest."

The matter-of-fact acceptance and lack of friends did not seem to affect Olivia, but it vexed Jack. She should be enjoying others her own age. In their adventures, she had in many ways seemed closer in age than the five years between them, but he realised he had been her only childhood companion.

His friends had found her agreeable and appreciated her talents at riding, shooting, and hunting. And she was a worthy adversary - for a girl. A once debatable fact was now undeniable... she was definitely a girl.

As he dwelled on it, he wondered why she had not been to London. She was at least fully seventeen; she should have come-out last season.

"Well, we must get you to London. You can meet friends, and there is so much to do, the theatre, museums, music, dance, and people - people everywhere. You would like the excitement above all things." Jack insisted.

"Oh, no!" Olivia said adamantly. "Aunt Annabelle says I am not ready. She says I need more refinement."

"What the bloody hell does she mean by that? I believe she enjoys your company and wishes to keep you to herself. How old are you anyway?" he asked, clearly without thinking.

"What?" She trilled. "First of all, you are never to ask a lady her age. If you were any sort of a gentleman, you would know these things."

Jack almost burst out laughing at her indignation. He held his laugh to a chuckle as the young lady holding court continued.

"And secondly, you know very well how old, you were present at my birth," she chided, giving him a look of annoyance.

That look, he shivered. She definitely needed time away from his mother. She would most assuredly disagree, but he had done her a bad turn leaving her with only his mother for companionship.

She had been correct. He had been right outside, waiting with her father and his own, while his mother helped with the delivery.

How long ago had it been? So much time had passed. He and his father were hunting with Lord Sinclair.

***

"My Lord, my Lord!" The groom was shouting as he approached with his mount and a ponied second. Both men turned in surprise; the viscount, about to take a shot, was not pleased as he watched the partridge fly away to safety.

"What is it?" The earl barked, clearly irritated by the interruption.

"Is Lady Sinclair me lord. Yore ta come quickly." The groom was giving instructions as he took guns and tossed the horse's reins to them.

"Oh, God!" Lord Sinclair's voice trembling.

"It will be fine, James, do not worry." Lord Birkshire patted his friend on the shoulder.

"Come, Jack, you and I will take this one," his father handed him up on a chestnut gelding, threw a leg over behind the boy, and the three were off.

There were grooms waiting at the front door as they dismounted before the horses had time to stop. One helped the boy to his feet, and the butler held the door as they flew by him, piling coats and hats on the poor man. When they reached the stairs, the men took them two at a time.

"Hurry it up, boy," his father called.

The three sat in the hallway for hours. Without warning, Jack's mother appeared from the doorway, smiling. She carried a small bundle of blankets. The men jumped to their feet. She walked over to the taller two and unwrapped the swaddling. Holding on to his father's arm, Jack stretched as tall as he could to peek inside. As his mother knelt, he was amazed to see a tiny, pink, little creature sucking on its fist.

***

How long ago that had been? He grinned as he thought of that wee face wrapped in the blanket.

"I remember," he elicited. "I think I was six when I first saw that little pink face trying to eat your own fist."

"You were not six…not yet. Mama told me."

Walking to the sofa opposite her, he leaned against the corner, draped his arm over the back, and once again propped one ankle on his opposing knee. Olivia, now seated at the other end, he deemed it safe to return to his previous comfortable position and had an uncontrollable urge to be near her. She was a tiny little thing when she was born and had remained quite petite. He searched for the little girl he left behind, the one that pulled at his heart and begged him not to leave every time he went away. First to Eton, next to Cambridge, and then, God, when he left for the continent two years ago, her sobs were more than he could bear. But now, what he saw, good lord, the pretty flaxen blonde, blue-eyed little girl, was now, well, now she was…

He had been staring at her but was not exactly sure what he was thinking. Then again, he was more afraid, he did. His thoughts were confused and uncomfortable. He had been searching for that tiny child he had missed. The thought of that young girl being gone unnerved and saddened him. If she had been replaced with this young woman, where did that leave him? Most of his last two years had been spent discovering himself, with no parent to moderate or challenge his behaviour or conduct. Living something of a lascivious, salacious lifestyle which, until now, seemed the lifestyle of most young nobles and admittedly satisfying. But where would that man fit into Olivia's innocent life? As he considered this...he sensed he would not.

CHAPTER 3

A few days later, rising early, Jack found himself alone in the breakfast room. The Times pressed and neatly folded, rested on the sideboard next to an array of fresh bacon, sausage, kippers, eggs, toast, chocolate, coffee, tea and a host of jams and marmalades. Driven by habit, he moved the paper to the table and filled his plate. He was accustomed to breakfasting alone with nothing but the Times and a hangover for company. His regular morning hangover, he did not miss, but he hadn't come to his birthplace for solitude.

Engrossed in the latest news from London and the war in France, he scarcely noticed his father's entry nor the raised eyebrow at the confiscated newspaper.

"I suppose I must accustom myself to my paper being second-hand if I do not make a purpose of rising earlier," He chuckled as he filled his plate.

Jack looked up at his father with a sheepish grin. "I assure you there is not a fold which was not pressed there. I yet have nightmares from my childhood, and your flatly ironed newspapers."

"It was not the wrinkles I minded as much as the jam," laughed his father.

The Earl of Birkshire was a large man who was still in good form despite being on the wrong side of his fiftieth year. The similarities between the two individuals were obvious. Chestnut brown hair, one streaked by the sun, the other aged with grey. Both had violet-blue eyes and handsome aesthetically chiselled faces with set, square jaws. The matched taut muscular builds, one the reigning incomparable Corinthian, the other eloquently renouncing the title due to the uncontrollable passage of time.

The earl had indulged his son with every advantage to ensure he was prepared for the day the earldom would pass to him. He had made it clear to his only son the position was not to be taken lightly. In his early years, he had been warned of the heirs, who found themselves ill-equipped when fate unexpectedly landed those responsibilities upon them. Jack hated it when his father spoke of such things. However, he too, had seen first-hand the results of powerful noblemen taken before their time, leaving a mere boy to step into large shoes. Their insouciant lifestyles dealt a heavy blow of inadequate preparedness, along with untrustworthy estate agents and overbearing guardians.

His courtesy title, Viscount Andovir, had not been given lightly, neither had it been taken for granted during his youth. He loved the land and made agriculture, land preservation and business acumen his primary studies at Cambridge. But in the past few years, he had discovered other advantages of his title extending past the interest of inheritance. In London, a title opened doors to fascinating and intriguing establishments of the illicit variety. Two marquesses as close friends enabled him to enjoy privileges beyond the imagination of a young nobleman who had spent most of his life learning about dirt and those who benefitted from it. Today, the viscount was to learn the inconvenience those pleasures could also present.

"How would you feel about assuming Eustace Estates as your own?" The earl launched the suggestion suddenly and without emotion.

Jack choked on his bacon. Where had this come from? Eustace Hall was a good four-day ride from London, three days if you changed horses. Hell no, he did not want to assume responsibilities for an estate that far from the life he had become accustomed to living in London.

The earl eyed his son's reaction as he took a large bite of sausage, then slapped a dab of strawberry jam on his toast.

Jack quietly laid down The Times and studied his father. He could not be serious. Unfamiliar with such paramount conversations with his father, he was hesitant. "Are you requesting or informing… respectfully, sir?" Jack was intently focused on his father's countenance.

"Which would you prefer? As Viscount Andovir, which you have been using a great deal over the past few years to your advantage, I leave the question to you. Do you wish the responsibilities or only the influence?"

Remaining silent, he continued to study his father's countenance. He was not certain if this was a test of virtue and honour or if his father was apprised of his past year's behaviours.

The viscount pushed his unfinished plate aside, suddenly no longer hungry. Finishing his last drop of coffee, more for courage than from thirst. He placed both his forearms on the table, peering at his father, the older gentleman stoic, with no indication as to his thoughts or suspicions.

"Man to man, or father to son?" Jack pressed.

"Interesting, shrewdness is new to your constitution." The earl rubbed his chin with slightly squinted eyes. "Did I mention I attended several sessions of parliament earlier this year?" The earl placed his own arms on the table, leaned in and raised his eyebrows.

"You did not." Lucidity forming in the youthful brain.

"I spent the entire month of January in Town, arriving in late December. There were important matters to attend, necessitating all the Lords' attention."

"I see."

He was now clear on the reasoning behind the conversation, but how much his father meant for him to rectify was another concern. He was certain his father had done much the same at the age of two and twenty. Where he had crossed into concerning his father vexed him.

"I am not at all certain you do see." The earl leaned back in his chair, never releasing his son's gaze. "I have not spoken to your mother, nor do I intend to do so. However, she has many acquaintances in London, and I do not intend to intercede on your behalf. She will be in residence there for The Season, and I will not have her embarrassed." The earl had successfully gained his son's attention.

"You have not made a cake of yourself at White's or Boodle's, never saw you in your cups, and you seem to have your head about you where gaming is concerned. Even your attendance to the lower gaming hells, you seem rather lucky at faro and recognise hazard is not your game, and I would have learnt of it if you were in the basket, which I have not."

Lord Andovir was silenced by the conversance being presented.

"But the foyer of the Theatre Royal is no place to be seen with questionable ladies, even if The Season has not yet begun."

Jack's eyes remained fixed on the earl, suspecting these were not rumours that reached his father's ear but supported, and it did not signify when it was the truth.

"Your mother adores the theatre and the opera; I will not have her made uncomfortable. Do we understand one another?"

"We do." The only acceptable answer was rendered swiftly.

"The other asseveration of which I take exception." He said as Jack held his breath, eyes never leaving his father's.

"The Carlton House Set." Shaking his head, "I know it is easy to follow the mode, not wanting to be left out, which is overlooked for a young man of your age and affluence, but for how long and how deep before one is lost in the thrill. I had such affairs, but times were different. However, some of the rumours are repugnant to me, so I must articulate my misgivings. I do not say a path of rectitude is required, but you must remember the gossip within the Ton." The earl noted the incensed countenance. "Now, do not look so reluctant. You must consider Olivia. She will be presented this year as my ward and your reputation reflects upon her. She is sure to be a diamond of the first water, at the very least.

Jack mumbled in agreement and grinned. The reaction was noticed by his father, who paused, then disregarded it. "Your mother will likely hear of your escapades if she has not already. I warn you; she will have her say."

"I am sure of it. How does my taking over Eustace Estates rectify my situation or my scandalous reputation in London?" Jack was curious as to how one related to the other.

"One of itself does not signify. However, it will provide an excuse at a given notice." His father gave his son a grin, a slight nod, and a wink.

"Aww!" Jack had clarity; responsibility could be wielded as a weapon if necessary.

His father nodded. The matter was settled between them with understanding. Eustace Estates needed attention, and Jack had always loved the place. He pondered the agreement between them and perceived wayward young men a bit better. A purpose is needed now and again. Lord Andovir now had a purpose and an escape. How it would affect the rest of his life, only time would tell.

***

"Aww, traditions." Jack strolled into the parlour finding his mother standing at the mahogany sideboard, placing selections of cakes on a small plate. Advancing to the table, he placed a kiss on her presented cheek.

"Do not expect the sweet confections every morning. I fear I must take notice of them." She said.

"Mother, you are as beautiful as ever. I see no concern."

"My dear boy, I will not be toad-eaten. But your mother's vanity appreciates the gesture none the less."

Her ladyship watched her son as he walked to the window, standing silently, feet slightly parted, hands clasped behind his back. A warm sense of satisfaction rose from her chest, a dashing young man in his neatly pressed muslin shirt, collar stiffly pointed, double-breasted waistcoat with buckskin breeches and brightly shining top boots.

"You must be riding this morning, quite the fop you are today." She announced proudly. Two years ago, he had left just a boy but returned, without doubt, a gentleman of the first stare.

"Is there news from London?" She quizzed. "You spent time there before coming home, so the prattles say."

"Same as always." He came to the country to remove himself from the city, not discuss it. After the interchange with his father this morning, a tête-à-tête with his mother was to be avoided above all things. Undeterred, she pressed on.

"Are there any of your recent pursuits you wish to share?"

Jack adjusted one of the pillows before sitting, again ignoring his mother's inquisition. She lifted an eyebrow; he glanced at her, raising a matching one attempting a look of innocent curiosity, which he was certain held a hint of guilt but remained silent.

His mother flicked her wrist with superior indignation. "You know, I have friends in London, and your father has been there recently,"

Knowing his mother to be quite the investigator, he chose his words carefully. "Pray do tell. I had no notion of it. Assuredly, I might have seen him at White's, and I have not." Two could play the supercilious game; she had been his teacher.

Before the charade could proceed, it was interrupted by the entrance of Miss Olivia Sinclair. Jack leapt to his feet and bowed like an overexcited schoolboy. The young miss, taken aback, offered her hand to the viscount. He took it and brushed a light kiss upon it before releasing it. Olivia found herself blushing pink.

Lady Birkshire, shocked by the entire presentation, nearly swooned. She had left the two savages much to their own devices in their youth, and she had never witnessed a display of societal propriety from either, much less toward one another.

"My dear, you look charming. Is that a new riding habit?"

Another observance which delighted her ladyship.

Captivated by the charming and handsome figure greeting her with such gentility, she had forgotten to breathe, let alone notice anyone else in her presence. Her aunt's voice broke the trance, and she peaked around Jack's tall form.

"Indeed, I bought this sometime past but only remembered it this morning. I do love a morning ride in the crisp cool air, you know." Wishing to conceal her purpose to capture the viscount's notice.

"Well, it looks lovely on you. The old one was a bit too youthful. You will find fresh chocolate and some of your favourite cakes. Emma must be in good humour. She has made all our favourites this morning."

"I daresay they are the viscount's favourites." She glanced at Jack with a devilish grin, "She makes no secret of her prejudice toward him."

"You tease me, my pet, and after my warm welcome upon my arrival."

Olivia scowled at him and sashayed by him, whisking her riding habit, which was a bit harder than a full skirt, but did not go unnoticed. Grinning incessantly, it was the first remnants of the cheeky little girl Jack remembered so well. Olivia partook of the hot chocolate, cakes and joined her aunt at the small table.

"I have been trying to find news of London. There is much to prepare before our travels. I must know what is expected upon our arrival, but my son is little help."

Annabelle tossed a glance at him and turned back to Olivia and the move to London for The Season. Olivia was more interested in her cakes than the London schedule. Aware of the disinterest, the countess directed her attention back to her earlier inquiries.

Olivia watching the interrogation, giggled, relieved someone else was under the scrutiny of the countess.

London held little interest to her until her aunt snapped at her perfect son.

"Do not change the subject, young man. I am aware you have been carousing about," she glared at him but still received no response.

Jack was fidgeting with the pillow, determined to play innocent and remain silent. He was certain whatever she knew, he could only expose his indiscretions by speaking.

"Very well, if you are not to be forthcoming, I will do so," she advised, losing patience.

"Please do." He grinned and leaned back in his seat, crossing one knee over the other.

"Lady Camilla Davis?" she blurted.

Olivia suddenly dropped her cup and whirled around. She had never swooned in her life, so the possibility she was about to do so was quite remote. Nonetheless, she felt a bit lightheaded and located the nearest chair. Now riveted by the conversation that clearly did not include her, and thankfully, they were unaware of her flushed visage as she stared at them.

"Oh!" Jack said nonchalantly, relieved he had held his tongue.

"Indeed," his mother scoffed, "It was my understanding you were courting her."

"Briefly," Jack said, trying to dismiss the issue.

"I am truly sorry to hear it," his mother sighed, "I am told she has turned into a very lovely young lady and her family, of course, beyond reproach."

"I suppose so. Admittedly, I was attracted by her beauty. However, it soon became a dead bore. To execute a conversation was beyond her ability. She disliked promenades in the park, 'susceptible to freckles, you know' was her constant retort, which I could not abide and most appallingly, she abhorred horses. It seemed she abhorred anything beyond the drawing room."

"Oh!" His mother gasped, "I was not privy."

"I mean, really, what female does not appreciate a beautiful stepper."

Olivia was stunned by such revelations as she touched the bridge of her nose, where she was certain a few freckles abode. But really, what girl did not like horses? More importantly, why would Jack seek the company of one particular lady if not seeking a wife? Her head began to spin. She knew he was expected to procure a wife - someday. But that was to be years from now, was it not?

The idea of another female permanently joining their... their what? Suddenly, she wondered what exactly they were... now? Jack had been away for the better part of five years, but she had never stopped thinking of him as anything but her own. He always had been. Her body stiffened as she realised Jack had seen the world, and made friends, apparently both male and female, while she remained at Birkshire with her cats, dogs, and horses. The thought quite disturbed her, and to attach a name to another female was more than she could bear. Her face warmed, her nose tingled, and her eyes moistened. She closed them to hold back tears, and a long-ago memory came flooding back.

***

She was thirteen, and Jack was eighteen. The summer was waning, and fall too soon would make its chilly appearance, and he was to return to Cambridge. If the weather held, they always planned a picnic for the last day at the lake. Olivia was melancholy; she hated when he left for school. It always left her heartbroken and lonely. Since her parent's death, she had an emptiness she never quite understood, but Jack seemed to fill the void.

The picnic was their time to say goodbye. Jack always made them special. Even as a small child, when her mama visited Lady Birkshire on Tuesday afternoons, he would grab some bread and cheese and back then, her nanny would spread a blanket in the garden just outside the library doors. It wasn't a real picnic, of course, but to her, it seemed one. As she grew older, they moved further away from the house until, finally, they were at the lake. Every summer, they would sit on blankets under the big oak tree that grew right at the water's edge.

The day was sunny and warm, and Jack spread the blanket across the grass. They dropped to their knees and rested on their heels. Jack began emptying the basket filled with sweetbreads, cheeses, and pastries.

"I wish you did not have to go," Olivia said, her eyes moist.

"I will be back before you know it, my pet." He reached over and wiped her cheek as one of the tears escaped. Still on his knees, Jack slid his forefinger under her chin, lifting her face to his.

"Please Olivia do not cry," he said softly, "I cannot bear it when you do. I like you better when you are saucy and abominable." He released her chin and stretched out on his side, propping himself on his elbow, "I will be back at Christmas; we will roast chestnuts, and maybe it will be nice enough to go riding."

"Christmas is such a very long time." She whimpered, lowering her head. She raised her eyes to his, brushed back tears and cleared her throat. "Did you receive my note?"

Jack quickly sat up, bending one knee, and resting his elbow upon it. The mention of the note instantly made him uncomfortable. What was he to say? He regarded her silently and searched for words. He had indeed received the note; it was slipped under his door. He opened it expecting the usual childish dribble.

"I will miss you terribly. Please keep this near your heart, so you will not forget me.

Your servant, Olivia."

She always left him one. However, this one was unexpected. He found at eighteen, he was ill- experienced to know how to manage such a request from a thirteen-year-old child. Especially one he loved and adored. He thought of its contents once more.

Jack, Please, say you will wait for me. I will grow up someday, you'll see. My heart belongs to only you.

Forever your servant, Olivia

Jack cleared his throat, trying to retrieve words beyond his years. Olivia's crystal blue eyes, wet with tears and filled with wonder, were focused on his.

"Olivia." He took her small hands and squeezed them.

"When you grow up, you will find a handsome young man who will love you as much as I do, but in a different way."

Jack's words were soft and tender, but he could see they stung the little girl, but he continued, carefully selecting each one.

"He will adore you and take care of you, just as I have always done. And you will love him even more than you do me."

He heard her softly whisper, "No."

She lowered her head, and he felt a teardrop on the back of his hand. His heart broke, and he struggled to continue.

"I will always love you, and you will always be my little pet, always," Jack pleaded.

Olivia jerked her hand from his, wiping her eyes.

It was not the words she wanted to hear. At that moment, the pain in her heart was one only a girl of thirteen could understand when a first love is crushed. Jack's hands fell to his knees.

She grabbed her skirt and wiped her tear-soaked fingers and face. She clutched the edges of her dress and struggled to stand as her feet swiftly began moving beneath her, one in front of the other.

"Olivia!" She heard him calling, but she just kept running.

***

The memory dwindled away as quickly as it had come. She glanced up at mother and son, thankful she had been ignored and given a moment to reflect upon the confusing thoughts which overwhelmed her. Why had she thought of that silly note now?

At thirteen, she had felt all grown up; writing that note had meant everything to her. Of course, she now understood thirteen was far too young to understand love, commitment and forever. For goodness' sake, she hardly understood the depth of commitment now. The confusing thoughts made her head hurt. But most confusing were the changes in Jack and why he had to return home, looking like…like…like a full-grown man!

Startled from her reverie by the conversation which now included her as both mother and son awaited an answer.

"I beg pardon; I am afraid I was wool-gathering."

Jack had moved to the trestle table, opening the pots, and searching for refreshments.

"Is she not lovely? She has worked so ridiculously hard the past couple of years." His mother motioned for him to take notice, "after your near ruination."

"What?" Both Jack and Olivia responded, shocked.

"Oh, you both know what I mean. This hoydenish child was almost impossible to turn into a lady." The countess motioned for Olivia to join them, and with annoyance, she proliferated.

"You had her wading into the fishpond in some of her best dresses at seven, fishing in the lake, baiting her own hook at ten, firing pistols, and teaching her to ride a horse astride."

"Well, actually, my papa did that!" Olivia interjected in Jack's defence.

"Oh fiddle, my son saw you as his personal plaything."

"I beg your pardon!" Jack appeared offended, then grinned at Olivia.

"You acted as though she was born for you, to do as you will. My Lord, it is a wonder I was able to turn her into a lady at all," she continued, "If it had been left up to the both of you, neither of you would be fit to find a wife or a husband. God knows I take responsibility for it, being lost in my own sorrow all those years. Then spoiling you both beyond all matters of sensibilities or rather the lack thereof, letting you do as you pleased."

Lady Birkshire noticed the pillows out of place as she rose from the settee.

"And what have you been doing with my pillows? Heathens, the both of you," she scolded, plumping the pillow, and returning it to its rightful place. Then as always, she turned to her two spoiled children and smiled.

"Never mind all that! If I know the two of you, the grooms are waiting with saddled horses, and I shan't see either of you until the light has faded. I wish to have a country house visit and ball."

"What the blood..., pardon mum, must we?" Jack groaned. The last thing he wanted was a house filled with those he had chosen to escape. He turned to gather Olivia's support and was unprepared to find her a pale shade of green and speechless.

"It will be in honour of your homecoming, an informal affair, with only a few chosen invitees, less than fifty." Olivia's eyes widened, and she slipped silently into the chair near her. The countess, noticing her despair, quickly retraced her words. "Well, maybe thirty. My child, it will give you a chance to gain the needed confidence before thrusting you into the London season. I should have taken you to London, where you could have known what to expect, but a country party will ease your nerves." Annabelle rattled quickly, hoping to calm the frightened eyes of the child staring back at her. "Trust me, it will be the perfect place to practice your first introduction. Moreover, you can dance here and gain experience before you are presented, which must be done before you can attend most of the London societal affairs."

"Presented? To the Queen?" her voice cracking and rising to an unbearable shriek. She wasn't certain which was worse, Birkshire House filled with strangers or going to London to meet the Queen. Good God, she would be a freak! The thought terrified her, and she turned to Jack.

Jack had literally bit his tongue to prevent his laughter but managed to retort. "Do not look at me. I am against it," he interjected, slinging his arm over the back of the sofa.

His mother glared at him and cleared her throat.

"Oh, dear God, making conversation…with total strangers!" Olivia moaned. Jack stifled another chuckle.

Olivia's thoughts spun out of control… It would be a nightmare. She wasn't good at her lessons and, until the last two years, spent most of her time avoiding them. She had excelled at history, but when she attempted to share it with her aunt, she was told most history was vulgar and inappropriate for a lady to discuss.

She had enjoyed French and had tried Italian, but when she mixed a few Italian words with French, her tutor, Madame de la Croix, flew into a rage and Italian lessons were immediately ceased.

She could not see a conversation going well, as she knew little else other than horses and hunts. Another censure she had received from her aunt. Some discussions in mixed company were considered churlish, and she reminded her that her actions might be considered coltish.

She had been isolated in Birkshire and allowed by her doting aunt to do as she pleased until she turned fifteen, then suddenly was to be turned into a proper lady. In her ladyships' defence, had she known of all Olivia's hoydenish ways, she would have been mortified and put an end to her pleasures long ago.

"Olivia!" Her aunt beckoned her from the daydream.

"I am sorry, my mind seems to be wandering."

"Come, sit, dear. You will help with the planning. It will be a wonderful experience for you."

"Me! I cannot; I have no..." Olivia said as she stared down at the pages her aunt had spread about the drawing-room table.

"Nonsense, I will be here to guide you…and Jack will help." She regarded her son, one eyebrow raised.

Rolling his eyes, he joined Olivia at the table. His mother hovered over them, pointed at columns with decisive instruction.

"The guestlist, I have included several daughters of friends in London. You both may invite whomever you wish. I will sit out of the way but available. Remembering there must be an equal number of gentlemen and ladies, the first rule you must learn. One hour of your time is all I request, then you may go."

Neither could see a recourse and set to work as they glanced at the mantle clock.

Lady Birkshire walked to her chair, gathered her embroidery, and made herself comfortable. She watched the two young people she loved more than life, discussing the guest list. Both appeared morose. Annabelle sighed and tried to focus on her stitching. She made three stitches and glanced over at the grumbling pair. She couldn't help but laugh. If they only knew, she thought.

She stared at Olivia; how much she looked like Marian, flaxen blonde hair, light, crystal blue eyes, and so petite, with skin reminiscent of a porcelain doll. Marian would be so proud of her daughter. Tears filled her eyes. Not a day passed that she did not think of and miss her friend. What she and Marian had gone through to bring these two babies into the world. Her embroidery fell limp in her lap as her mind fell into the past.

***

Annabelle Catherine Grayson Norrys and Marian Elizabeth Catherine Hamilton Sinclair could not remember a time they had not been friends. They shared lessons together, entered London society together, and married best friends. They had experienced all of life's blissful moments together. Regrettably, they also shared the most sombre. The realm of motherhood had eluded them both.

Neither Annabelle nor Marian would accept the prospect of never having a child, as much as women, as to the duty of their titles. More times than not, their afternoon teas were filled with conversation and tears about the shared heartbreak neither could forget.

Annabelle found herself with child for a fourth time. With careful observation and rest, she gave birth to the most handsome, amicable baby boy.

With hidden envy, Marian loved this child nearly as much as Annabelle. John Jacob Anthony Norrys was the happiest, healthiest little heir they both ever laid their eyes upon! By the time Jack was five, he was learning to shoot, hunt, and fish and accompanied his father everywhere.

Annabelle and Marian were at the local village, shopping for ribbons, and a new candle shop had opened. They went in. The ladies had not been in the shop but a moment when Marian dashed out the door. She had exited so quickly that Annabelle had not noticed until she saw her sitting on a bench through the front glass. She quickly followed her friend. Approaching Marian with concern, she stopped, then gave her a mischievous smile.

"Why Marian Elizabeth, when were you going to tell me?" she retorted.

"Tell you what?" Marian still trying to suppress the need to expel the tea and crumpets they had eaten earlier, her skin a greenish tint.

"Do not try to hide it. I know you too very well," Annabelle scoffed.

Marian tried to smile through her pale lips. "Very well," Marian pulled her friend to the bench. "I wished to keep it to myself until I… I could not bear the pitied faces again."

"Marian, of all things, and myself, someone who would understand better than anyone."

"Please forgive me," she sighed. Marian's eyes watered from embarrassment.

"How far along?" Annabelle whispered, taking Marian's hand into her own. "I am not certain, nearly six months."

"What!" Annabelle screeched. Several strolling shoppers turned their heads and stared. "I mean, how on earth? I mean, why on earth have you not said something?"

Marian placed her free hand over Annabelle's and lay her head on her best friend's shoulder and murmured. "You know exactly why!"

Annabelle leaned her head on top of Marian's, and the ladies sat together in quiet solitude.

Two and a half months later, they were wiping tears from one another's faces, staring down at the most precious little girl with a tattering of blonde sprouts coming from her head and the lightest blue eyes they had ever seen.

The little girl was beautiful but very tiny. The midwife was standing at the foot of the bed when Marian looked at her and asked about the baby's small size. The heavy-set woman who had delivered fifteen years of babies in the area chuckled.

"Milady, that's the most beautiful little chip I ever laid me glimms on. She may be a wee bit early, but lands sake, ya' can't have missed them bellows of 'ers."

Annabelle walked into the hallway with the tiny bundle and pulled the blankets from the pink face in her arms. "Now, say hello to your little girl."

"A little girl?" The two men, in unison, exclaimed.

Then she looked at her own little boy at her side, his arms crossed in disgust and disappointment.

"A girl!" he groaned. "They're no fun!"

***

With tears streaming down her face, Annabelle could not help but giggle at those memories. She brushed away her tears and smiled. She glanced at the two miracles, fussing, and making decisions. It seemed Jack had made peace over that disappointment seventeen years ago. Annabelle leaned back in her chair and tried to focus on her stitches once again.

CHAPTER 4

A fortnight passed quickly. The afternoon was bustling with carriages beginning their arrival. By the time the clock struck 5:00, the expanded drawing room was filled with guests, and the atmosphere was perfect.

Compliments were abundant regarding the flowers, the food, the drink, and the impressive string quartet hired for the occasion. Although years had passed since Lady Birkshire had hosted a grand party, she had not lost her touch.

The earl made his own contribution to its success by opening the game rooms. The billiard tables were refreshed with new cloths, leather pockets and sticks refreshed with new leather tips. The nearby card room tables were cleaned and polished for lively matches of Whist, Loo, and Casino and the liquor cabinets were stocked with scotch, burgundy, brandy, and port.

Lord Andovir, not to be outdone, readied Birkshire's finest thoroughbred hunters for a gentleman's hunt race. The grooms spent days ensuring the course was both challenging and competitive. Several of Jack's friends, all top sawyers, had accepted invitations, and he looked forward to besting them in his favourite childhood meadows and woods.

The first evening's dinner found Olivia seated between two of Jack's closest friends. Lord James Sheffield and Lord Thomas Worthington. She knew Sheffield from his many visits during his youth. Olivia had not seen him in several years, but their friendship was easily rekindled, and he was delighted to see her changes. Andovir had shared how nervous she was, to ensure his assistance in setting her at ease.

Lord Worthington, the heir to the Duke of Derbyshire, was seated to her left. He was also a guest of Lord Andovir on many occasions and was an acquaintance of Olivia. Both her dinner partners were more than pleased to see her again, and the three were delighted with the arrangement.

"Lady Olivia, will you join the Hunt Race tomorrow?" Sheffield queried.

"Please, Lord Sheffield, it is Olivia. I think our long acquaintance enables us to dispense with such formalities, at least here at Birkshire House."

"Only if you call me James. I agree our long friendship exceeds such protocol. At least here, as you say, where we have many memories. Which brings me back to the question. I believe I am due a rematch. After your trouncing the last time, I was foolish enough to make a wager with you." He gave her a sly grin.

Olivia could not help but giggle, and her cheeks turned a pale pink. There was no mistake in his manner. Lord James Sheffield was pleased to have been asked to make the now mature Olivia comfortable this weekend.

"I had forgotten," she reflected, "but I have received permission to join the race."

Olivia glanced across the table, where Jack was seated, to ensure he was not listening. He seemed to be engaged with the young lady to his right. She hoped he was too involved to overhear her. She had promised not to complain regarding her restrictions for the race.

"I have been constrained to ride the side-saddle. So, you are sure to have the advantage." She whispered. Sheffield could not help but laugh aloud and leaned his head toward her.

"If you remain the accomplished equestrian you were as a child, I will accept the advantage. Was the restraint made for the male ego or something far more nefarious?"

"Far more nefarious, I dare say." She glanced over the centrepiece as Jack's eyes caught hers. She blushed, hoping he could not see in the candlelight.

"Just so! I suppose if you are to go to London, you should practice using the contraption."

"I suppose, but pray, the entire ordeal caused me much frustration."

James could not help but chuckle, remembering just how very much of a hoyden she had been growing up. "I am certain of it!"

Their ease of comportment was as if only yesterday when they raced neck to nothing across the meadows together.

Lord Worthington, overhearing the exchange, quickly joined the discourse.

"Am I mistaken, or may we have a chance to regain our membership in the Four Horse Club tomorrow?"

"If your membership depends on arriving back at the stable before me, do not count your guineas just yet, I assure you. I may not have sat the side-saddle since I was a babe, but it does not mean I am not accomplished enough to beat the two of you." Olivia stated, where both could hear the challenge, she extended.

Both men laughed out loud, accepted the wager, and commented on their advantage. Jack, unable to ignore the laughter, glared at both his friends. They were having far too much fun.

Jack was being held captive by Lady Davenport, whose encounter with an enamoured chicken in the village was endless. It seemed the chicken was so besotted he waited for her exit from every shop and chased her into the next. Every moment of the ghastly confrontation was detailed. His thoughts waned into penning a novel, pondering the work to be entitled, The Five Ways to Kill Your Mother.

The seating arrangement was worsened by his companion to his left, Miss Elizabeth Jameson, whose lengthy tale consisted of a full account of fifty loaves of bread baked the previous week for charity, including the batch thrown out due to the horror of confusing the salt with sugar. During this saga, Jack revised the title of his novel to Ten Ways to Kill a Countess.

The evening of cards, billiards and musicales stretched late into the early hours of the morning, causing Olivia to oversleep.

In frustration and haste, she slipped down the servant's stairway unnoticed, through the back garden and out the gate. But when she slung open the door at the back of the stables…

"What the bloody hell!" A familiar voice came from the other side as the wooden slab was caught abruptly. The door was jerked from her hand, and she recognised the tall figure glaring down at her.

"Good morning, Olivia. Pray, may I ask what the hell you think you are doing sneaking into the stables?" Jack had both hands on his hips and one eyebrow raised suspiciously.

The sight of him startled her. Lord Andovir looked dashing. The white leather breeches with side buttons at the knee, the white muslin shirt with black riding coat, white riding gloves, beaver hat, perfectly tied neckcloth and, of course, the Hoby Hessians buffed to a stellar shine, she could see her reflection. Olivia held her breath for a moment before remembering she had been accused of sneaking into the stables and snapped back to the situation at hand.

"I was not sneaking. I only wanted to reach Spartan's stall without, without…" She thought about it and really could not think of a good reason why she had.

"Without what?" he asked, raising his arm to the edge of the door with his right-hand towering over her. His other hand was still on his hip, postured with the intent of intimidation. Still in a foul mood from the prior evening's dead bore, too much scotch and no luck at the billiards table, he was certain this little chit was up to mischief.

Olivia stood innocently in silence, she had only wished to avoid the uninterested female guests, but now she appeared guilty, of what she was not at all certain of, but guilty none the less. "I really do not know," she finally admitted.

"You were not attempting to swap your saddle," he said suspiciously, his eyes never leaving hers.

"I was not. I truly was not." Honestly, Olivia had not thought of it. How could he think it of her?

A moment later, the countenance of the familiar form in front of her, she knew fully how he could. He knew her better than anyone, and had she not wagered with the encumbrance, she might have thought of it. But the odious actions of this bully, strikingly handsome as he might be, he would never know of it.

"Be assured I did not. In fact, if you must know, my wager was made with my impediment of the blasted side-saddle." Olivia's voice was filled with indignation and haughtiness.

"Why does that not surprise me." Jack raked his hand through his hair.

Between his horrid evening with his own party plus watching the gaiety from Olivia's, his frustration had crested. Although it had been at his insistence, he was irritated with the attention she received from Sheffield and Worthington, he had asked them to put her at ease, but for God's sake not to make love to her all-damn night long. They had enjoyed the burden a bit too much while he was left to entertain several boring young ladies. At least, he hoped that was all there was to his annoyance.

He knew she had not been trying to swap saddles. Sheffield and Worthington had boasted later in the evening regarding their wager and appreciated Jack's good sense with the restriction. But he had been searching for her. He had planned the obstacles with his top sawyer companions in mind, not her. He was having second thoughts regarding her taking part. The final jump was to make the race, but he feared it would be dangerous in the side-saddle. He had not given it much consideration until the breakfast discussion and the strength and accuracy the last jump would need.

"I wished to discuss the jumps before the race, so I am glad I caught you alone."

Jack stared at her, covered from head to toe in wool and leather. Even in all the riding attire, one could not help but notice her petite frame. The jacket, not yet buttoned revealing the light muslin bodice, clearly indicated she was definitely, no longer a child. Why did he keep noticing these things? He swallowed hard and directed his attention to the race. She looked at him in surprise. Her eyes twinkled expectantly.

"I want to warn you about the last jump," he said, trying to shake his thoughts from the muslin bodice.

"I had not anticipated you participating in the race when I added to the last jump. You have not even tried that new saddle, have you?"

Jack took her arm and pulled her around where she faced him directly, "You must listen to me, Olivia. I know how competitive you are. Sheffield and Worthington told me about the conversation at dinner." Olivia drew her brows together, staring at him as he continued. The tiny hairs on the back of her neck stood on end. She was not going to like this.

"There is a hedge in the northeast meadow, south of the barley field, you know it?" he paused.

"Of course, I do." She retorted.

"Very well, do not try that jump."

"What!" Olivia jerked her arm from his hold, "I do not believe it! What are you asking!"

"I am saying there was a water hazard added to the other side of the stone wall, and I do not want you to take that jump," Jack caught her arm again and pulled her to him.

"You are jesting, are you not?" Olivia was trying to hold her temper and pull away, but Jack's grip tightened.

"No, I am not," he demanded, "You must promise me you will not try it."

"I most certainly will not," Olivia snapped. "I may not have sat a side-saddle in…in… aeons, but it is the latest of its kind, and Spartan is the finest jumper in England. I am skilled enough to make a double and…" Olivia was twisting and trying to pull from his grasp. Both arms holding her now, he turned her to face him. "I am asking you, Olivia, please do not try it." Jack wasn't certain if his concern was due to her being female, his sister or something more, but he was near panic.

"Give me one reason I should not," she wailed.

He released his grip. "Because I have asked you not to do so."

He was trying to remain calm, but damn, she made it difficult. He felt as though they were back in their childhood, and she was hell-bent on showing him she could manage anything. But this wasn't their childhood, and she could be badly hurt.

She pulled away again and crossed her arms, "No, that is not good enough! You never wanted me in this race. You wished it between you and your friends. Is that the reason you forced me into that...that contraption?" He said nothing. "Is it?"

"Do not be absurd. With your skills, you little chit, you could beat the whole of us with or without it." Jack was trying to hold his temper, but her obstinance was making it damned hard.

"Mother's exact words... if you allow her to ride in that race, and anything, anything at all happens to her, I will never forgive you." Jack was pleading with her to understand.

"Olivia, she was unusually serious. She wanted me to refuse you. She had nothing on her mind but your best interests and safety. But she drew the line. The side-saddle or not riding was my choice. Olivia, things are different; you are different."

"Why would she ask such a thing of me? I am not different." She knew that was untrue, but she was angry and peevish.

Jack could only see the spoiled ten-year-old. He could not believe she was acting so childish. It was the last thing he wanted to address, how things were different with so many of the upper ton as guests.

"Olivia, you're acting like a child," he snapped, "this party is for your benefit. You are no longer an adolescent, and this competitiveness of yours is unbecoming of a young lady."

As soon as the words left him, they were regretted but irretrievable. Unsure if it was fury or hurt that he saw in her eyes. He deserved them if fury, but if they were hurt, insufferable.

He raked his hands through his hair as they stood in silence. Minutes passed, and neither uttered a word. He thought it was best to just leave it. He had said his peace and could only hope she would listen. He murmured something about seeing her on the course and walked away.

He felt like hell talking to her so, but he was struggling with this change in their relationship. She was a young lady; he could no longer treat her like the little girl he left behind. Frustrated over the small figure, not one of a child, but bloody hell, the sharp tongue seemed the same stubborn, obstinate, headstrong ten-year-old! Damn her insolent hide. He had sealed her fate; she would take that jump, side-saddle, and all. God help him if she were hurt. He would never forgive himself. He would have to remain behind her.

Olivia slung her arms around Spartan. She felt the tear-soaked hairs on his neck. She was so angry. "How could he? How could he say such a thing?" she susurrated. "I am not a child. I am not!"

Olivia watched as the groom took Spartan and put that horrid saddle on his back. She hated it; Spartan hated it. They were both accustomed to her weight being carried evenly astride. She was reminded of Jack's words, or rather her aunt's. Maybe they were being fair. Neither had seen her ride in ages and she had not been on a side-saddle since... she could not remember. Maybe it would be better if she did not take the jump. But Spartan could make it. She knew he could. He was big and strong. Doubtful, she thought perhaps she would not.

It was the final obstacle at the end of the course. She would know how she was managing the earlier jumps by then. She knew the leg hold would be completely different, but she rode every day. She was strong; indeed, she would make her decision when she got to the double.

She adjusted herself in the saddle, and as her long-time groom handed her the reins, he stopped just short of her hands.

"Miss Olivia, please remember your pressure points with the pommels. You must hold differently with this saddle." She could see the concern in his eyes as he released the reins to her.

"I will, I promise." Then headed Spartan in the direction of the first meadow.

The field of horses was larger than expected. Olivia tried to mind her manners, but when the gun went off, she forgot everything but riding Spartan.

In the beginning, the awful saddle gave her trouble. However, the two soon fell into an agreeable union. Olivia continued to remind herself this was a party, and she should restrain her competitive nature. She really had good intentions until Lord Sheffield came near with his playful taunts. He knew how to tease and provoke her, and of course, he did.

Olivia continued to push Spartan harder. As they made the last turn toward the final heath, she looked back and saw James only a few lengths behind her. She slowed Spartan to a rhythmic canter. Jack's words repeated in her mind. She turned to see James and Thomas move to take the final hurdle. She knew they were on two of Birkshire's finest Hunters. The double would be easy for them. Every genteel and ladylike part of her was saying, stay in the flat. At the last minute, instinct and uncontrollable competitiveness took hold; she direct reined Spartan to the obstacle course. Spartan settled into an even rhythm to make the leap. She knew in her heart, she could still bypass it, she really could, and she really should. It would be the right thing to do.

As the jump grew nearer, she could feel Spartan's muscles tighten. He had the hedgerow in sight and was preparing for the approach. There was never a question if he could make the vault. He judged the effort necessary to clear it, adjusted his line, pace, balance, impulsion, and length of stride, and was focused on his point of take-off.

Spartan was a well-trained and experienced hunter-jumper; she knew he was ready for it and would clear it with ease. She felt his foreleg take the one last step, engage his hind legs forward under his body and sit on his hindquarters, with his hocks bent as his forelegs thrust against the hard dirt, one after the other. Both hind legs thrust powerfully against the ground, sending them both up and forward. Olivia was unable to take her usual two-point stance, she squeezed her thighs against the pommels, but they were already weakened from the earlier jumps. As the large gelding left the ground, his neck extended forward, and his shoulders rotated, bringing his front legs up. He folded his forelegs tightly backward.

Olivia could feel Spartan's body travelling up, up, and over, arcing his body, and extending his neck forward and down as his shoulders rotated. She could see in her mind the motion of Spartan's hocks, stifle, and fetlock joints tightly flexing, with the hocks pulled up behind his hindquarters. She knew exactly where his arc would come.

She had to pull her legs together against the two pommels as he lowered his neck for the landing, extending his foreleg. Olivia tried to hold against the fixed and leaping head pommels, but instead, her strength was waning, and all she could feel was air. She felt her left leg move away from the leaping head pommel.

As Spartan's body pivoted forward over both forelegs, creating a brief moment of suspension before the first hind leg touched the ground. She knew she needed to squeeze her right leg downward and against the upper pommel and her left leg upward into the leaping head to create a strong grip, but the unused muscles were depleted. As his hind leg landed well forward under his body, followed by the second hind leg, she felt her body lunge backwards, then forward.

Spartan landed his jump beautifully with balance, coordination, the correct lead and without missing cadence. However, Olivia did not!

The hunter's grand size, length of stride and balance provided Olivia, at the last moment, an opportunity to regain somewhat of a corrected position. As ungraceful as it was, and with the strength from pure adrenaline, she somehow remained in the saddle.

Olivia slowed Spartan to a slow canter and could feel the sting of her upper legs. She knew she was going to pay physically for this behaviour. She knew she was going to reap the brutal contempt from Jack. However, she could not help but grin. It had been a difficult obstacle and dangerous. But she made it, bruised but unhurt!

Olivia was exhausted when she reached the stable with Spartan. Her legs were shaking, but she was grinning as she replayed the jump over and over in her head. She was walking down the alleyway smiling as she reached the tack room. She entered to leave her riding crop, but there was no one about. She deposited it on the desk and was thinking of her wager with Jack's friends and let out a giggle to herself. Removing her glove as she turned to leave, she looked up at the figure blocking the doorway; she froze, and her face went pale.

"I am glad you find this so God damn funny!" Jack's voice was cold, his eyes hard. She watched as he stepped into the room and slammed the door behind him.

"I knew you would be upset with me, but I made it." She chortled, "You should have seen us…"

"I did see you!" He roared, cutting her off.

"You did?" she whispered reluctantly.

"Yes, damn it to hell, I bloody well did," he said, trying unsuccessfully to control his wrath.

Jack had never been so angry in his life. His hands were shaking, sweat pouring from his brow, his heartbeat hard and rapid, his lungs were painful, his breathing difficult. His emotions were out of control, unable to escape the continual replay in his mind of the near catastrophe.

He had watched in horror as Spartan set up for the obstacle. He knew Spartan would make the jump but was uncertain if Olivia had the strength left to stay in the saddle. He watched impotently as she approached the massive stone wall, shifting her body to compensate. All he could do was watch powerlessly and pray she could manage it. He watched her small body violently thrown backwards and forward; her neck jerked in every direction like a ragdoll. Then she slipped in the saddle. He had very nearly emptied the contents of his stomach when he saw her legs lose their grip. He had never felt more useless in his life and all he could do was watch.

"It was a bloody challenge you could not resist. It was a mistake to allow you to ride in the damn race. Then like a fool, I tried to force you to relent despite the danger and any regard for those who care for you. I should have said no when mama demanded you ride side-saddle, but she worried for your reputation. Trying to appease you both damn near got you killed. Jesus Christ, Olivia, what the hell were you thinking!" Jack turned toward the door in frustration.

Olivia had never seen him out of control or so angry. She watched as he ran his hand through his hair, dropping his broad shoulders in defeat as though he was searching for words and trying to collect himself.

His voice softened, his breath still laboured, "Damn it, Olivia, if you had fallen, you could have been badly injured." He paused, still speaking softly. "Or worse, you have no idea what it felt like, being so totally helpless, watching you struggle."

"But I did not fall off," sounding more defiant than intended, but still not understanding the magnitude of her actions or his fears. "I was able to get my legs back against the pommels. I am sure to be uncomfortable for a few days."

Jack's temper rose again, hearing her instinctive obstinance. She did not understand. Hell, he did not understand… his lack of control…his anger; it was not the bloody jump… it wasn't her damn stubbornness…it was the thought…His body stiffened. Dear God, it was the thought of… losing her.

The incipiency of comprehending life was meaningless without her in it overwhelmed him. Good God! The revelation dazed him. He could not live without her. He swung around, studying her frail frame. Until this very moment, he had not been aware, since the day she was born, that she was an extension of his life.

He stepped toward her and reached for her. She flinched but dared not move. Grabbing her shoulders, his fingers biting into her riding jacket as he tightened his grip. Jack's violet eyes pierced her crystal blue ones, which were now wet with tears.

She was so small, so delicate, so damn beautiful. He closed his eyes, trying to regain his composure, but visions of the five-foot stacked rocks, her lifeless, mangled body, shattered from the impact of the stone wall, blinded his thoughts, and his grip tightened.

He was hurting her, but Olivia remained stunned and silent; she had never seen him so aggressive, and when his eyes flashed open, they were black with fury. It was the first time she had ever been frightened; the blood drained from her face.

"I am sorry," she tried to whisper, but it was barely a whimper.

Jack was filled with a mixture of confusion, fear, and an unrecognised emotion. He vacillated between the fear of losing her and the relief that she was here, safe. It seemed judgment and common sense had vanished, replaced by pure unrestrained emotion. He wrapped his arms around her and pulled her to him. Without warning, he slightly pushed her away, gently wiping a wisp of hair from her cheek. He lowered his head and placed his lips to hers. His heart stopped, and he pressed harder. He embraced her tighter as though his selfish desire wanted to bury her within him. He wanted, no, he needed, to hold her, engulf her, own her. It was an uncontrollable need to feel her body next to his own to ensure she was truly unharmed and safe.

Releasing her lips, he was suddenly aware her body was limp. He could hear her whimpering like a frightened rabbit, trapped and waiting for the skilful hunter to finish her off. Her soft whines nagged and tormented him. Regaining some of his wits, he realised her suffering and released his grip, allowing her a moment to regain her strength. He lowered her to the nearest chair and dropped his arms to his side, her body shuddered with tears; eyes cast to the floor. His voice was low, quiet, and filled with regret and remorse. He heard himself struggle to whisper. "Are you hurt?" His voice racked with self-loathing and disgust at a person he did not recognise.

"No," her shattered voice softly answered.

He stared at the tiny figure, arms stiff, both hands grasping the seat of the chair, tears trickling to her lap. He stood over her, filled with self-hate for causing so much torment. He made vows to protect her, and within a heartbeat, he had destroyed all the valour he had ever shown. He had allowed fear and anger to control him and was not certain how or if she could forgive him. Or worse, if he could forgive himself. Jack raked his hand through his hair one last time, stood straight, opened the door, and walked out. Leaving her sitting alone in the empty stable.

It took Olivia a moment to gather herself. Jack had never spoken to her with so much wrath, and when he had grabbed her, she was not at all sure what rage was, but assuredly that had been it.

Hands shaking, she removed her gloves. Placing them on top of one another, she stood, wiping the tears from her eyes, attempting to regain her composure. He had not hurt her; she'd known he never would.

But as she thought about what had transpired, he had shocked her. She barely remembered him clutching her to his body, and he had kissed her… but why?

As she left the stable, she recalled the confrontation and was vexed by his anger. Olivia had known he would be agitated. He had been before, but not like this. Instead of being proud of her success, he was furious and enraged. As she approached the back entry, she was trudging along, her arms swinging angrily, brow furrowed, and huffing. The more she thought about it, the more ill-tempered she became.

"How dare him walk out on me without a word," she muttered, knowing full well she had been more than ready for him to take his leave. "Not one word, raked his bloody hand through his hair and walked out." She mumbled. The mishap with the jump was over. She and Spartan were unhurt. Why on Earth would he be so angry?

Olivia took the back stairs to the family wing muttering unladylike comments under her breath.

What happened to his insouciant, devil-may-care disposition? Olivia was becoming distressed, deciding her anxiety was due to her exhaustion and dusty attire. The sticky, clammy riding habit was causing her discomfort. Upon entering her chamber, she met her maid.

"I am hot and damp. Get me out of this horrid thing." She snapped.

"I took the liberty of preparing your bath," Sarah assured her.

Her maid removed the sweaty riding habit that clung to Olivia's body as if it were fused and tossed it to the floor. The chambermaid delivered the final water for her bath. Olivia stepped into the warm liquid, then promptly and deliberately submerged under the warmth of the water, head, and hair.

"Lady Olivia," Sarah gasped and in sheer panic, reached for her, "Whatever are you doing?"

The maid pulled her head from the bath. The startling grip caused Olivia to swallow a deal of water, emerging coughing and choking. Sarah undeniably disturbed by the behaviour.

"Miss!" Olivia cleared her throat and found her voice.

"I am fine. Only exasperated. It seemed appropriate to drown myself," She tried to explain and calm her maid, who was noticeably distraught.

"My goodness, whatever could be upsetting you so?" Sarah, indeed, was shaken.

"It is nothing. We only need to put me together for the evening. I must appear at my best from head to toe. I assure you I am perfectly fine, it is nothing a handsome gown, and the perfect coiffeur will not repair."

Her dunk in the tub and near choking had somewhat cleared her mind. She would arrive at the party aglow and remorseful, and all would be forgiven. She surmised this in her own immature mind. The viscount was merely overwhelmed with responsibilities. Otherwise, he would not have been so out of sorts.

Olivia had chosen a pale pink silk gown with an empire bodice and square neckline. The neckline was trimmed with white lace and hemmed with pink tassels. The sleeves were of the newest Paris fashion, short and puffed, along with matching long pale pink cotton gloves. Her slippers were pink, adorned with a small rhinestone shoe buckle. A short wrap cape was sewn to coordinate the gown. It crossed at the bodice with button fasteners at the shoulders to complete the ensemble.

Once again, Sarah masterfully piled the flaxen curls atop Olivia's head with pink satin ribbon weaved throughout and soft ringlets framing her face.

Little more than a few hours ago, she had been dusty, dirty, and clammy. Her flaxen locks were sticky with unladylike perspiration. Now unrecognisable from that girl, she stared into the glass.

"Oh!" she cried, startled, "is this me? I hardly recognise myself."

"It is you! But you are no longer a girl, milady. You are indeed a woman."

She swished her gown one way and then the other. "I cannot believe it's me," she giggled in astonishment.

"I hope my aunt and uncle approve."

"I am certain they will."

"And…" she paused, "I do hope Lord Andovir will find me properly sophisticated and polished."

Olivia was humbled by her appearance. She studied the reflection, astonishingly aware of what Jack must see. While she felt like a little girl, she no longer presented as one. For the first time in the finery of a lady, she saw a young woman. She remembered the disappointment in Jack's eyes. It caused her heart to race. His remarks regarding her behaviour were telling. She stopped moving, lost in reflection. This was indeed no child or even an insolent young girl.

The way Jack had reacted to her the day of his arrival, commenting on how different she seemed. Recalling the fury in his eyes when he lost his temper in the stable. Olivia began to comprehend; this was what Jack saw when he looked at her.

Oh God, she must speak with him. She prayed tonight he would see her as she now saw herself. She could be a lady, and he could be proud of her again, and maybe, just maybe, she could be… It was… it was too much to believe.

Olivia had tears in her eyes as she remembered the many times Jack had reminded her—*you were born to be a lady. Never forget that!*

Few memories remained of her parents, but she knew her father was an earl and her mother's father a duke. She was to become a fine young lady and marry well, but she was also to be happy. At this moment, happy she was not. She had disappointed her closest and dearest companion and hurt him with her selfishness… but he had kissed her. She blushed, thinking of his kiss, the embrace. She touched her lips, and her heart skipped a beat as her face grew hot and pink. Oh, God!

CHAPTER 5

Jack paused in front of his mother's bedchamber; taking a deep breath, he knocked softly. Christina opened the door and was startled to see the viscount.

"Christina, if my mother has a moment," Jack stated quietly.

The maid looked at his haggard face and weary posture. She had served the countess since the viscount was a boy and knew she would see her son without delay. She opened the door wide, allowing him entrance.

"I'll let milady know you are here."

Leaning against the dark wainscot wall, he exhaled the breath he had only just realised he was holding.

"Jack, I do not believe I have seen you in my bedchamber since you were a little boy."

The countess swept into the sitting room; her initial smile quickly vanished. She watched as the slumped figure against the bedroom façade pushed himself from the mahogany panel. A woman in her late forties, she was still quite lovely. Her stature was one of consequence, aware of propriety but never standing upon it with her family. Tonight, her coiffure, lightly powdered to mask the newly forming grey, was intricate. Her dress was adorned with crystals, silk, and ribbons. A whiff of lilacs reminiscent of his childhood passed a brief smile across his lips.

"It can wait," he hesitated. It could not, but…

"Nonsense. I am never too busy for you, dear." Seeing he was troubled; she patted the seat of the small sofa as she sat.

The countess watched his ashen face, as he walked across the floor. "Christina has turned your mother out well tonight, has she not?"

"Indeed, Mother, you look beautiful... as always," he placed a light kiss on her cheek.

"You are very quiet and look as if you carry the weight of the world on your shoulders."

The young viscount cleared his throat. She sensed apprehension and quietened, allowing him to gather his thoughts.

"I wanted to make you aware, I will be leaving first thing in the morning."

The countess held her composure and said nothing, collecting her own thoughts, before addressing her son. "What has happened? You were to accompany us to London. You have not quarrelled with your father?" she hesitated.

"Pray no," he assured her. "I spoke with him earlier; he understands, it seems better than I, there is no explanation, it's only..."

Taking his mother's hand, wishing, childishly, it had not been gloved. He desired a mother's comfort but was too old to expect it.

She would not understand, and how could he explain something he did not yet accept? Searching his eyes, she perceived the pain and confusion in them.

"Well, I am confused and unhappy, but…?" She checked herself, fighting every instinct to question further.

"I must return to London. I regret leaving, but I know I cannot stay." He said stoically.

Inhaling a deep breath, he lifted sad and vexed eyes to hers, he was expecting a great deal of his mother to embrace his sudden departure without explanation.

"I can only apologise and hope you will someday forgive my impertinence. I will stay for the ball, not to cause you embarrassment. Please forgive your disgracious son," he lowered his head.

She knew her son was confused and hurting. She would ask no more. Disappointed, she quickly removed her gloves and took his hand in hers.

Jack suddenly felt five years old and wished he could curl into her arms and bury his face in them.

"My heart is broken, but not for me but for you." She said.

His mother patted and then, released his hand. "Very well, make an appearance tonight, and I will see you in London."

"You never cease to amaze me." He stood, kissed her hand, and took his leave.

As he quietly quit the room, his mother stared at the closed door and wondered if she would indeed see him in London.

***

The main saloon was filled with guests as Lady Olivia

approached the main staircase leading to the grand entry hall to make her first appearance in society. Lord and Lady Birkshire, sensing her presence, turned, and peered up in approval. She descended the staircase, and the earl stepped forward, extending his arm,

She felt a rush of calm exhilaration overwhelm her as she positioned her gloved hand on the forearm of the Earl of Birkshire. He placed his free hand over hers and squeezed with assurance. "You look radiant, my dear."

Olivia understood the magnitude of the moment... her moment. She took the final few steps into the ballroom, leading to her new life.

Lord Birkshire paused, holding tightly to Olivia's arm, as she stood at the top of the grand entrance into the sunken ballroom, unable to breathe. The elegantly dressed guests turned to face her and the earl. She peered around the room at the unknown and unrecognisable, but without a doubt, representatives of London's finest houses. She searched for a familiar face and found only three. At the far end of the long room, dressed in their finest, standing side by side. Each holding stemware filled with France's finest champagne, the three lifted their glasses to her in unison, but only one with the elegance of a prince deeply bowed...Viscount Andovir.

When they reached the floor, without incident, the earl smiled and led her toward the orchestra, taking their place for the quadrille. The orchestra struck the first note. He bowed to her, she to him, and to their respective corners. The earl took her hands in his, and Olivia, with his lead, took her first step dancing at an assembly. The young miss epitomised the belle of the ball. Favoured for every dance, she was graceful, her manner and politeness exquisite. Lady Birkshire turned to Lord Birkshire expressing her delight and declared Olivia ready for her first London season.

Lord Sheffield and Lord Worthington, enchanted with her transformation, quickly secured dances. She was noticeably seen in the company of one or the other throughout the evening. Pleased, Lord Birkshire, having profound respect for both families, expressed his desire to see them calling on his ward in London. He laughed and commented, you know she could do worse than a duke.

Lady Birkshire grinned and agreed, commenting she thought it would please Jack if Olivia were to be agreeable with one of his close friends. In raptures regarding the success and comportment of her ward, her husband's rigidity to her comment went unnoticed.

"Olivia, when will you be arriving in London?" Sheffield handed her a crystal flute filled with lemonade.

"Thank you, my lord." Lowering her eyes as she accepted the glass, then fluttered her lashes open to peer into Lord Sheffield's eyes. "It is my lord?" She responded. Meeting her eyes with his own, felt his heart and breath catch.

"I know you are the heir and yet a Marquess, but when you assume the dukedom, you will be your grace, correct." A blush rose to her cheeks, unsure whether she was flirting or appearing quite ridiculous. She felt the latter until...

"I – I beg your pardon," James choked, mesmerised by the crystal blue eyes, and fluttering long dark lashes she had turned upon him. Without warning, he found himself unnerved. The hoyden he'd helped bait fishhooks and the equestrian who had eaten away at his masculinity had disappeared. He was now lost in the intensity of those liquid blue eyes and the irresistible apparition of a young lady of seduction and charm. James, The Marquess of Sheffield, seemed to have lost his God given ability to comprehend the language to which he was born.

"Your title," Olivia repeated, quite at ease with her long-time friend, "when you assume the dukedom, you will be addressed, your grace, is that not correct?"

He was captivated by the cocoon that had emerged into a beautiful butterfly right in front of him. He had a new appreciation for this chameleon. Finally, he comprehended not only her question but her attempts at flirting. The effects of her charm and the simplicity of her request had left him feeling rather stupid.

"Just so!" Slightly shaking his head, managing to gather his wits. "However, I thought it agreed we were to call one another by our Christian names." Quickly recovering his rakish grin.

"Pray, oblige me as I prepare for London. I am doubtful to meet those who will be old friends." Olivia's long eyelashes swept across the tops of her cheeks in a slow blink.

Good God! A slight dizziness raced through Sheffield's head. Her attempt at a small flirtation had knocked him quite off his game. As he took her arm, leading her to the dance floor, he tried to determine how much of this evening he would not be sharing with his best friend.

He was the only man in the room aware of the madness affecting his friend. The friendship which placed him in the position to watch the theatre unfold, was now threatening to be his own undoing. This was to be nothing more than a bit of fun, ensuring the young lady easily made her debut into the world of high society. However, it suddenly occurred to him he should watch his own heart. This young miss was about to steal it, along with the affection of every other male in the country of England and beyond. He was unable to resist the thought; this fair maiden would make a fine and proud duchess. Then prayed he could successfully keep his heart from falling for this incomparable. He bowed to Olivia and swept her away in a lively country dance.

CHAPTER 6

The dusty road to London had been dampened by a light rain. The precise amount to quiet the dirt, while simultaneously preventing the weight of mud-caked hooves to impede the three bits of blood, which bore the top sawyers of the prestigious Four-Horse Club to London.

"Not a bad ride today?" Sheffield offered his opinion to anyone who might care to listen.

"I find it quite enjoyable. The rain settled the dust, along with amiable temperatures," Worthington agreed.

Lord Andovir said nothing. He hadn't uttered a word since the trio left the Birkshire House gate. Any attempt to engage him was met with silence.

"We must be dead bores!" Worthington cocked his head toward the quiet rider.

"Does he know we are riding along with him?" Sheffield's words were spoken rather loudly.

"Doubtful!" Worthington returned.

"I say, old boy." Sheffield trying to rouse him. "Andovir, I say, are we quite so disagreeable?"

Andovir acknowledged the direct address. "Beg pardon! Not the thing today, a dead bore, I am afraid."

"Just so! He's not deaf, Worth, just ignoring us." Sheffield smirked. "Says much about our station, does it not."

"Indeed, I suppose we should be thankful our fathers are in good health. More time to improve upon our ducal command!" Worthington retorted.

"Indeed!" Sheffield snorted. "A quizzing glass, is the thing with Ratcliff, works every time for the duke. All he must do is curl his gnarly fingers about it, and silence."

"True, my father the same, but I dare say, I thought we were trying to draw him out, a quizzing glass is not required for Andovir's silence," Worthington reminded.

The viscount gave his friends a half smile. The two shrugged, resolving the aberrant behaviour, the blue megrims. The three rode in silence until the toll gate came into view. Sheffield cleared the remuneration for all three to Mayfair, handing the tickets round as they waited in silence for the pikeman to open the gate.

Andovir was still dwelling on his contemptible actions of withdrawing from home, whether borne of honour or cowardness. However, his removal from Olivia's presence was necessary. The uncontrolled anger, out of character for the viscount, angst him. She had always been coltish but never reckless. He blamed himself for encouraging her behaviour throughout her life, finding the precocious actions fun and cute for a child of ten. Then he thought of the broken little girl of six, the one lost and alone. Jack's heart began to ache as he recalled those horrid days. He was at Eaton when he received the news.

***

Jack was about to make his way to the breakfast hall when he was summoned by the headmaster. He scratched his head, "what now?"

"Come in and close the door." Headmaster Joseph Goodall

motioned.

Goodall's reputation of being a mild disciplinarian had been tested by the viscount, and his now sober countenance did nothing to ease the young lord.

"I received a letter from your father."

"Sir?" Andovir said startled.

Mr. Goodall cleared his throat. "He is well, as is your mother. I will commence with the missive." Jack sat erect and attentive as the provost began.

"It is with the deepest regret notification is by currier. It is with utmost haste my son; Lord John Norrys is to return to Birkshire House."

The headmaster paused and looked up at Jack. Seeing the confusion in the boy's eyes, he continued. "Lord and Lady Sinclair were lost in a carriage accident. Please inform him Olivia is safe. Your servant, etc., etc." The headmaster ceased and lowered the note to his desk.

The room was deafeningly quiet, and the young viscount slumped in his chair motionless. He removed his handkerchief, straightened it, and wiped his face. "My apologies, sir," Jack quiesced. Unsure how an eleven-year-old boy was to respond, he only nodded, stood, and before taking his leave, turned to the headmaster.

"I must go to my mother and..." he gulped before dizzily grabbing the back of the chair.

"Are you quite, all right?" Goodall enquired.

"Yes, sir," he paused. Lacking the understanding of such pain, how was he to protect little Olivia from this?

***

"I beg pardon?" Jack muttered, realising he had been woolgathering again.

"Should we not be coming to Maidenhead and The Bear soon?" Sheffield said again.

Jack pulled out his pocket watch, scanning the late evening sky, agreeing it should not be much farther. They would allow the horses to rest, feed, and water. The men would enjoy a night's meal, drink, and rest.

They settled the horses with the ostler, procured rooms at The Bear and enjoyed a meal in the tavern across the road. Sheffield and Worthington talked of nothing but the weekend party and the events awaiting in Town. They made every attempt to engage their friend but were met with silence. Even an upcoming dinner at the Carlton House did nothing to gain his attention. Another round of ale was ordered, and neither man was surprised when Andovir declined, announcing he would see them at breakfast.

Crossing the dusty road and making his way to the well-established coaching Inn, he overheard a little girl crying. She was sobbing and pleading with her mama to take her home. It appeared to be the child's first journey, with little comprehension of a short visit and distressed of never returning home. He entered his room, leaving the suffering little girl and the mother's useless explanation behind.

He settled into the freshly scented linens, hopeful of rest. His mind wandered back to the little girl's tears. It was dreadful to witness such anguish. His eyelids became heavy from the long day of travel, and this little girl's distress was soon overtaken by dreams of more than a decade before.

***

Jack walked the quiet halls of his once cheerful home, now filled with sorrow. His mother, who had collapsed at the loss of her dearest friend, lay in her bedchamber for weeks remembering nothing, completely lost in sorrow and grief.

The sight of Olivia was heart-breaking; tiny blue eyes filled with constant tears streaming down tiny cheeks, face pale, crushed in sadness. Her nights were filled with walking night terrors, her body drenched in sweat, screaming for her mother, her father, her Aunt Annabelle, all those she could no longer see or touch. Awake, she shrieked and begged to see her aunt, fearing she too had gone away and there was no one left to hold her.

Jack's dream recalled the horrors that had been lessened by the passage of time. He was tossing and turning, the stress and misery trying to wake his body, but the unconscious images continued.

Weeks passed, and there was little change in the suffering of either. Anger and hateful behaviour had taken over the once precious little girl, her tantrums affecting the entire household, already in chaos.

Seated in the family hallway, Jack watched as Olivia descended the stairs with her nurse. Reaching the second floor, she jerked away, running to his mother's bedchamber. Her screams deafening as she passed Jack, taking no notice of him.

He jumped to his feet and followed behind. Her tiny hands grabbed the knob, slinging the heavy door open with little effort. Olivia froze at the sight of the woman lying motionless between the 4-posts. Jack halted behind, not uttering a word, or reaching out to her.

Olivia quietly and slowly drew closer to the bed and

whispered his mother's name with so much grief in her voice he would never forget it. His heart was breaking, but he made no effort to stop her, only watching in silence, believing whatever she was doing was needed. And maybe, it was something his mother might need as well. Olivia reaching the bedside, began to weep. She could barely see over the tall mattress at the lifeless figure.

Jack perceiving a presence, turned his head to observe the nurse with hands clasped to her mouth. He put his finger to his lips, and she nodded as they both stood quietly watching the little girl try in vain to reach the woman.

The little eyes searched the frame heeding the wide wooden side rail, placed a tiny foot atop and tugged at the cover, pulling with all her might, and found balance with a knee onto the bed and pushed into the feathered mattress. She crawled next to the unaffected figure, snuggled lengthwise and lay her head on the female's chest, sobbing softly.

Jack saw his mother move for the first time in weeks. He saw her shift position. She raised her head, turned, and embraced Olivia, cuddling her to her breast. She uttered her first words since the accident. The nurse gasped and quickly smothered her sound.

Both watched in awe as Annabelle kissed the little girl's hair, her forehead and then her tiny cheek. "Oh darling, Aunt Annabelle has you. She has you, and she will never, ever let you go. Do you hear me, Olivia?"

Jack had never heard a voice so filled with anguish and sorrow, but the little girl's head nodded in response. His mother then whispered words he would never forget.

"Marian, I promise, I promise." His mother manoeuvred the tiny creature closer and laid the blonde head on her shoulder. A sense of peace spread over Jack as they fell asleep.

The nurse put her hand on Jack's shoulder and motioned him to come away with her, softly closing the door.

At the landing of the second floor, Jack sat on the step and glanced back toward his mother's door, then cradled his head in his hands and closed his eyes.

***

Jack awoke sheets drenched in sweat, and his pillow held evidence of tears he had not cried in years, recalling his promise made on those stairs. He had pledged his own oath to Olivia. He promised, no matter, to take care and watch over her, always.

CHAPTER 7

The bedchamber topsy turvy, Olivia slung open another drawer stretching her arm to the far back, but nothing. She threw open the small drawers below the mirror, empty. She rushed around in frustration. Where had she hidden them? She could not, would not, leave without them. She had searched her escritoire, her armoire, and her chest. The potpourri mixture of wood, flowers and spices filled the room from the constant manipulation of the furniture, and she was growing agitated.

Equipages loaded with trunks, portmanteaus and ban boxes, along with weary grooms holding the heads of the impatient horses, waited nervously in the drive. Word from the foyer had been sent three times; the caravan awaited her. But her precious letters? Those she had kept tied in the small ribbon that had grown soft and faded with time were gone.

Once more, she examined the bottom drawer, the hiding place that had not changed in ten years. Olivia knelt on the Aubusson carpet and pulled the bottom drawer, swelled from the recent rain. It tugged against her. In frustration, she jerked, and the drawer stopped just above her knees. Reaching as far as her arm would extend, she felt a wisp of tiny binding.

Stretching and wiggling each digit, she wrapped two fingers around the loop of ribbon, gently pulling until the bundle relented. The letters tightly secured were stacked, and tied in a pale blue ribbon, a gift on her seventh birthday, sapphire blue then, to match her eyes, he had told her. She tucked them into her reticule, patting the bag. Jumping to her feet, she headed off, stopping and glancing around the room with a sombre smile. She was leaving this room a child but would not return as one. Her breath caught, and she swallowed hard at the memories. A tear attempted to escape, but she brushed it away, smiled and quietly closed the door.

"I am coming, I am coming," She cried as she ran to the stairs.

Sarah waiting there, snatched the reticule. "I will take your bag Miss Olivia, or you shall never make it down the staircase in one piece."

"Do protect it with your life." She called as she flew down the stairs. "I am here!" She called breathlessly.

"Slow down, my child. I would like you in one piece," Lord Birkshire cautioned and rolled his eyes.

Graham, attempting to hide a grin, watched as his lordship shook his head, smiling as the young girl dashed by, saying her goodbyes. The earl turned to the old butler accepting his hat, coat, and cane and whispered. "Do say a prayer, Graham. I fear I shall need it. They will be the death of me before I am to return," he said, giving the old butler a wink.

***

The following afternoon, they arrived at Birkshire Place, the London home of the Earl and Countess of Birkshire. The symmetrical design of elegant Greek architecture was constructed of brick and covered in stucco. The exterior was embellished with marble pilasters, and the exterior corners adorned with decorative friezes and cornices, with horizontal bands of marble near the roof line. A cascading flight of steps rose to the massive front entry masking the basement below. The front façade consisted of narrow windows exclusive to the sides, with bay windows on the second floor. The third and fourth floors were enhanced with double glass doors opening onto small balconies.

Preparation for the family's arrival had been underway for weeks by the permanent staff. The four-story dwelling was dusted top to bottom, Holland covers removed from furniture and large framed wall paintings conveyed from storage. The morning of arrival, fires were lit in the bedchambers to be occupied. On the main level, drawing rooms, the family dining area, the library, and in the Earl's study, hearths were aglow to rid the dampness.

The large town coach came to a halt in front, and the staff graced both sides of the entry steps. Several maids straightened their skirts and aprons, their arrival just in time after scurrying out the door.

Her ladyship smiled, remembering the scruffy little boy around the block, who, at the sight of the Birkshire crest, dashed through the alleyway at a dead run. She imagined a shilling waiting in Gray's white-gloved hand as he snatched it and took off laughing down the street. The Butler, Alexander Gray, standing tall and stately, as a footman let down the coach's step.

"My Lordship, my Ladyship." Gray addressed them in an austere monotone and bowed.

Olivia winced at the formal manners rarely observed at the country house. There were bows and curtsies, not mere nods from the estate staff. Even those coming from the country estate held to a higher standard of formality in London.

Sarah quietly giggled as Olivia sighed at the protocol and propriety. Her mistress would do well here, even if she did not believe it yet.

The butler assisting in the removal of coats, hats, and gloves proudly watched as Lady Birkshire paused in the grand foyer, tilting her head to gaze at the walls and three-story ceiling. She genuinely loved this house, its pomp and circumstance, the furnishings, the centuries-old paintings. It was truly magnificent. She slowly turned in place, admiring every inch, only snapping from her trance at the sight of Mrs Grimes, the housekeeper. A congenial woman in her mid-forties employed at Birkshire Place as a chambermaid at sixteen. She was now the housekeeper of seven years. After more than five and twenty years, her efficiency and knowledge were eclipsed only by her loyalty to the family.

"How are you, Mrs Grimes?"

"Very well, my lady. I hope you will find everything in order."

"I have no doubt of it, Mrs Grimes." Annabelle took the housekeeper's hand and squeezed it affectionately. "It is nice to be back."

The housekeeper smiled. There were few in the aristocracy who treated their staff with such warmth and generosity. With a happy heart, she followed her ladyship down the hallway to the library for last-minute changes and instructions, knowing how fortunate she was to have the honour of serving this family.

Olivia entered the vestibule; the sheer beauty of the place captivated her. She had not been here since she was a child. She stared at the paintings and admired the fresh-cut flowers that filled the antique vases placed with precision on the Demilune entry tables. She breathed in the aromatic fragrance; it was obvious the flowers had been carefully chosen that morning. Their light, sweet, and touch of citrus aroma filled the entrance hall.

Olivia was twisting like a ballerina, soaking in the beauty and magic around her, as she made her way up the stairs into the small drawing room. Gray interrupted her delightful and childlike wonderment, clearing his throat.

"Yes," she said softly. Her cheeks were a bit pink from being caught whirling about the room.

"May I take your cloak and inquire if you would like tea? Lord Birkshire will be in his study and Lady Birkshire in the library."

"Yes, please," she answered timidly.

Embarrassed at being caught dancing and mindlessly retaining her riding cloak in the drawing room, she scolded herself, 'what a great beginning,' she thought.

Gray assisted her off with her cloak and quietly exited, leaving the doors slightly open. She returned to the exploration of the room. Nothing was casual here; everything was of the finest quality.

She strolled from one window to the next, her hand lightly gliding across the upholstered furnishings and peering at the different views from the windows overlooking Park Lane. Some things remembered, but most she did not.

Satisfied with her tour, she took a seat on the sofa, stretching both arms across the back and stretched her legs in an unladylike and rebellious fashion. She giggled; she could be a little hoydenish here if no one were watching. She heard someone coming, quickly straightening, and adjusting the linen of her skirt.

It was only a footman bringing tea. She relaxed and sighed.

"Pardon, milady, the cook wishes you to know sweet biscuits will be ready shortly."

She was quite hungry after the two-day journey, never caring for the food at the Inns, even at The Bear, but she had been spoiled by the Birkshire cook.

"My precious Emma, I knew she would have them ready upon our arrival." Speaking only to herself.

Olivia was quite satisfied with her condition, sitting on the sofa with her tea awaiting fresh biscuits.

She was feeling grand and happy, quietly listening to footmen scurrying up the stairs with trunks and baggage. She could hear Christina and Sarah giving orders as they monitored trunks and portmanteaus. She giggled, overhearing Baxter, his lordship's valet barking orders. He sounded so rough and demanding when he spoke, but she knew better. The kindly old gentleman accepted nothing less than perfection for the lord of the manor, even if were to be for only a day or two.

She enjoyed being a spectator as the energy of a full house came to life. She attempted to relax, thinking this was to be exciting. Tomorrow, they would visit the modiste for fittings. There were ball gowns, theatre gowns, walking, morning and day dresses, milliners for gloves and the slipper makers. A visit to Miss Starke, the milliner on Conduit Street, for bonnets, new ones must be procured for rides and promenades in the park. Her aunt had also promised a visit to Lock's. Technically, a men's hat shop, but it was where ladies could buy a proper hat for their riding habit.

Olivia's thoughts were thoroughly occupied with the details of the next few days. Chortling to herself, a figure entered the room. She sensed it and glanced up to see the footman deliver Emma's promised treats. Olivia sat her teacup on a nearby table and proceeded to the marble top credenza holding a silver platter filled with confections. She smiled at the footman, who nodded, bowed, and excused himself while Olivia surveyed the plate and its selections.

"My goodness," she muttered, "Emma must be thrilled to be in London."

There were cream and chocolate *petite duchesse*, buttered pasted puffs and jam-filled tarts. Overwhelmed with choices, she finally settled on a strawberry tart. As she bit into the morsel, she made a gratifying noise, leaving a bit of jam at the corner of her mouth.

Alone in the parlour announced, "Oh, Emma, you have outdone yourself," barely audible with the confection filling the space and delighting her taste buds.

"You should tell her so. She adores compliments, you know," came a voice from near the entry.

Olivia nearly choked on the pastry and whirled to see a familiar figure leaning against the wall, just inside the doorway. A handful of fruit tart half in, half out of her mouth and jam lingering on the corner of her lips, she quickly removed the tart, swallowed hard and for a moment was at a loss for words.

The viscount was leaning casually against the door, arms and legs crossed with the toe of one top boot resting on the other. He had slipped in with the footman, quietly watching her childish examination of pastries. How could he ever be angry with this delightful creature? At this moment, he could not imagine. Straightening his stature, he walked directly toward her, his gaze never leaving her.

Olivia, unable to take her eyes from his, watched his approach. Frozen in place, her heart was racing. He had been viciously angry at their last encounter, leaving for London without a word. She stood like a statue, arm bent with a half-eaten tart still in her hand, strawberry jam on her lips.

Jack was smiling as he drew nearer but stopped suddenly. He had been heading toward her with such desire and hope of redemption. The amount of passion and yearning startled him and caught him off-guard. He had wanted to grab her, take her in his arms and kiss the jam from her lips. He took a deep breath. What the devil was wrong with him? These sudden outbursts of unhealthy emotions had to be controlled.

Both stood in silence, staring at one another. Then as if a dam burst between them, in unison, blurted, "I am sorry!"

Olivia found the tart still in her hand, dropped it to the small side plate and quickly brushed her fingers against the napkin alongside it. She dashed around the table with unbridled affection, threw her arms around his neck, raised herself as high as she could on her toes and kissed his cheek. There were tears in her eyes, and they trickled down her face, now mixing with the jam at the edge of her mouth.

"Oh," tasting the salty mixture of jam and tears on her lips, "I am a mess." Olivia reached for the serviette just as Jack felt the sticky mess on his own cheek and began to laugh. He could not help but remember his homecoming, wanting to avoid another mishap.

"Oh, no, no, no, let me have that." Snatching the cloth from her hand, placed one hand on her shoulder as he wiped the corner of her lips right at the point where they met. He was so gentle as he blotted and wiped the soft corners. She looked up, his face so intent as he masterfully wiped away the sticky mess.

Feeling those blue eyes focused on his, dropped his own to hers. A bolt of electricity shot through Olivia. Snapping her gaping mouth shut, she lowered her gaze. He released her shoulders, turning the serviette and wiping the mixture of tears and jam from his cheek.

Neither wanted to be the first to move, both missing their childhood intimacy and secrets once shared.

Focused on a wall hanging, unable to face him, compunction prompted Olivia.

"I have been miserable. I had planned to apologise the very next day, but when Aunt Annabelle said you had gone, I was inconsolable. I acted abominably, rude…"

"Reckless, irresponsible and thoughtless," Jack broke in, smiling.

She turned her eyes to him and nodded in agreement. She saw his smile, but she remained embarrassed and lowered them.

"It was the reason I left so quickly. But I should never have done so."

"I suppose it was also the reason you did not dance with me." She cut in but did not look at him.

"I had never been so angry with you, or out of control. I only thought to put distance between us. But I should not have done so. At least not without saying goodbye."

She raised her eyes to see the shame on his face. She knew him too well. He had not meant to be hurtful. Her light touch on his arm assured him she knew of it. Her own actions had brought the same shame. He took her arm, leading her to the sofa. The uncomfortable but honest truths were always their deepest bond.

"Olivia, this is not going to be easy. I do not know how to befriend a fully-grown young woman."

Long lashes fluttering open she innocently replied. "Well, I do not…exactly know… how to be a fully-grown young woman."

Jack burst into laughter. She always had a way of making his difficult moments seem so ridiculous and silly. He wrapped his arm around her, and for the first time since he returned to

England, he felt the sibling affection they had always shared. She was the most adorable thing he had ever laid his eyes upon, and she had no idea the effect it had on him. What a success she was going to be in her first season. Untouched by prudish manners and the haughty, pretentiousness of the young ladies brought up in London, who honed it as well-bred. The young bucks were going to fancy her freshness and honesty.

Jack promised to take her riding in the park and to the places she had heard about as a child. She looked to him as an older brother and confidant, and he must not forget his place. He could not bear to lose any part of her due to his uncontrolled affection. He had not untangled the raw emotions he had discovered but clearly understood he loved her too much and had to forget the unexplained desire and in time be satisfied with a sibling bond. The one thing they both knew with certainty… they needed one another.

CHAPTER 8

Viscount Andovir stepped off his curricle in front of the stately manor, glancing at its façade reflecting upon the Birkshire legacy which he was borne. He knew every room and passageway throughout the hallowed halls from childhood play. Someday, he would be responsible for not only the house but the staff dependent upon it for their livelihood. The responsibilities of his father sometimes overwhelmed him, but those same thoughts also seemed to keep him grounded. He smiled turning back to the sporty carriage and offered his hand to Olivia.

Taking his offer, she replied sarcastically, "I thought for a moment you had forgotten me."

"Never, my lady." His eyes sparkled with undeniable charm. Assisting her to the pavement, he watched as she brushed the muslin folds of her walking dress, making sure each one was in its place.

He offered his arm. "I was only thinking of childish games played in the halls of this old mansion."

"You mean chasing me down them, trying to pull my pigtails."

They both chuckled at the memories. "Until your mama snatched me up by the collar, reminding me you were a tiny little lady and should not be made to run down vestibules or any other open area."

"I do not think she would have been pleased with many of the things we did as children." Olivia chortled.

"Most likely not." He chuckled, remembering the long-ago crawls through the small spaces, exploring the attic, only having to explain later how four-year-old, little miss Olivia's dress had gotten so very dusty; even with hoydenish conduct, her dress was always of utmost concern.

"I love exploring London with you; Hyde Park is so lovely, and that balloon ascension today, oh my goodness," she clasped her hand to her chest, "it was exhaustingly exciting. I dare say, I almost lost my breath as they released the ropes. I could never be so brave." Olivia said, shaking her head.

"I told you London was exciting, and there is far more to see. We have only begun to see the sights."

Jack had taken her on several excursions about London. He could think of many reasons he had done so but tried not to dwell on the most significant. He had almost forgotten their ease of one another and the joy of her company. He was determined to become acquainted with this delightful half-woman/half-child she had become.

Their childhood was buried in a long-ago past, and they were desperate to maintain their relationship. The imbalance of the years between them had caused far too much pain recently, and they resolved to find a companionship worthy of two children, who had long since passed through childhood.

Jack discovered she was far brighter and astute than she had claimed. Lessons in his absence had done far more than prepare her for entry into London's society. Her knowledge of England's history was quite shocking, only eclipsed by her loquacious excitement of sharing it.

Upon their visit to the Tower of London, she was quite animated. Fascinated, she prattled throughout, "The White Tower was built in 1078 by King William II, well, it was actually designed and built by Gundolf of Rochester, a Norman Bishop, and The Bell Tower in 1190 to warn of impending attacks. The Wardrobe Tower was finished in 1199 for the Royal Garments and Crown Jewels. Then in 1209, King Henry III constructed the Wakefield and Lanthorn Towers, and King Edward I constructed the mint. That is why the Yeomen Warders are here."

"You mean the Beefeaters?" The viscount interjected as she became a walking book of knowledge.

"How common of you." She retorted, giggling, "Only you would give reference to the Italians. I suppose they are proud of their contribution to the label."

"You know there was a great deal of torture inflicted here and executions."

"Not really, so very much torture." She stated with great authority. "Actually, the wealthy and nobility could bring their own servants. King John Balliol was allowed to bring his servants, hunting dogs and even his wife before he was exiled to France in 1299.

"Good God, woman, you've become a virtual bluestocking!"

"I have not!" She whispered emphatically, "keep your voice down, and for goodness' sake, do not let Aunt Annabelle here you call me that. Once, I told her about the beheadings, specifically Henry VIII's wives, Anne Boleyn in 1536 and Catherine Howard in 1542, and she nearly swooned… literally." She stated, quite emphatically. "Then she proceeded to instruct me in the virtues of a proper lady, and one did not speak of such vulgarities. I stopped talking of the history lessons by my governess, who seemed to like the macabre and shared many of the tragedies in our history."

"Oh God, I can just imagine Mother's face when you spoke of Henry VIII's wives stepping up to the block." Andovir nearly bent with laughter, and Olivia softly chortled.

"I think it is time I take you home. How about a stop at Gunter's?"

"Oh, I would like that above all things."

A few days later, he escorted her to Egyptian Hall to see William Bullock's collection of animals in their natural habitat. As they entered the passage to the Pantherion, the viscount was again entertained by Olivia's enthusiasm and naiveté.

"How fascinating. I feel as if we are in a real cave, do you not?" She looked up at him, eyes wide.

"Indeed, gazing at the rocky surface of the walls, you can almost feel the nippy feel of the inside of a cold, dark cave." He said mocking her, but she took no notice.

"Makes me shiver thinking of it." Just as she was rubbing her upper arms, the cave-like hallway opened to a tropical forest filled with exotic plants and preserved animals, along with the painted backdrops appearing almost real.

"Oh, my heavens!" Olivia was bewildered at how anyone could recreate such an environment so lifelike and natural. However, her love of animals left her with mixed emotions regarding the displays.

There was a lively conversation on the carriage ride back to Birkshire Place regarding the preserved elephants, rhinos, and giraffes, along with the exotic birds and fish. However, she was thoroughly fascinated by and rattled on about Bullock's ethnography collections, how the discovery of weapons, costumes and other artefacts could provide so very much information regarding cultures long since passed. Jack realised how much of her life he had missed.

As always, their outings ended at Gunter's confectioner's shop. In fact, she had become a regular at #7 Berkely Square every afternoon, the flavoured ice becoming her favourite treat.

The viscount's double life, however, was beginning to show signs of wearing on him. It was difficult being principled and respectable by day, only to be drawn into the ignoble and immoral life with his friends until the wee hours of the morning.

With the responsibilities toward Olivia, he no longer had the pleasure of sleeping until three in the afternoon. He must make changes soon. Justifying, he had escorted her to all the promised venues and frequented Hyde Park, ensuring her comfort and proper etiquette. He had promised to escort her and his mother to the theatre this evening, but afterwards, he was going to restrict his chaperone events to the balls. His mother would not resent leaving her to the musicales and small dinner party gatherings.

He had been noticeably absent at Jackson's and Cribbs and had become too well acquainted in the gaming hells on St. James. He had noticed his pockets a bit lighter at the Faro tables, surmising his lack of sleep affecting his purpose, but his luck was no better at the Hazard tables, where a bottle-head could manage. He decided he was only fagged to death and required more time in his bed chamber. Yes, after tonight, he would make some needed changes.

Capitulating to her strictest social etiquette, Olivia found herself keenly aware of her tendency to gape as they entered the grand saloon of the Theatre Royal Drury Lane. When her eyes rose to the magnificence of the Rotunda, she felt the need to place her hand on her chin to ensure it remained closed. She had never seen such luxury in a public venue. Eventually lending notice to the patrons gathered near her, she was aghast by the splendour of fine satins and silks, along with the shimmering jewels which adorned the ladies of the Ton.

Settled in their private box, the lack of musty air and the stagnant smell of ageing fabric astonished her. As she discreetly surveyed the deep, thick draperies and thickly upholstered chairs, the viscount saw the bewilderment on her face.

"Everything is new." He remarked.

"Oh, was it in need of it?" She asked.

"You could say so, I suppose." He chuckled.

"Whatever do you mean?" She drew back, turning to face him.

"It burned to the ground in 1809 and only reopened in 1812."

"Oh, dear. I was not aware of it."

Jack leaned over and whispered for only her hearing, "Your interests were held by Henry VIII, decapitating his wives' heads. This was a few hundred years later, I am afraid."

Olivia's eyes widened; her entire body stiffened. She darted her eyes toward his, and the viscount almost laughed aloud. Olivia, being chastised repeatedly, had gathered, discussing body parts, any body part, in mixed company was vulgar. Suddenly feeling quite shameful, he proceeded to recount the details of the fire and the recent restoration. Giving her time to regain her demeanour, only to be rebuked regarding his choice of private theatre box on the prince's side rather than the King's side.

"The prince has a rather questionable reputation, you

know." She told him with great assurance.

He chose not to remind her of the King's insanity or share that his association with the Carlton House Set was how he had procured such a prestigious loge and it had come with compliments from the prince himself. He instead alluded to the fact, they would not be sitting so close to the stage, and she would be facing the prince's private loge the entire evening otherwise. She quickly determined from the stories told of the particular theatre enclosure in question that this was the better choice.

At intermission, Olivia was surprised by the commotion of mingling. It seemed to be an entirely different type of entertainment which occurred during set changes.

Turning her attention to the knock upon their own box, she was delighted to welcome Lord Sheffield, who quickly made himself comfortable taking the seat next to her.

Jack was preoccupied with something in the pit area, Lady Birkshire chatted with another lady of consequence, who had joined them, and she was being quite ignored. "Oh, James, it is lovely to see you. I had no idea you held an interest in Shakespeare."

He frowned as he released her hand after lightly brushing his lips across her glove. "I do not care a farthing for him. Quite boring and cannot understand most of the gibberish."

"Oh." She leaned back in her chair, vexed. "Then why... for what purpose..."

"It is the thing, my dear. You will find there are many things one does because it is expected within the upper class." He saw her perplexed countenance, "I did not mean to set your back up because you were the reason I came."

"Me?"

"Yes, you. I wanted to ask you to go riding in Richmond Park tomorrow. I heard mention that Spartan was delivered to the Birkshire mews; thought you might like it."

"Oh, yes, I would like it above all things."

Lord Andovir recovered from his interest in the pit, turned to acknowledge his friend and was relieved to hear he was taking Olivia out the following day.

"That is a smashing idea, Sheffield. Spartan needs a good outing after his long journey into Town. He will want to stretch those oversized legs of his."

The three all agreed it would be a nice ride. Just as quickly as he had involved himself in their conversation, he disengaged and excused himself. With little notice, Olivia and James continued their intercourse regarding the day's events.

When James excused himself from the box, Olivia inquired of her aunt regarding the lady's retirement room. The countess motioned to Christina, who had accompanied them for just such a purpose. Olivia exited the box, following Christina's lead. The Rotunda and the Grand Saloon showed signs of those making their way back to the pit and boxes. She glanced at Christine with concern but was assured she had plenty of time. She noticed a corridor leading off into the darkness.

"Where does that lead?" she queried.

"To the green room, there are actually two of them," Christina said.

"What are they?"

"Oh, rooms where the actors can relax and prepare for their

scenes." She said, regretting her answer.

"It seems very dark leading to them. Are there no candles to light the hallway?"

Christina paused and cleared her throat, gathering her thoughts and selecting her words carefully. "I suppose actors do not need their way lit and prefer no one else enter there."

She knew very well why the corridors were in darkness. Most did, but this young miss had no need of that knowledge. She would find out soon enough on her own.

Returning and opening the door of their box, Olivia glanced curiously to the darkened corridors once more, noticing movement beyond the curtains that framed the dim hallway. She hesitated before entering, observing the shimmer of a satin gown pushing back the lower portion of the drapery. The movement exposed two figures embraced firmly against the wall. The chestnut-haired man had his knee firmly clamped between the woman's long legs, his hands pressing the woman towards him, and his head buried... oh... Olivia knew she should look away, but she could not. Something had her frozen in place. As the young man's head slowly made its way up to the woman's neck, it was obvious the satin-gowned female was quite enjoying his scandalous behaviour. Olivia regained her mobility, and just as her feet moved inside the door, she identified the chestnut-haired rake. With the swiftness of a cat, she closed the door and took her seat just as the actors took to the stage.

When the viscount returned to the box, the play had begun, and her attention was safely focused on the stage. However, her peripheral vision did not fail to catch the addressment of hands being raked through his hair and the tug at his waistcoat before he reclaimed the chair beside her. He said nothing, and she made no effort to glance in his direction.

The remainder of the play were fragmented pieces of a well-known saga she had long ago committed to memory, but the intermittent visions of a scene, clearly not meant to be a part of Shakespeare's script, kept her quiet and perplexed. She had never seen two people hold one another so closely or intimately. Her instincts told her she could not ask the sole person; those uncomfortable requests had always come easily.

The carriage ride home was quiet, and at the late hour, no one noticed her captivation with the closed shops and strolling pedestrians. When they arrived at Birkshire Place, the ladies were let down by a footman, the viscount giving no excuse as to his quick departure, and little heed was given by either lady.

Laying in her bed, unable to fall asleep, the images returned of Jack embracing the woman in the darkened hallway. Maybe she would ask Sarah, she was older, she might tell her. She rolled to her side, placed her clasped hands under her face and fell into slumber.

CHAPTER 9

The morning light shone through the window of the viscount's bedchamber; streaks of bright sunshine crossed the wrong side of the massive dark panelled, four-poster bed. In his state of arrival and the darkness of the room, he had failed to pull the thick velvet curtains. Keeping one eye tightly shut, he squinted with the other. Jack rolled to his back and stretched one muscular arm over his head to block the brightness torching his eyelids. An ache shot through him. Oh, God. The raised hand quickly latched onto his crotch. The rock-hard appendage stood proudly like a flagpole, the discomfort of it made him grab hold like a fragile antique. How many mornings had he awakened like this? The dream suddenly crossed his tired, monstrously hungover brain.

Over the past few weeks, the recurring dream had been a welcome relief to the losses he was racking up at the gaming hells on St James and the overabundance of brandy, which no longer obscured the reality of his present condition. The worst part, he awoke before the woman in those dreams was revealed, but bloody hell, it was a nice dream. Slumber seemed the only place he could find peace of late.

Attempting to return to his sleep, he found it impossible. Not even the relief of his discomfort had enabled his return to it.

"Finley!" The viscount managed to bellow to his valet, who he knew without a doubt was just on the other side of the door in his dressing room. Most likely pouring the champagne concoction over the hessians he had carelessly discarded in the corner; at whatever ungodly hour of the morning he had drug himself in.

It only took long enough for his valet of seven years and childhood friend to set the single hessian to the side, lay the cloth next to the bottle of champagne, and enter the room. Finley, not much older than the viscount, was much more than his valet, especially over the two years of freedom and peregrination from boy to man. He had pulled, pushed, and carried the viscount out of brothels, gaming hells, and taverns, dodged areas of war-torn Italy, Spain, France, and Belgium, sometimes bloody, sometimes not. He was an overly large man, which signified on more than one occasion when he was tossed into the fray, attempting to protect the viscount.

"Where the devil has you been? And why the bloody hell did you not pull my curtains? The damnable sun burned my eyeballs opened this morning."

Finley said nothing and just waited for instructions. His lordship never welcomed the mornings, even late ones. They were usually laden with headaches, stomach ailments and sore muscles. This morning would be no different. The valet had learned from pulling the older boys off him as a child in the streets of the village outside the Birkshire estates, this one was scrappy and privileged, but they had somehow developed an odd friendship. One was borne early on from Finley's pity of the viscount for being an only child, and the other being envious of the four brothers and three sisters of the valet.

"Prepare my bath."

Finley walked to the heavy rope and yanked it, then turned to a small cabinet, pulled a decanter, a small glass and a small packet of powder and mixed the two contents. Sitting the glass on his lordship's bedside table, still without uttering a word, he returned to his boot polishing, leaving the viscount struggling to reach the small heavy glass filled with the elixir that would make him whole again.

"God dammit, Finley, could you have placed the blasted glass any further away?" He drank the foul tasty drink and dropped back into the linens. "Oh, God, that's worse than death."

As he slid into the oversized tub of steaming water, he motioned to Finley. Have my chestnut readied and brought round. I need to pay a visit to Somerset Street."

"This time of day? You are a brazen one, are you not."

The viscount gave the valet a scowl as he walked out the door.

An hour later, as he left the doorsteps of the frequented house on Somerset, he was more frustrated than ever.

"What the bloody hell is Clarice doing taking a walk in the park at this time of the blasted day? Has the whole bloody world lost its senses."

The viscount mounted his steed and headed to the park to locate his bit of muslin. He needed to start visiting her more and White's less. It would be a damn sight cheaper.

***

On the other side of Hyde, down Park Lane, a young flaxen-haired miss was pulling on her new riding gloves and chattering away at her own personal confidant, who was placing a final pin in her tight chignon, which was fastened at the nape of her neck.

"Is this habit not glorious?"

She stood and turned to face the full-length looking glass. "Sapphire blue has always been your most becoming miss."

"I had no idea there were so many colour choices for a riding habit."

Sarah turned to fetch the new hat with the long sapphire scarf floating off the back. The match was perfect with the riding habit the modiste had designed and fitted to the small but shapely figure it adorned.

"I will see you in the park. I must retrieve Spartan before his groom sees fit to take him around the block."

The hat was positioned precisely, a tiny tilt to the right, and the young lady was off to meet her large, black fine bit of thoroughbred blood.

It was too early for much activity in Hyde Park; only those members of the Whip Club and other avid riders chose to ride at this hour. The children, escorted by their governess or nurse, also found pleasure in the park before it was overrun with fashionable ladies and the dandies, who found children a distraction. Above all, a cute, mischievous child at play seemed to garner more attention than the feathers and baubles of an impeccably designed bonnet and flowery walking dress.

However, Olivia found the children delightful. They usually had their *animal de compagnies* along, and they were fascinated by Spartan's massive build and gentle nature. Always enjoying her sequestered rides, Olivia never failed to stop and allow the courageous child, who would dare come close enough to rub the lowered head of her prized gelding.

Today there was a little girl walking along with her nurse, pushing a baby carriage, with what appeared to be a well-dressed cat nestled inside a pile of pink blankets. Olivia could not help but draw a bit closer to examine the odd state of affairs.

"My, I do not believe I have ever seen such a site, my dear."

Olivia smiled down at the beaming child as the little girl crooked her neck upward to view the small young lady in blue riding the enormous mount.

"This is my baby." She proudly announced. "She is always dressed in her finest for our outing in the park."

The nurse peered up at Olivia, dropping a slight curtsy, bowed her head, smiled, and then quickly turned her attention back to the tiny female.

"That is necessary for a promenade in the park. You have dressed in your finest as well, it appears." Olivia was delighted by the formality of the small one.

"Oh, yes, mama says it is of most important never to leave the house without regarding our manners and... oh, dear, I cannot remember the rest." She glanced up at her nurse for assistance.

"Propriety." The nurse whispered.

"Oh, yes." The little girl continued. "Pro...pr...iety."

"Indeed." Olivia agreed, giggling.

Olivia and the small child exchanged a few more niceties, then parted ways. She was elated by the interchange and was riding along, unaware of anything around her, thinking about the little girl and her cat. As she made her way back through the park, she noticed the same little girl next to a tree wailing, the nurse attempting to calm her, the tiny carriage overturned just a few feet away and the mollycoddled cat nowhere in sight.

Olivia, unable to ignore an animal in destress, turned Spartan toward the apparent misfortune. As she drew closer, the large tree where the little girl's eyes were fixed contained on its second large limb what appeared to be a small creature adorned in a long gown dangling from its neck, draped over the large bough.

"Oh, dear, what has happened?"

The nurse knelt in front of the small child raised her eyes to the sapphire-cloaked miss.

"A tragic accident, I'm afraid, some boys were playing stickball, and the orb landed in the carriage."

"Oh, I see." And she very well did see. Her very own Frederick never took to sudden interferences with his naps without a disaster looming.

"And the boys did not offer to help, I see."

"Oh, goodness, no. Apparently, they had been warned of playing stick ball in this part of the park and scattered like rodents."

"And…and…poor Miss Puss is frightened to death." cried the little girl, trying to hold back her tears.

Olivia smiled down, asking if she might lend her assistance in retrieving the poor Miss Puss from the tree.

"Oh, can you? I would be ever so grateful."

There was no way she could resist this mature beyond her year's child. "At your service, mademoiselle."

The little girl smiled and peered up at her nurse. "That's French, and she called me a miss."

The nanny tried to hold in a giggle. Olivia directed them

away from the tree as she maneuvered the big hunter under the lower limb. She ducked under the large bough, with a firm heel to Spartan's side, as he quietly sidestepped, moving his hip close to the trunk.

In amazement, the nurse and the wide-eyed child watched as the lovely miss easily stood on the saddle and launched herself to the lower tree branch. Then in bewildered admiration, they held their breaths as she softly spoke to the small cat and lifted it from the upper branch. One hand on the trunk, the other firmly holding the impeccably dressed cat, she wedged one foot against the upper pommel and slid back to the saddle, of course, landing astride the contraption.

The nanny quickly approached the massive horse as Olivia gently handed the cat down to her and attempted to address her awkward and inappropriate position on her gelding's back.

"Oh, my lady, you should not have."

The nurse glanced around, and the only audience in site seemed to be preoccupied with other interests.

The little girl taking Miss Puss from her nurse was busily restoring her to her carriage with a much happier countenance.

"Thankfully, it appears no one is the wiser." Olivia brushed off her habit and straightened herself properly in her saddle.

"If you please, address with the little miss, this is not the proper action of a lady, and she should not share the experience with anyone. I fear, if word reached my aunt, I would not be found in good graces."

The nanny was grateful and assured her she would explain to the now happy child this was one incident she should remove from her thoughts and never speak of it again. The nurse thanked her. As she turned Spartan back to the original course, the tiny girl was waving vigorously, and shouting thank you, my new French sapphire friend. Olivia prayed no one would be the wiser.

As she trotted Spartan back to *Route de Roi*, she was pleased her new little friend thought her a French mademoiselle. Maybe if the story did slip, no one would think of her. They had not properly introduced themselves, so she had no need of a name passing her lips. However, the damnable sapphire riding habit she had been so proud to adorn earlier in the day might be a problem.

Moments before the cat launched itself with all its glory into the oversized oak, there had been another scandalous event at the edge of the line of trees in the background. The viscount had met his ladybird in the thick brush and had her slammed against another large tree, skirts gathered around her waist when he glanced up at the distant commotion. He ignored the wails of the child and continued his pleasure being taken in the hidden safety of the trees. But just as he was about to straighten his own attire, he glanced up to see an unmistakable figure on a prime bit of blood being manipulated against a rather large oak.

"Oh, good God almighty, you must be bamming me!"

Clarice pulling her long skirts back into place, twisted her head around the tree to follow his lordship's focus.

"Oh, my." Even an ill-bred courtesan knew the sight was not appropriate.

"Clarice, I must bid you adieu." Said the viscount hastily.

Quickly fastening his fall and putting himself in order, he snatched his hat from where he had placed it and made his way to his horse tied nearby. By the time he managed to address his own issues and walk his chestnut to the edge of the wooded area, the sapphire miss and massive horse were gone.

"Damme, that little chit, wait until I get my hands on her!"

His day had just gotten a bit worse. He mounted his thoroughbred and headed out of the park toward Park Lane.

Gray met him at the door taking his hat and coat. "Is Lady Olivia returned?" His tone was not at all directed at the butler, and as usual, the butler took no offence to the angry growl.

"No, my lord."

"Is my mother?"

"No, my lord, it is her morning at the orphanage."

"Thank God!"

Jack heavy-footed his way to the blue drawing room. Upon arrival, he poured himself a brandy, sat in the large leather wingback facing the door, crossed a shiny top boot across his knee and waited. His elbow propped on the chair arm holding the heavy glass filled with amber liquid, his expression one of a large cat waiting to pounce upon an unaware mouse as it walked into the trap.

He heard the light click of ladies riding boots making their way up the hallway. She was tugging at her sleeve as she entered the room. She saw Jack seated in the wingback and smiled.

"Good morning." she beamed.

It had been several days since he had been to the house, and she was pleased to see him. When he made no response, she looked up again. His eyes were bloodshot, and she noticed he was a bit dishevelled from his usual neat appearance.

"Are you well?" she asked, not broaching any further into the room.

"Would you be so kind as to close the doors?" His voice was controlled but stern.

She turned and closed one door and then the other. Holding the knobs that now met, she inhaled a deep breath, then slowly turned to meet his gaze. His anger had subsided a bit, and the brandy had put him in a bit better mood, but he knew full well this had to be addressed.

"I see you have a new habit?"

She watched him closely, unable to determine his disposition but erred on the positive. "Yes, is it not pretty? I had no idea one could find..."

"A tree-climbing habit." He interjected.

Oh, dear God, how did he know already? Surely, he was not riding in the park. He was never out this early unless he was meeting her. They had not agreed to meet this morning, had they? No, she would have remembered it. She inhaled another deep breath, exhaled, and quickly crossed the room toward him.

"Oh, Jack, I was only a second, and there was no one around. The nurse was watching, and I could not stand doing nothing when I was the only one who could rectify the situation so quickly. And the poor little girl was so very distressed, and Miss Puss was frightened to death, and it would have been ages before she would have come down on her own and..."

"Stop!" He moaned, holding up one hand to her. "My head cannot tolerate your ramblings this early?"

She stiffened at his impudence. "I beg your pardon. If you were unable to tolerate me this early, you should have gone to your own house to nurse your headache rather than come here to start a fight with me."

Jack put down his glass and rubbed his face with both hands, rubbed his temples and raised his eyes to meet hers.

"You are correct, and I do apologise. But dammit, how many times must I warn you about your behaviour. If anyone had seen you, good Lord, it would have been back to Mother before she could return home today."

"But no one did. What would you have me have done differently? There was a poor little child crying her eyes out…"

"I know. Her sobbing was most disruptive."

That caught her attention. She cocked her head. "Where were you?"

He suddenly realised he was in no position to disclose that information. "It does not signify."

"I believe it very much signifies. If you heard her cries, why did you not help her rather than leave me to put myself in such a position? Which I was well aware would have been scandalous had I been seen."

"Well, it does not." Again, rubbing his temples.

"I disagree."

Jack uncrossed his leg and stood, taking his glass back to the cabinet from where it came and headed to the door.

"Please do not go." The soft voice pleaded.

He stopped. He always stopped… for her. Of all the women he had met through the years, proper and improper, she was the only one who could make his heart stop beating. His head fell back, and he turned to her.

"I am sorry." She whispered. "I did know better, but…"

He made his way to her, clasped her arms, and pulled her to the settee, sitting beside her.

"Olivia, you have been presented to the Queen, you have received the most coveted invitations to the best houses and balls, and you are considered the incomparable. The entirety of the Ton is waiting for you to falter." He raked his hand through his hair. "I should have been with you. And you are correct. I should have been in a position to save the cat for the little girl."

"Why were you not in a position to save…"

"Never mind that it shan't happen again. I will be riding with you from now on. Why was a groom not with you?"

"Sarah was meeting me… Oh, dear, I forgot about Sarah. I suppose when she does not see Spartan, she will return home."

Jack released her hand and leaned against the sofa's back, dropping his head to it. "I now see what father was trying to tell me."

"Whatever do you mean?"

He lifted his head and faced her.

"I mean, he said my behaviour would be a reflection on you, and it appears that is so. I owe you an apology. I will take care to correct some of those actions and take better care of you."

"I really do not think I need anyone to take care of me."

"I beg to differ with you. You have always needed someone to watch over you."

She wrinkled her brow but was in no mood to argue further.

"Give me a day or two. There are… things I must put to order. Then I will escort you to museums, the theatre, Vauxhall, anywhere you wish to go."

"To the art gallery? I hear it is magnificent."

"And the art gallery. But promise me," he squared her shoulders to him, "no more climbing trees," she shook her head, "no more riding in Hyde Park alone," again a head shake, "and no more racing Sheffield in Richmond Park."

"Oh, you heard of that too," she said quietly.

"I did." He raised an eyebrow and smiled down upon her, "he seems to forget himself when he is with you. Promise me."

"I promise."

He kissed her forehead and rose to leave. "Jack."

He turned back to her.

"Will whomever you were with remain quiet?"

He could see she was truly aware her actions were inappropriate, and he was certain it would not happen again… if she could help it.

"You have no need to worry about it. No one will say a word of it." He assured her.

"One other thing."

She lowered her head, and her cheeks turned a rosy pink. He could see she was hesitant. He hated that so much had come between them in the past few years. He was beginning to dislike who he had become.

"Do you..." she stopped, "never mind, it is really none of my concern."

"What? It is obviously something you wish to know. We have never been unable to ask one another whatever we wish."

He walked back to her and took her hand. She pulled it back and turned away from him. "I cannot ask you if you look at me. I should not ask at all, but..."

"Ask, for if you do not, it will drive me mad wondering."

She turned back and faced him, but her eyes were cast downward. She hesitated, deciding whether to ask what she was desperate to know.

"Do you have... a... paramour?"

"A what?" He took a step backwards.

"You know a..."

"I know what you mean and why on earth..." Now he was the one wanting to turn away.

"I saw you." She whispered shyly.

"In the park?" Panic struck him, and Olivia clearly noticed but answered before she had time to think.

"N-no, at the theatre." She lowered her head again, realising he had been at the park as well.

Evidently, with what she had come to learn over the past few days were women of easy virtue and loose morals of the lower class who made their wages becoming companions of aristocratic men. She was not exactly certain what that involved, but crushing one's body against another must have been a part of it.

He gathered himself and assured her it was not something they should discuss, but he most assuredly did not have a...oh lord...a paramour.

No, he did not have a paramour, as one usually set up a mistress in her own house and provided her with a life of luxury. He had become an overindulged man of drink, spent too much time in the gambling hells and the brothel on Somerset Street, with one usual doxy, after Henrietta Clark, the lady abbess of the high-class bordello, who had guided the boy into manhood but did not have a mistress.

Titled gentlemen of his age were allowed the indiscretions, overlooked as a rite of passage. But now, his actions had crossed into Olivia's world, and God forbid, she had been the one to discover it.

Oh, God! He had been her hero, protector, the white knight in shining armour and in one careless, no two by his own admission, moments had become a black knight with no armour at all. She had stripped him of it with one innocent question of which he knew she had no real understanding.

He left her confused but still innocent. He made his way across Grosvenor Square and wondered if Lucifer had any regrets, as he now knew how it felt to fall from grace.

CHAPTER 10

Jack had managed to avoid most carrefours, but now he stood at the brink of his first and most important. The life he had made in London over the past few years had been satisfying and agreeable. He understood; however, it had threatened no one, not even himself. Now his salacious lifestyle imperilled his reputation, along with the Birkshire name, legacy, mother, and most of all, Olivia, who seemed to remain on the verge of his every thought.

He had tried to keep her at arm's length in his libertine thoughts. He tried pushing himself further into the decadent lifestyle, including private hedonistic parties with the Carlton House set, romps into exclusive brothels with their high-class courtesans, like the White House in Soho Square and his favourite on Somerset Street and pushed his luck at the most exclusive gaming hells. He had never been considered a real gambler, but he had lost a great deal over the past weeks. All in an effort to push Olivia back where she belonged, a sibling who had never been a sibling at all. It had failed miserably.

It had been a comfortable life until now. Her re entry into his world had destroyed his selfish, parsimonious comportment, and he needed a change. It was time to do so, well at least change a little, perhaps, maybe. God help him.

Finley was shocked when the viscount wandered into his bedchamber before 2 a.m. He looked at him curiously with a strong urge to touch his forehead for a fever. "Shall I call for a doctor?"

"Arse!" Andovir glared at his valet.

"What is one to think when you are normally not seen until daybreak, smelling of whores and liquor." Finley retorted smugly.

"Why is it I put up with you again?" Andovir sat on his bed and lifted his top boot to his valet.

"Because I know all your damnable secrets and have since you were out of leading strings," He stated flatly as he pulled off his master's boots.

"Thought there was a reason for it."

Finley laughed and helped the viscount out of his tail and waistcoat.

"I am three- and twenty-years old Finley, no longer a boyish irresponsible fool."

"That happened just today?" Finley smirked.

"You know, you are a real bastard." The viscount grumbled, unbuttoning his fall.

"It comes with years of pulling you out of scrapes," Finley said candidly.

"Prepare to become bored, my friend."

His valet scoffed at that as he watched Andovir pour a glass of brandy and sit before the fire. He was deep in thought, and his valet figured he was deciphering how to go about his next move. He had worked for the viscount for years, and this was nothing new. He moved like a chameleon in and out of the divergent phases of his life. But he could not imagine him ready to settle down, not yet.

When the viscount awoke the next morning, he had not had his normal lust-filled dream of the past few weeks. Instead, it was more of a memory resurrected, one he had not thought of in years. It was becoming evident; he had never thought of Olivia as a sister. It was a charge cast upon him by his parents, who had always loved her and, once their dear friends had passed, easily stepped into the parental role. But he had been her white knight and protector, not a brother. The forgotten memory was more indication of it.

***

"You will never catch me," Olivia squealed and laughed as she ran up the hill from the lake.

They were enjoying the early summer sunshine, she nearly fifteen. He was nearing manhood, exhibited by the lean, muscled physique stretched across the large blanket. They had finished their favourite picnic lunch of meats and cheeses. He now lay on his back, head resting on clasped hands, eyes closed, basking in the fresh scents of evergreens, wildflowers and pasture grasses bursting with new growth, a welcome break from the damp, musty smells of a building centuries old, where he had been stuck for months.

Olivia could not resist his peaceful, vulnerable state. She quietly gathered a pile of old, decomposed leaves. She heaped as many as possible in both hands and threw them across his outstretched body, giggling, swiftly jumping to her feet and dashing up the hill.

Jack immediately responded by bolting after her. Her challenge quickly answered when he caught the flowing skirt that floated behind her. She tumbled to the ground, lying face down in a meadow of English countryside bluebells, laughing with glee. Jack straddled her small frame and flipped her onto her back with one quick move, his hands pinning her arms to the ground. She was panting and laughing, her hair dislodged from the pins that once kept it fastened in a neat chignon at the nape of her neck. Jack's laughter turned quickly to an amusing grin as he stared down at her. She was trying to catch her breath, the newly forming breasts heaving up and down. Jack was silent and the grin slid from his lips as he noticed the heavy breathing.

Time stood still as he noticed the body lying beneath him. It was no longer one of a little girl but a developing young lady. Her long blonde hair curled across her shoulders, and the small but pronounced bosom between his hands. He had recently become aware of the girlish shape of others of the gentler sex, learning to appreciate and desire them. His urges began to awaken as he scanned the curves of the small creature beneath him. His eyes moved from her neck to her mouth, and without warning, he felt an overwhelming urge to lower his body and taste the plump pink lips smiling up at him. He looked into her crystal blue eyes, which held a look of curiosity at his silence.

A flash of recognition ignited his thoughts. Olivia, this was Olivia. He jumped to his feet, yanking her from the ground, ignoring the throbbing sensation that was building within him.

"Are you all right?" Olivia, stunned by the quickness of his actions, looked at him with concern. Perplexed by his uncontrolled reaction to her, managed a somewhat governed response.

"Yes, but you need to go to the house immediately."

"But why, and what of the basket and blanket?" Her innocent eyes were peering at him in confusion.

"I will get them. Just go before it rains," he muttered without a glance at the clouds for confirmation.

She shrugged, and he watched as she walked up the hill.

"What the bloody hell was that?" He chastised himself as Olivia's figure topped the hill. He had a difficult walk back to the blanket. A dip in the lake might help. Instead, he sat on the throw, attempting to unravel the confused emotions surging through his body.

She might as well be his sister. But she was not, nor had she ever been... his sister.

***

Since it was early and he was not blessed with a hangover, he decided to make his way to Birkshire Place for some of Emma's bacon and famous coddled eggs. He ambled into the empty breakfast room. The early meal was laid on the sideboard, and the silver receptacle holding the coddled eggs beckoned. Filling his plate, the Morning Post caught his eye, and it would be his company. Folding it to fit comfortably in one hand, he shovelled eggs with the other. Laying it to the side momentarily, it flopped open, and a parchment floated to the tile next to his chair. Glancing down, the odd title captured his attention, 'All About Ton.'

"What the deuce" he muttered, followed by the reminder of the gossip writers in London. They lived for the rumours and whispers of The Season.

Under his breath, he snorted, "What a ridiculous waste of time."

It seemed there were more tattler papers than actual newspapers. Jack glanced around, but no one was in sight. He snatched the paper from the floor. Curiosity clouded his sober judgment; he skimmed over the thin paper. Typical tales, who's who for The Season, those who were thought to be dandies, nonpareils, pinks, tulips, announcing the ladies in their first season and chastising those in their third and fourth, as either too picky or too intelligent. Without warning, he felt the heat rise from his chest to his throat.

"What the bloody hell?" He boomed.

He continued to absorb the script, stopping, and readdressing each line. He slammed the paper upside down on the table with a thud, covering it with his hand as if it would make the words disappear. Red- faced, he felt his temples pounding inside his head. He could not believe it. Surely his brain was coddled along with the eggs, which had instantly lost their appeal. Good God, this was worse than any hangover he had ever endured. He turned the paper right side up to analyse it again. But only the paragraph that had stopped him mid-bite.

Jack's jaw clenched painfully as he re-read the lines.

"It has come to this author's attention that we have quite the treat this season. I have become aware we have a rare gem. She is, by birth, a member of two of England's prestigious families. However, tragedy took both her parents at a very young age. This fair maiden was, however, blessed with the advantage of becoming a ward of yet another of England's Aristocracy. She has spent little time in London, being protected and well-hidden in the countryside. This author is told; however, she has been provided with the best tutors and is more than prepared to enter London Society. We have not yet personally seen the fair maiden but are told she is exquisite and can easily take her place with London's finest young ladies and is assured to be considered 'A Diamond of the First Water.' We were privy to the account of her impeccable presentation to the Queen. While others fumbled and struggled with their oversized hooped skirts and over-adorned large feathers, she seemed to have floated her way to the perfectly orchestrated curtsy of which her majesty took obvious and delightful notice.

It has also come to this writer's attention for all you gentlemen currying fancy this season she has been bestowed by her late parents a rather flush dowry and is quite full of juice. It appears we may have found the rare diamond of The Season. However, this author is withholding opinion until we see for ourselves if the country bumpkin can, indeed, cross the threshold and truly withstand the resourcefulness of London's most ambitious mamas and desperate young ladies."

"Bloody hell, this is a damn nightmare, a damn bloody nightmare." Jack crumbled the paper and threw it across the dining room. Where was everyone? He needed to expend his frustration on someone, anyone.

"Good God!" he bellowed.

Taking a deep breath, knowing there was nothing to do at this instant. But as soon as his mother was up, he would have to advise her of this vulgar turn of events.

Exhaling, he was grateful to have taken breakfast at Birkshire Place if his mother had seen this without preparation, without the presence of someone to comfort her. Comfort her? He needed serious comfort himself. Good God, he took a hell-uv-a time to mend his wicked ways.

Did she really have a large dowry? Good lord, if she did, every poor bastard looking to secure their estate would be on bended knee, the old ones, the young ones, and everything in between. The peerage was filled with unqualified aristocrats whose estates and properties had been run into the ground and found themselves remarkably close to losing them to Howard and Gibbs. A large dowry was always the key to salvaging their stupidity and irresponsibility.

Jack had a fresh pot of tea brought to the drawing room. Tea hell, he needed brandy for this. He picked up the revolting crumpled paper from the floor and headed in that direction. He was staring out the window with a cup of brandy-laced tea in hand at the ungodly hour of 10:00 am. He was mindlessly raising and lowering the cup to his lips, unsure if he had taken the first sip, fearing even a small one would choke him to death.

His throat was tight, jaw clenched, trying to think. The betting books would be a start, and at clubs like White's, there would be rumours of suitors searching for a honey fall. In an hour's time, in his solitude, he had turned into a regular Bow Street Runner.

He was deeply engrossed in his thoughts when Lady Birkshire entered the parlour. She was a little surprised to see him at this hour. When he took no notice, she cleared her throat. Startled, he quickly turned to find his mother lounging on the sofa.

"I did not hear you come in," acknowledging her and placing his cup in the saucer.

"Obviously, what brings you out so early?" She smiled.

"You have no notion," Jack said as he walked over and took the seat next to her."

The foreboding tone did not escape her, the smile waned. The Season had only just begun, yet she sensed impending misfortune.

"I will not be pleased?" his mother sat her cup back into its saucer.

"Hardly!" He uncrumpled the sheet, folded it neatly where the paragraph of interest was exposed and handed it to her.

She looked at him confused, then glanced down at the crumpled parchment. She scanned the page.

"The last section, I will save you the time," he sneered as he walked back toward the window and stared at the street filled with servants bustling about in search of the costermongers.

The countess fell silent. He knew his mother was reading it again, just as he had done. She was attempting to discover how this author had gleaned the information and whether it sounded confirmed or pure speculation.

Finally, she looked up and calmly asked, "Your thoughts?"

"Is it true?" He stared into her eyes, knowing she would never outwardly lie. His mother's lips parted, then tightly closed, and she winced.

"So, it is." No longer a question and her silence indicated it might be worse than he imagined. "Good God, Mother, how did this happen?"

"It happened when she was orphaned by wealthy parents, and a duke with only one grandchild and little entailed in either. Except, of course, the family homes and surrounding land."

"Does Olivia know about her dowry?"

"No. Your father only recently found out the details. See what a mess thing become with only daughters. The poor duke's lengthy line goes to a younger brother and the earl's passing to a cousin. However, I must say Kit has done well with it, and he adores Olivia. But he, too, remains a bachelor and who knows where it will go should he not marry and produce an heir. That, of course, only explains how she came about so much land and fortune. Nathan Rothschild, the London Bank man, was left in charge of it and has apparently doubled and tripled it."

"Damme, what are we to do now?"

"I suppose I should send for your father. When he found out, he hoped no one would discover it. It is one reason he never told Olivia."

"Or me."

"Well, dear, he has said, you have not exactly been dependable over the past years. Who knows who might get wind of it…" she stopped, not wanting to offend her only son.

"I beg your pardon?"

"I am sorry." She said, "You are only living the life expected of young noblemen."

"Well, you will be pleased to know I am trying to correct some of it." He retorted.

"I am glad to hear of it, especially for Olivia's sake."

"Hopefully, nothing will come of this, but I will search for anyone in deep." His mind was racing. "Do not notify father yet." Still thinking, "I will visit Standish. He will be filled with the latest news and is always talkative. He will know who has been asking around about this season's crop."

"John Jacob, Olivia is not a tomato, you know." She flashed disapprovingly.

"I beg your pardon. I was not thinking of her in my description.

His mother was about to assure him, she knew he had not, but at that very moment, the little heiress waltzed into the room.

Lady Birkshire immediately turned the conversation, "Have you had breakfast, my dear?"

"Indeed, I did. I would not miss Emma's eggs." She

quipped.

"They are the best." Jack smiled.

"I was informed of your early arrival. You could not have waited?"

"I beg your pardon, Emma's eggs wait for no one," He laughed, hoping to hide his frustration. His mother's quick glance assured him no word was to be mentioned to Olivia.

Jack placed his cup and saucer on the side table. "Well, I must be off."

"So soon?" Olivia pouted.

"I have inquiries to make." Then quickly thought. "But have yourself ready at 3:00, and I will take you for a drive."

"Oh, I would like that above all things."

Pledging her 3:00 readiness, he was off, leaving two bewildered females behind.

Olivia walked to the window overlooking Park Lane and watched Jack mount his chestnut. He was the most handsome man… she had ever seen. A tingle suddenly raced down her spine. It was not a cold chill but an unknown sensation.

***

Later that afternoon, as the Birkshire carriage rambled past Piccadilly Street toward The Strand, Olivia was fascinated by the sites. A multitude of questions were directed toward her escort regarding one place, then another. He could not help but laugh at her childish enthusiasm. After more than four years in the West End, he was seeing it again as he had when he first explored it. He asked the coachmen to drive by St.

Paul's Cathedral and did not quite understand his own reaction to Olivia's reverence of it.

The carriage halted in front of #32 Ludgate Hill, the shop of Rundell and Bridge. The viscount leapt from the equipage, and as the steps were let down, he extended his arm to the eager young miss and escorted her into the shop.

Olivia ceased walking and talking upon entry. "My heavens, I have never seen so many shiny things in one place."

He smiled as though they had been swept back in time and he was showing the six-year-old little girl his boyish trinkets and treasures. She strolled through the shop, stopping in amazement at the encased jewels.

"Oh, Jack, see the snuff boxes. They are most exquisite. I have never seen such things." She said.

"Thinking of taking up snuff, are you?" Jack grinned.

"Certainly not!" She giggled and lightly tugged at his sleeve. "But can you not see the shock on your mama's face if I did."

They both laughed, imagining the horrified face of the countess.

A rather large, locked case with a jewelled necklace had garnered her attention. She was astonished.

"You like that one?"

"It is quite resplendent, is it not? It must be for a princess or a duchess."

Jack began to laugh. "Have you not noticed the ladies adorned with such flair and imposing jewels at the theatre and balls?"

"I have not noticed at the balls, and the young ladies could never wear such things."

He had forgotten all the strict rules and guidelines for the young ladies during their come-out. No, these were for the ladies of nobility whose husbands had them adorned for their own show of wealth, not that the ladies minded, of course.

"They remind me of Mama's Sinclair and Hamilton jewels. Of course, the Sinclair jewels were kept by my cousin, but I am not at all certain what happened to the Hamilton Jewels. I had quite forgotten them until seeing these. I was a little girl, and so many of my memories of Mama and Papa have faded. I wish it were not so." Olivia's face turned downward in sadness.

Seeing the melancholy, he quickly diverted her attention to the next case filled with earrings more fitting her present station.

"Do you like sapphires?"

He pointed out a petite pair of earrings with a sapphire stud and a drop holding two tiny diamonds.

"Oh, yes, those are beautiful. I indeed do like sapphires. Aunt Annabelle let me try a pair of hers; she says they make my eyes sparkle."

She lifted her face up to meet his, the deep crystal blue eyes with long fluttered eyelashes beckoned and he easily concurred with his mother's observation. He glanced back to the case as the swell within his heart overwhelmed him. He was interrupted by a shop assistant making his way to assist.

"I must see the clerk. Stay right here. I will return directly."

Jack motioned the agent to meet him away from his companion. He gave the man direction, then turned back to

Olivia, noticing a young lady and gentlemen standing at her side. The three were admiring items in one particular case. Olivia and the young lady were conversing over the contents.

"Oh, yes, it is the most breathtaking trinket I have ever seen. Is it the one you have chosen?" Olivia seemed quite swept up in intercourse with her new acquaintance.

The girl was handsome and fashionably dressed and did not appear much older than Olivia. The young man by her side had made every attempt to dress like a dandy. Jack had drawn close enough to hear the conversation between them.

"Oh, no," the young girl exclaimed, "it is much too fine for me."

She turned to look at her beau. He took her hand and promised one day he would provide her with one as sublime. The ladies said their goodbyes and the couple departed.

As Jack stepped next to her, he saw the case contained betrothal rings. "Are you wishing for rings, pet?" he teased.

"Of course not. But I must say, these are the most beautiful rings I have ever seen. All different shapes and exquisite stones."

"You know these are betrothal rings, do you not?"

"Oh," she blushed, "I had not. But you know, I should have. I was speaking with a young lady just now."

"I saw as much." Amused by her affability.

"Yes, well, it has only just occurred to me that is what they must be seeking. Do you not agree?"

"I do. They seemed very much attached."

Yes, I think so too." Her eyelashes fluttered.

"Which ring had you both captivated?" It was a dangerous question, but he wanted to explore Olivia's taste in jewellery. Funny, it was one of the few things he did not know of her.

"The one there." Olivia pointed to a gold filigree band with a ruby, a sapphire, and an emerald set within three separate small circles of gold and a circle of diamonds around the three. It was not at all ostentatious or pretentious but was obviously of superior quality and premium.

"It is quite stunning." The viscount was not a connoisseur regarding jewellery, but he was more than knowledgeable of rare jewels and gold. The piece was exquisite. He was impressed by Olivia's elegant and fine choices, although not altogether surprised.

The clerk approached with two small packages. Jack discreetly slipped both into his pocket and expressed to the attendant he would come around tomorrow and retrieve the remaining selection.

Olivia strolled a bit longer, looking at the fine clocks and other exquisites, then pronounced she was tiring and was quite ready for Gunter's. Jack took her by the arm, nodded to the clerk indicating their business for the day was complete and escorted her to the carriage.

Once inside, she straightened her skirt and settled. The viscount took the seat across from her, tapped the side, and they were off. Watching Olivia, her countenance was a bit weary, and her clear blue eyes less bright, showing signs of a long day and trying to hide a small yawn.

"How exciting this was. I cannot believe so many beautiful items in one shop. The small one in the village would never have such things. I was a bit overwhelmed."

"Are you certain you are up for Gunter's? We can go another day. You can rest before dinner."

"But you will not dine at Birkshire, and I am not ready to be rid of your company." Although fatigued, she was enjoying her time with him.

"I have places to attend tonight, but if I dine at Birkshire, would that be acceptable? It appears you need a respite."

She agreed to this, as she was quite tired. She would go straight way to nap and meet him for dinner. Jack escorted her to the door, handing her off to Gray, turning to find his gelding brought around by one of the grooms. As he mounted his prized thoroughbred, he felt pleased with himself for his accomplishments of the day. He reached in his pocket to ensure his packages and set off toward his townhouse with a smile.

CHAPTER 11

The viscount arrived for dinner, as promised, immaculately dressed. He wore a superfine dark blue tailcoat, a double-breasted waistcoat, and a white muslin shirt with a starched raised collar. His cravat was a scrolled multi-coloured design that appeared quite dashing with the waistcoat. His tight buckskin-coloured pantaloons exhibited his time spent in the Jackson Saloon, along with clocked stockings, black shoes, a beaver hat, dark gloves, and a cane.

As he entered the drawing room, Olivia's mouth gaped but she quickly caught herself and snapped it shut. She had also taken great care to look exceptional. She chose a sapphire blue satin gown that enhanced the stunning shade of her eyes, blonde ringlets left to frame her face and a few dangled down the nape of her neck.

Lady Birkshire entered the room a bit irritated, pulling at her sleeve, but when she glanced up at her two dinner companions, she halted at the sight. She swiftly announced they should have dined at Vauxhall. Further stating it was regretful she was the only one to appreciate the aesthetics of the evening.

The dinner conversation was exclusive to the upcoming ball at Almack's. The countess had decided it was time for Olivia to make her appearance at the more public assembly hall and enter the official marriage mart.

Olivia displayed a disgruntled countenance, and the countess did not consider Jack's enthusiasm any better. But plans were made for Lord Andovir to escort them from Park Lane. She made it clear she wanted to arrive early, having

Olivia announced to a lesser-than-full assembly. Jack nodded in agreement but provided little more to a matter neither he nor his mother wished to discuss in great detail. The dinner passed quickly, and after retiring to the drawing room for a quick brandy, he took his leave of the ladies, assuring them it was not the company which ushered him on his way, as he had business to attend.

Both ladies surveyed his attire with a look of wonderment regarding his questionable business, dressed as he was, a Tulip of the Ton.

The viscount had reconciled himself enough so, to make changes in his circumstances. If he was going to be a proper escort for Olivia and his mother without drawing unwanted attention, he must address his behaviour. Aware of how London Ton's tongues wagged, he thought he had been discreet. But if Olivia, a naïve child, had noticed, God only knew how much trouble it might be to restore his reputation.

He had walked to Birkshire Place, intending to head directly from there to his destination. Not a long walk, and he drew less attention on foot and was less likely to be recognised. Most of his acquaintances and friends wouldn't give a farthing of his visits to Somerset Street, but it very much mattered to him, and he had no appetite for more rumours and gossip.

Lord Andovir strolled down Duke Street, crossed Oxford and onto Somerset. The side street was not well-lit. Lamps remained oil, whereas the streetlights on the main thoroughfares had been altered to gas. He glanced back toward Duke, saw no one and strolled to the entrance of the stately old mansion. As he approached, the massive door opened, and the elderly butler greeted him.

"Good even'n milord," the little man bowed best he could, "we wufn't 'spectin' you tonight, I don't believe we wuf. But I will ring milady and get 'er straight away."

The old butler shuffled down the hall. Jack removed his hat and gloves and laid them on the side table inside the parlour. Glancing around the room, he remembered the first time he entered years before. It was going to be strange letting go of this part of his life, but it was time if he intended to restore his reputation. As he stared at the familiar paintings, he heard movement behind him and turned.

"My Lord, it is good to see you. We have missed you."

A woman in her forties waltzed into the room, extending both hands to him. She wore a bright red gown adorned with large stones, precious gems encircled her neck, wrists, and sparkling baubles on every finger. Her blond wig was stacked high upon her head, with an elaborate tiara embellishing the massive pile of curls. Painted lips and knowing assertive eyes left no doubt she was the mistress of the bordello. Clasping his hands in hers, she kissed his right cheek and then his left.

"You look exquisite tonight, my dear. The cut of the cloth fits you well, especially those pantaloons. Tres risqué!" She raised an eyebrow and smiled, admiring his muscular legs and the tight fit of the stylish pants, especially at the fall, with which she clearly gave extra attention.

"Thank you, Henrietta, you've always been very kind."

"I can see by your countenance you are not here to see Clarice."

"No, not in the manner which you speak. I have come to see you and a moment of her time if I may."

Henrietta could see by the polish of his delivery Lord Andovir had come to say goodbye. The madame had seen many of her clients come and go and easily discerned the look and mannerisms of young men.

Lord Andovir had been a mystery from the beginning. She was not surprised. Brothels gave way to wives or paramours at this age. Especially this lord, after her training which she had stretched far longer than most, he had been a most determined student and one whose mere presence could still make her wet with passion. But when Clarice Townsend had presented herself on the bordello doorstep looking for work, having met on difficult times at an early age, Henrietta liked her from the start. She was a pretty little thing, and Henrietta knew her star pupil had the skills to pass along the experience required to transform a simple ruined young girl into a successful ladybird.

Henrietta allowed Lord Andovir a moment to say his goodbye. Clarice was a wisp of a girl. Chestnut hair, grey eyes, and plump lips. Had it not been for her fate, he thought she would have been a naturally pretty girl. The heavy makeup covered her youth, but it also covered her features. He never asked her age; certain he did not care to know. The viscount pulled one of the boxes from his pocket and handed it to her.

"It is just a token of appreciation. I owed you more than an empty gesture."

Clarice opened the box to reveal a lovely pair of pearl earrings. She thanked him, wished him well, raised to her toes and kissed his cheek. He, in turn, took her hand and kissed it lightly, noticing a moist glint in her eye.

Lord Andovir returned to Henrietta in the parlour and retrieved the other box. Again, he thanked her for turning a young, naive boy into a man. She stepped to him, her low-cut bodice and exposed breasts pressing against his coat; he flinched as he felt her hand clamp tightly about his fall; he did not move.

"Are you certain you would not like a more… private goodbye."

The offer was too arduous to decline, the gleam in his eye was her answer. She tugged at the fall, released it, and turned toward the hallway. He followed.

The enormous bedchamber was filled with mirrors, books, fainting couches, and draped in fine French chintz. As he surveyed its ostentatious décor, he recalled those first years here. She had given him lessons in how to touch and please a woman and make them scream with passion and desire. She directed him how to serve a virgin to make it pleasant, where one would not loathe the act, resulting she had said, in he and his wife's pleasure in the marital bed.

Her years of experience, the art of lovemaking and expediency, found her swiftly standing before him completely nude before he could change his mind. He stripped himself bare as quickly, requesting one last lesson. A final test for the years of instruction in the Asian art of lovemaking… and so she obliged him.

An hour later, she was sitting in the dishevelled linens draped at her waist, as he walked across the room to retrieve the second box. She watched as the unadorned, taught muscles of legs, arms, and shoulders of what could only be described as Adonis himself, made their way back to her. Her blond wig, now gone, and her red locks lay over the luscious bare breasts, which had pleasured many of London's noblemen. She was the best, and they paid dearly to enjoy the pleasures.

"How much do I owe you?" He asked, before passing the small case to her.

"My love, it is I who owe you for one last pleasure. I in no way could let you walk out my door without tasting you once more. Your last test, as you called it, has been my privilege and pleasure. You have been my finest creation. I hope whoever reaps the reward of my loss, appreciates what they are to receive."

She opened the box to reveal an extravagant diamond bracelet. She thanked him and expressed she would treasure it always. She made no effort to leave her luxurious bed and only lifted her hand to him. He kissed it, dressed as she watched. Then, without a word, quietly closed the door behind him.

As he wandered down the hallway, he knew he would always be welcome within these walls. The old butler shuffled towards him, handing him his hat and gloves, expressing he too would miss his lordship.

The viscount strode onto Somerset and Duke Streets, down Oxford to St. James. He was headed straight to White's…it was indeed time…to get foxed!

CHAPTER 12

The following Wednesday, the manor on Park Lane was alive with excitement. Maids were running through the house, up and down the stairs, obeying one command, followed by another, ensuring every detail was met.

Olivia was tugging at her dress, pushing pins into her hair, and Sarah was making every attempt not to strangle her and resist the urge to tie her to the chair.

"Miss Olivia, please remain still and stop your fidgeting."

"I am sorry. I did not think I would be so anxious.

After all, how could this possibly be worse than the presentation to the queen?" Olivia let out a sigh,

"It is your first time to Almack's. Unsettled is to be expected."

"Is it?"

"Exactly so," Sarah tried to reassure her.

"It is not as if I am just out of the schoolroom. I am nearly eighteen, for gracious sake."

"And pray, what difference can that make. The first time at Almack's is still the first time," Sarah smiled as she slipped the final pin in her hair, "there, perfect."

Olivia stood and walked over to the mirror in her dressing room. She swayed at the sight of the person staring back at her.

"Oh, gracious!" she gasped.

There was a knock at the door, and Olivia gathered her skirts and turned to see her aunt enter the room. The countess leaned against the bed in a delightful half-swoon and gave her a nod and approving smile.

"You look beautiful, my dear."

From the tips of her slippers to the thin, diamond tiara tucked inside her hair, her aunt circled her with admiration. Sarah had masterfully weaved her blonde strands in and out of the small crown, then piled it tall and tight around her head.

"The gown is gorgeous. I am glad the modiste suggested the white satin. It complements your complexion," she studied the gown with approval.

She took Olivia's arm, smiling, "Are you ready?" Lending support, she turned toward the door. "Where are your gloves," her aunt's eyes were scanning the room.

Olivia pointed to the bed. Long, white ones lay neatly next to one another. Lady Birkshire walked to the bed and motioned for her niece. She slipped into them, then into the outreached hand of her aunt. "Let us be off."

Olivia strode out the door toward the staircase. Once at the landing, she glanced at the foyer. Her heart began to race, and she froze in place.

At the foot of the steps, leaning against the bannister, one elbow propped on the newel post, stood the viscount. Attired in a black superfine double-breasted tailcoat, a ruffled white linen shirt, a stiffly starched collar, dark kersey-mere waistcoat and neckcloth, light tan knee breeches, white clock stockings and black shoes with ribbon ties; he was striking and a tribute to his Corinthian physique and on this night a tulip of fashion.

The site took Olivia's breath away, and that same unexplained tingle returned. It raced down her spine, all the way to her toes. Her knees weak, she leaned into the bannister as she wiggled her toes inside her slippers. She had no idea what had come over her.

Jack pivoted, gazing upward, stilled and slowly released his deep inhale. Gathering herself, she descended the stairs. When their eyes met, it was as if there was no one else in the room. He extended his arm, and she gracefully placed hers upon it for support.

"You are absolutely breath-taking," The viscount whispered, unsettled and barely audible.

"Do you think so?" Her own voice quivered.

"I...I am certain of it." He clasped her fingers, tucked her hand in the crook of his arm and escorted her into the drawing room. Releasing her, he reached into his pocket. "I have something for you."

Olivia's eyes brightened at the sight of the small box withdrawn from his pocket. With shaking hands, she slowly opened it. "Oh, Jack, my earrings!" Tears filled her eyes, the very ones from their adventure to Rundell and Bridge.

The viscount smiled and admired the dress, her hair and the earrings complimented her already beautiful face. The blue eyes shone brighter between the sapphires. Lord Andovir took her hand, placed it on his elbow and escorted her out the door.

The carriage ride was quiet and uneventful. The air was crisp, and the viscount noticed Olivia pulling her cape around her. "Are you cold?"

"Only a little," she responded, "I think it is only nerves." He placed a blanket over her and smiled, again reassuring her it would be fine. The equipage turned onto Kings Street and began to slow. Olivia stared out the window as the building drew nearer. Noticing her clenching her hands together, the viscount reached across the conveyance taking one and lightly squeezing. A rush of warmth streaked through his body from head to toe. He was tired of denying what she did to him, just the touch of her hand.

"My pet, you are going to survive the evening, I assure you." He smiled; she nervously giggled.

As the carriage came to a halt, footmen dashed about, opening doors, and assisting ladies. Her eyes filled with wonder and amazement, overwhelmed by the number of people.

Mr Willis was in his honourable position as the famed doorkeeper and bowed them inside.

The night was as much as anyone could expect under the latest circumstances. The viscount was less concerned with the mamas and their daughters as he was with the sons, who had made ducks and drakes out of their early inheritance or those whose fathers had dipped too deep and looked to their sons to save the family from ruin. His evening was quite disturbed as he scrutinised every potential suitor.

However, as Olivia's escort, he knew the season could be disastrous for him in London's Marriage Mart. In the past five years, the viscount had declined most all the invitations to private balls, much less Almack's. The *Haut Ton's* bachelors understood attending balls, especially the Wednesday night assembly at Almack's, meant only one thing to the mothers of unmarried daughters.

The Ton's matrons were exceptionally cunning, promptly discovering the eligible among them. The masterful mamas with two or more daughters had no choice but to become a Meister in the art of catching husbands. The young men stood no chance against the ambitious and spent their time in ballrooms avoiding these experts. God forbid if the poor bachelor had a title, money, or both. Those poor fellows became no better than wild game animals to be hunted. As for the Ton mamas, they were both shrewd and masterful huntresses.

Of course, there were the gentlemen cast into their destined roles by fathers meeting untimely deaths, leaving their young heirs saddled with responsibilities and little time for frivolities. If not blessed with a mama to manage the domestic staff and social affairs, they became the hunters, matching wits with the mamas. Then there were those needing to salvage mishandled estates and some to elevate the family's position into the peerage. The strategy and tactics of all within the marriage mart was a challenge whether seeking or avoiding the leg shackle. However, those pursuing their fortunes would not be tolerated by the viscount.

If that wasn't enough, the bachelors content with waiting until their late twenties and nearer to thirty before desiring marriage, also had to be watched so as not to compromise a naïve and inexperienced debutant. Then there were the second and third sons, who had to find means of support among London's strict Ton rules, which usually meant ferreting large dowries from those mamas hoping to improve the family's bloodlines.

Good God! How did the papas manage to ensure their lovely daughters found suitable matches, without being compromised or ruined? Instead of the Marriage Mart, Jack decided betrothals at birth to be the thing, if he were to be blessed with daughters. Of course, that was something to worry of much, much later. Olivia was his focus at present, and her flush dowry destined her to be a paradigmatic candidate.

"Oh, Lord," Andovir shook his head, having an overwhelming desire to run his hand through his hair, and took a drink. A large hand slapped his shoulder, and a masculine figure drew up.

"Don't want to muss your hair," came a familiar snort from behind. "I know that demeanour. Why the frustration?" Sheffield's Corinthian build, sculpted from the same fencing and boxing clubs as Jack, removed his hand from the shoulder of his friend and stepped to his side.

"God help us, Shef."

"What's the chit done now?" The marquess asked exasperatedly. He knew if it was trouble- it was Olivia.

The viscount could not help but snort "Gone and found herself flush in the pocket and swimming in lard."

"Good God, no!" Sheffield suddenly took on the same frustration. "Pon my soul, you need to wrap that girl up in fine linen or step aside where I can do so. This will not do."

"Never been so exasperated in my life!" Andovir shook his head.

"What's to be done?" The two were like brothers, and both had affections for the little blonde hoyden. "Needs to be back in the country."

"It is a damn intolerable scrape. The earl and the duke would turn in their graves if either of us interfered with her first season."

"And your mother would skin us both alive."

"Just so." Andovir nodded.

"Does she know of it?"

"No, do not want her to know. She ain't quite the thing, you know, expect she will fly into the high dudgeons or fall into blue devils. Knows nothing of the unsuitable. You see how she is."

"Devilish unpleasant situation. Deuce take it, we can't make a mull of this." Andovir said.

That's the worst thing we could do." Sheffield agreed. "You need to make an offer."

"Christ, she sees me as a brother, always telling me so. She would be more likely to accept an offer from you than me."

"Then you would skin me." The marquess started.

"I shan't say I would enjoy it, but I would."

"Does anyone know of the dowry?"

"Don't read the gossip, do you?" Andovir blurted.

Sheffield nearly choked on his drink and then let out a belly laugh, only a marquess could manage. "Hardly! Oh... do not tell me a gossip got wind of it."

"Must have greased some tattler at the bank, I figure."

"What is to be done?"

"We watch for all the gammy fortune hunters and keep them away from her."

"And what army have you gathered?" Sheffield mocked.

"Only trust the four of us."

"Meaning Worth and Hawthorn?" his lordship moaned, "ain't near enough, but I can spend more time calling. I slacked off a bit. I didn't want you to get the blue devils with me hanging about so much."

"Never mind that now. She will not like it, but she is to have a gaggle of guards for the remainder of The Season. And damme, if I am not already having the mamas flutter their fans my way, dragging their misfit daughters in their wake. Good God, what have we come to, Sheffield?"

"One night at a time, Andovir."

The m e n strolled around Almack's, bowing their heads at the ladies, trying to keep the *incomparable* within their sites.

***

The following morning Olivia slept until half past noon. Her day dress and ribbons organised, and toilette prepared, Sarah walked to the window and flung the heavy drapes aside; a loud moan came from the bed linens, and the cover was pulled over the sleeping creature's head.

"No, please." She groaned from under them.

Sarah laughed and scurried over to help the chambermaid with the water for the bath. They both looked up to see a wave of sheets and coverlets flying toward the end of the bed. They both softly giggled. Olivia sat up, her dressing gown halfway around her waist.

"I heard that," then moaned. "Oh, my head."

They adored Olivia. She wasn't pretentious, pompous, or haughty. They watched as she tugged at her dressing gown and slid to the floor, catching her foot on one of her slippers.

"Go ahead, laugh at my expense. I am miserable, and you are mocking me." Struggling to find her slippers. She bent over, peering under the bed.

"There you are," she said, now on her knees, pulling out the lost slipper, "even my slippers are jesting me this morning." Sarah grabbed the hairbrush and waited for her.

"Your hair is a mess. Why did you not ring for me when you came in?"

Olivia glanced up at her, "at four in the morning? Are you mad?"

Sarah looked puzzled, "How did you get out of your gown?"

The young miss rested her elbows on her vanity, chin in her hand, and looked at her reflection in the mirror. Good Lord, I am a mess, she thought, then glanced at her maid, perplexed.

"I have no idea."

Sarah pulled her hair back in a chignon with side ringlets and slipped the soft blue muslin day dress over her. A row of tiny flowers embroidered the empire waist, and a tiny row of blue-covered buttons fastened the back and sleeves. The ribbon around her chignon reached the top of the bodice. With a small light pat at the final button, she declared. "There, you are perfect."

Picking up her rose water spritzer, squirted it twice. "Now I am done," and headed to the drawing room.

Now fully awake, she was excited and giddy. The ball seemed like a dream. When she reached the foot of the stairs, she whirled around, reminiscent of the night before. She was giggling as she sauntered down the main hall.

Reaching the drawing room, she saw the butler returning from the entry with a long box. She blinked, squinted, and blinked again. Were they flowers? She was afraid to hope. Gray stopped, holding the long carton, noticing her in the hallway and nodded.

"Good morning, miss. These came for you." He said dryly.

"Me?" Olivia clapped her hands, bouncing in delight, "Really?" she aghast. The steward raised an eyebrow at her enthusiasm.

"Really," dryly mocking her, hiding his grin. It was nice having young life back in the house.

"I'll have one of the maids put them in a vase and bring them into the drawing room with the others," The butler said flatly.

Olivia started to yawn and quickly clamped her mouth closed, "The others?" She dashed to the drawing- room before Gray could answer.

Grabbing both doors, she flung them open. Several vases filled with carnations, lilies, and chrysanthemums suffused the room with the balmy smell of cloves and an earthy, herbal fragrance. Strolling around the room, stopping at each one and locating the cards tucked neatly under the edge. Not sure what to do, she trailed her forefinger on the small cards. None moved into view, but she chortled in delight.

"Something funny over there?" came a familiar voice behind her.

She turned to find Lord Andovir leaning against the door with a cup of, well, she was not certain and didn't care. He looked handsome with his shoulder leaning on the door with the toe of one top boot crossed in front of the other.

"Oh, Jack, have you ever seen so many vases of flowers." She rushed toward him, giggling. He straightened as she latched on to his free arm.

"I should say not. It looks like a damn hot house in here." He smiled at her. "It appears you made quite the impression last night."

He removed her arm and strolled past her to the sofa, reclined, draping one arm over the back, crossed one leg over his knee, in his typical fashion and watched as she turned back to investigate the arrangements.

"You think so?" she asked seriously.

He shook his head, "You are such a funny little chit. You have no idea how lovely you are, do you?" Olivia pulled one of the florets from its vase and turned to him as she sniffed its fragrance.

He wanted to die at the sight she presented. God, she was exquisite.

"Well, you always tell me so, but when you say it, I am not certain if you are not mocking."

"I beg your pardon." The words cut the viscount. How was he going to share his feelings with her, if she did not even trust his compliments? She was enough to drive a man out of his senses.

"You know what I mean. You always say so," She was perplexed by the hurt registering in his eyes. "What are you doing here so early?"

Olivia still sniffing the flower and twisting the stem between her fingers.

"I came to see you. Should I have sent flowers to be the first of your afternoon callers?"

"Do not be silly." Olivia looked at him curiously, "I am not nearly pretty enough for you to court." She bounced to the sofa, bent a knee underneath her dress and sat facing him.

It was not the line of suitors with which he had to contend. It was the worst sort of competition, Olivia herself. Just as he was about to say his peace, his mother entered.

"Good morning, my lovelies." The countess's smile as bright as sunshine, after a long night of mixing with the best the *haute ton* had to offer. But more than likely, she was pleased after sizing up the season's line of available debutants and was ready to plan her next move on behalf of her charge.

"Oh, my. I should say you had a successful evening, my dear. How are you feeling this fine day?"

Easing her feet to the floor, unnoticed by the countess, she winked at Jack and sat up straight. "Much too excited. Are they not all beautiful?"

"Indeed, they are. I wonder how many will come calling today?"

"Too many." The viscount mumbled, but his mother gave him no notice. "Jack, you seemed to be out of sorts this morning."

"No, Mother, there is nothing to motivate me this early. Actually, I only need a word with you if you have a spare moment?"

"Certainly, I'm yours until I must make a few morning calls."

The two meandered off to the library, leaving Olivia to admire and sniff each one of the flowers in each one of the vases.

Slipping into his father's study instead, the viscount relaxed in an oversized leather chair and his mother behind the desk.

"I entered Lord Sheffield into our confidence." He said reluctantly, "I hope it is not objectional. I felt it was necessary."

"I am sure your father would not mind. He trusts your closest friends."

"Sheffield is as bothered by this new circumstance as I and will assist in keeping the literal wolves away."

"Good. I have been studying it. Olivia is very naïve. She has been protected and thus does not understand how desperate a potential suitor can be."

"Rightly so. Which begs the question I have been wanting to ask since my return."

His mother looked at him sheepishly. She knew his query and was not at all sure if she would be forthcoming with her answer.

"Why did you wait to bring Olivia to Town?"

"Truthfully?" His mother winced.

"Of course," Jack already had his own suspicions of the honest answer.

"You see how she is; she would have made friends easily and been influenced by the pretentious and pompous. And, knowing it, I wanted to keep her to myself a bit longer." She turned and faced her son. "It took years for me to recover from the loss of her mother. I often wondered what had happened to my mind. By that time, you and she had built a world of your own. Then after you were gone, we both were lost, and we found comfort with one another in your absence. She did require much polish and refinement after playing Robin Hood, soldiers or whatever else occupied the two of you."

"Robin Hood?" Jack interrupted, bemused.

"The riding astride, shooting, all those things that seem to fascinate you both so very much," she snorted.

"It wasn't that bad. I was just teaching her to shoot, ride and protect..." Jack stopped short.

"Protect? Protect what?" She looked up, startled.

"It does not signify," Jack said flatly. "It is only... she is so bloody innocent and knows nothing of the world. It seems you would have brought her into London to obtain her footing."

"I know. It is my fault." The countess smiled and sat across from him. "Unlike most mamas, I do not wish to see her off with the first man who comes along. Truly I do not wish to see her carried off at all. I know it is difficult for you to understand." She looked up, her eyes moist. "She is all I have of Marian, and when she marries..." She stopped and cleared her throat, not wanting to think of it.

There was the answer, and he understood more than she knew. He bore the same heaviness with his own muddled feelings. He nodded and gave his mother his arm, assisting her to her feet.

"My wish as well. I hope none come up to scratch, or if they do, she will not have them." His honesty intrigued his mother.

She looked at him curiously.

It appeared they agreed regarding Olivia's suitors. When they opened the double mahogany doors of the study, Olivia tripped over herself, nearly falling to the floor. She steadied herself, grasping the wide wainscot trim in the hallway in her attempt to retreat. Then she stopped and put her hands on her hips.

"You said the library."

"Reminiscent of the past?" Jack laughed and turned to his mother.

"Indeed, some eavesdropping. Only the blonde pigtails are missing." His mother laughed.

"Oh, the times I would run by and catch one of those pigtails, those intolerable screeches," Jack said with a grin.

Olivia turned on her heels, nose in the air and marched into the drawing room.

"Even the storming down the hall into the parlour." He called after her stomping heels as he and his mother smiled at the memories.

"I hope you do not have any knitting needles in there. She might use them on us both."

She took her son's arm, and they waltzed down the hall laughing regarding the child neither wished to relinquish.

CHAPTER 13

Olivia's first caller of the afternoon was Lord Sheffield, which was no surprise to anyone. The marquess had always been besotted by her, even as a child when she bested him at fishing, shooting, and riding. But when he laid eyes upon her at the country party, he fell head over heels in love with her, even knowing Lord Andovir's feelings. He had also promised the viscount to keep watch over all the potential suitors until the little hoyden had the opportunity to make the choice between duchess or countess, the two friends were determined it would be one or the other.

Knowing he genuinely cared for her, the first call was pleasant and eased the remainder of the afternoon for Olivia. Lord Sheffield stayed promptly for his half-hour, bowed, kissed her hand, and quietly encouraged her to relax and have a delightful time. He gave her a wink when no one was looking and bid her farewell. She thought without doubt, if she had to choose a husband this day, she would be a marchioness on her way to becoming a duchess. She truly adored James.

Her next suitor was a gentry's son. He was heir to a great estate in Herefordshire. His father owned a large herd of Hereford cattle and engaged in exporting the breed around the world. Mr William Beale seemed exceedingly kind. However, she found his intention, once he procured a wife, was to return to Herefordshire and run his father's large estate. Olivia found this most disagreeable. She was sure she had heard enough regarding cattle to last a lifetime.

Lord William Paget, the 2nd Earl of Loynton, she found aloof and unpleasant. His speech became grinding and boring. He was quite arrogant, she thought, and his half- hour seemed an eternity. Not entirely certain of his age, but imagined he must be near two scores, at least.

Lord Ralph Barrymore seemed quite pleasant, she had not the pleasure of dancing with him, but he made a point of requesting a place on her card at the next ball. He was the only one, except for Lord Sheffield, who had not bored her the entire afternoon. He was the second, or did he say third, son of the 5th Marquess of Hatton in Aberdeenshire, Scotland. When she noticeably hesitated at the mention of Scotland, he assured her he had a substantial inheritance and would not remain there. Lord Barrymore was of strong nature and seemed less bound to limit his attendance to a half hour. When Olivia acknowledged the other two gentlemen in the room and included them in her attention, he took his leave, albeit with regret. He was clearly smitten with her.

When the last caller left, the countess deemed the afternoon a success. Commending Olivia on her decorum and pleasant nature, after learning the little socialite found most of the gentlemen in question to be quite odious. There were eight gentlemen callers, all conducting themselves with genteel manners. Her ward, although truly kind to each, appeared bored senseless by the end of the day. The countess, aware of her exhaustion, suggested she retire to her bedchamber to await dinner.

The entire afternoon had vexed Olivia, and she requested, with no objection, to take dinner in her room.

She crept up the stairs and crawled into her bed quite ardently fagged to death.

***

The next few weeks, Olivia attended Almack's on Wednesdays, the theatre, musicales, and several private affairs each week. The countess hosted an Alfresco luncheon in the garden, the weather cooperated fully, and the roses seemed to know exactly the moment to bloom into their full glory.

Olivia made many friends and, at first, seemed to enjoy their company at the events. Until one of the musicales presented a sudden shock. She had anticipated being a part of the audience, but it ultimately ended with her behind the pianoforte.

Lady Birkshire's dear friend, at the last minute, inquired if Olivia happened to play, as one of her daughters had taken ill. Of course, the countess expounded on the hours Olivia had put into lessons and glowed with pride in her aptitude.

Olivia had not been pleased. She dreaded being the centre of attention but managed to suffer through it. It was quickly becoming apparent 'The Season' was not at all what she had envisioned. But upon further reflection, thought maybe it was exactly how she had imagined it would be.

The May morning was slipping away, and Olivia made no effort to leave her room. Sitting at the escritoire, arduously tapping her fingers on the polished mahogany, the other elbow propped under her chin, she stared over at the empty pot containing cold hot chocolate. She had grown tired of London and the monotonous grind of one dance, one dinner, one carriage ride and one promenade after another. She rarely had time for Jack's company, and he was acting a bit odd. A great deal of her time was spent with strolls and carriage rides with suitors. She fancied her time with Lord Sheffield, but Lord Barrymore was ever present and had become a bit of a nuisance. She had turned him down on the several hints and suggestions to offer for her, but his growing persistence was irritating. However, she continued to accept dances from him keeping him dangling on. She had no knowledge of teasing or trifling with someone's affection and thought little of her own actions.

She pushed back the chair and strode to her bed. She crashed backwards onto the counterpane, grabbed one of the pillows and pulled it to her chest. Tired of dressing in satin and lace, constantly smiling, and if she had to make one more curtsey, she felt as if she would scream. Maybe she was only fatigued; maybe she only needed a few days respite and wondered what her aunt might think of it. Olivia threw the pillow back to the top of the bed and scooted to the edge. The only way she would know was to head downstairs and ask. She took one look in the mirror and groaned, strolled to the vanity, and picked up her hairbrush. She rang for Sarah, and within seconds, the maid was stroking her long locks.

"Just a simple chignon, nothing elegant. I am only to speak with my aunt. I do not expect and certainly hope I do not have any callers."

"Are you feeling well, miss?"

"I am fine. I think, I am a bit tired."

Sarah tied up the chignon with a pretty white ribbon, and she was off.

The countess was sitting in the drawing room next to the window with her embroidery. Annabelle glanced up as her young ward entered the room.

"Good morning, dear. Are you well?" she said as she easily pushed and pulled the needle through the hoop.

Olivia cocked her head, watching how painlessly her aunt worked the embroidery needle. She could never enjoy it as much, then quickly returned to her mission.

"I am well. But I do wish to have a word," With conviction, she continued to stroll to the chair next to her aunt.

"Oh, dear." The countess dropped her hoop to her lap and looked up. She was quite accustomed to Olivia's pertinence. It was nothing new. It only seemed to be growing along with the child.

"Aunt Annabelle," Olivia said softly but cautiously, fixing her eyes on her aunt's face.

"Yes, dear? Would you like some tea? There are fresh cakes on the demilune, along with fresh tea and chocolate." The countess attempted to distract her long enough to brace herself for what was to come.

"No, thank you." Not wishing to be interrupted or lose her courage. "Would you be terribly disappointed, or I should say, would you at least consider," she was finding this harder than she expected.

"Oh, Olivia, just say whatever it is, child. I will not swoon or snap at you, whichever it is, you think I might do," she scoffed.

"Very well, I wish to go home." She clasped her hands and laid them in her lap.

"You do?" her aunt turned to face her. "Is there any particular reason?"

"It is a dead bore, or maybe I am only tired. Always sitting around waiting for the next boring caller to try to impress and please me." Olivia blurted. "And if Lord Ralph Barrymore asks for my hand one more time, I will scream."

"What?" That took her aunt by surprise, then she laughed, "Of all the things I expected to hear, that was not one of them."

"I was afraid you would be disappointed, and now I have made you cross?" Olivia slumped in the chair, stretching her legs out in front of her.

"No, no, nonsense. And do sit up straight." Annabelle quipped, "I am as ready as you to leave London."

"You are?" Olivia straightened in her seat with delight, "when can we leave?"

"You are such a capricious child. I can never keep up with you." The countess smiled.

"But I am ready to go home. I am tired of all the London promptitude and alacrity."

"Tired of being on your best behaviour, ay'?" Lady Birkshire could not help but laugh,

"Well, yes, that too," she said in a sombre contrite whisper.

"It is only May, and there are still a few weeks left to the height of The Season, but we may take a few days in Brighton if you like. You must not fall back to your old ways of Birkshire Estate. Furthermore, I do not imagine your uncle is ready for us to cut up his peace. How does Brighton sound? There will still be parties and gatherings, but you can relax a little. Hmmm?"

Olivia's eyes flashed with delight. She had not lost the childish excitement for anything new.

"That sounds wonderful." she wrapped her arms around her aunt. "I have never been to the shore, you know. I hear it is rejuvenating, as there are salt baths and beaches, and – and – oh, I overheard Jack and James... I mean Lord Sheffield, speak of Prince Regent spending time there. Shall we see him, you suppose? I am not at all certain how they know such things, but they seem to be quite aware."

"Yes, well, you really should not be eavesdropping on their private conversations, especially if they speak of the…the… well, their connection with the prince."

The countess knew exactly how they were aware and did not wish for Olivia to have any knowledge of The Carlton House Set coming to her ears.

"Whatever do you know of rejuvenation? You are much too lively a girl for such speech." She chortled at her small ward. She too thought a few days on the shore, sounded exactly the thing.

Annabelle opened her mouth to assure her the arrangements would be made, but in haste, Olivia scurried out the door. The countess inhaled and exhaled slowly, thinking she was the one in need of rejuvenation. It had been an exhausting season. It seemed the gentlemen who were calling were too young, too old or… Annabelle shook her head slightly, a bit chuckle headed. And the ones that were brought up to scratch…no, no, a thousand times no. It was time for a moment's halt to the confusion, and the seashore was just the place.

The trip to Brighton was planned, and in two days' time, the arrangements were made, and carriages loaded. Maids and footmen were dashing about as Olivia entered the main hall. The door to the library was open, and she followed the familiar voices smiling as she peeked in.

Lady Birkshire and Lord Andovir were focused on piles of papers. "May I come in?" she asked, noticing the stack of documents.

"Of course, come, come, child," Her ladyship retorted, never looking up.

Olivia watched mother and son as they shuffled through files. Her arms folded over the back of the wingback chair, and she stared at Jack. His chestnut brown hair was a bit longer than usual, and much of the sun streaks had vanished, although they had suited him, but what did not, she thought. The line of his jaw was strong. Her eyes travelled the short distance to the white muslin shirt, which could not hide his muscular arms. He was the perfect Corinthian, she thought as she watched him accept papers from his mother, placing them in different stacks. His hands were large, fingers stout, and they looked as if they could oversee anything. He was the strongest man she knew and the most handsome. It had always been easy to linger on his aesthetic features. Not one of her callers was as handsome as he.

Olivia's eyes eased back to the tanned and elegantly defined lines of his face. His cravat was a bit loose at the neck. He bent over the desk exposing the concave indention of his throat. The slight up-and-down movement of his Adam's apple mesmerised her. She imagined her nose pressed up against it as it moved. Goodness, what had made her think such a thing? At the same instant, the strangest feeling came over her.

There it was again, that tingle and burning sensation that was becoming quite annoying. What was it? She was not certain she liked the sensations and hoped she was not taking the influenza, not now. They were heading to the seaside for heaven's sake.

Her thoughts were interrupted by her aunt's instruction to ensure a stack was carried to Henry Standish immediately. It suddenly occurred to her that Jack would not be joining them. Olivia's heart sank and decided to leave them to their duties.

"I will wait in the parlour," she sighed. Neither looked up in acknowledgement. She rested her hand on the large mahogany door and glanced over her shoulder at the two buried in paperwork, and taking no notice of her, she exhaled heavily and quit the room.

Olivia slouched indelicately into the chair just inside the small saloon and fashioned her legs straight in front as each arm flopped across the arms and closed her eyes.

It was not long before Jack entered taking no notice of her sullen stupor just inside the entryway.

He turned to leave and observed the disinterested boorish form with eyes closed. "Why so forlorn?" He asked.

"I beg your pardon," she mumbled, sitting upright.

"Something is amiss," he smirked, raising both eyebrows, "or am I mistaken? Is this cheerful when you are about to set out on an adventure of your own choosing?"

"Never mind, I am just ready to be off." She said blandly.

"That is what mother said. I was a bit surprised. I thought you were having a time of it."

"I suppose I was, but it has become a bore, and I have never seen the shore, you know."

She sat up and leaned forward, even finding a curt smile.

"Bored? I should have taken you riding in Richmond Park. I am not sure why I have only just thought of it."

"No, no, that would not do. James has often taken me there, and it is still not up to Spartan's requirements, nor mine. It is not the same as in the country."

"I know, but it is not that offensive," Jack sympathised.

"It is. It is not the same at all. There are too many horses and people with which to be aware.

"Olivia, you sound upset. Did something happen?" He sensed something more was going on.

"No, of course not, it is only a dead bore. Dancing, theatre, musicales, playing that wretched pianoforte in front of hundreds of people. It… it is…" she trailed off.

Jack laughed, "It is called The Season, pet. It is what they do in London."

"Well, I find it boring and stupid." She said sedately.

"Come now, Olivia, do not be so unpleasant. You are going away for a few days. "You sound a bit childish."

She flew out of the chair, and all five feet of her glared up at him. "Childish? You did not just call me childish," she hurled acridly.

Jack raised his eyebrows and looked down at her. He crossed his arms and cocked his head left and then right. Olivia was scowling at him.

"And now you are being insolent." She accused.

"No, I am trying to think when you went from a civil young lady to a brat." He said cynically.

Clearly frustrated, tears began to form in the corners of her eyes.

"Fine," she lashed out and sat again.

"I know it is silly, but I thought, I mean, it never occurred to me you would not… oh… dash it all… I became a brat the moment I realised you were not coming." She said demurely.

Jack dropped his arms to his side and peered down at her, and quirked the side of his mouth, trying to understand.

"I am sorry," she muttered, dolefully lowering her head, and wiping the tears from her cheeks.

"To Brighton?" he said perplexed. "You know I have responsibilities. I am minding father's business."

Olivia looked up at him. He really had no idea. Could he really be that distracted? She inhaled and let it out as he patiently awaited her answer.

Trying to hold back tears, not at all certain herself why she was in such a pet. Raw emotions unravelling, overwhelming, and she was no closer to untangling them. But she did know he had much to do with her despair. Everything she had thought London to be, it was not. Her dream of a London season consisted of spending time with Jack. He had been away for two years, and she envisioned dancing with him, promenading in Hyde Park, early morning rides and the theatre, Vauxhall, all the things she had heard tales of, but with Jack. Which they had done together when she first arrived. She had missed him terribly. He had come home changed, and she liked discovering the boy, who had turned into a man. Then these stupid, strange men, lined up for dances at the balls, started making calls, filling her afternoons expecting her to talk with them, inviting her to go for walks and carriage rides. There was no time left to spend with the only person she had hoped of being with after two years of separation. She shook her head, trying to make sense of it all.

"How old are you?" She looked up at him and whispered.

"I beg your pardon?" he asked vacuously.

"How old are you?" she insisted.

Jack decided the best thing to do was to indulge in what he considered pettiness. "Three and twenty," He declared.

"And except for last summer, how many summers have we…" she appealed, "have we…" she broke off.

Jack tightened his lips and cut his eyes to the ceiling. Suddenly the candle was lit in the darkened room. "Aww," he murmured.

Now he was getting somewhere and understood the little minx. He swallowed, took her shoulders, and lightly pushed her towards the back of the chair, her chin tucked to her chest. She was determined not to let him see her tears. He knelt in front of her and took her hands in his.

"Olivia," he lifted her chin to meet his gaze, his strength too much to resist. She closed her eyes. "Open your eyes, Olivia," Jack's voice was soft but stern. "Now."

She did, and tears rolled down her cheeks. A gut-wrenching pain struck his heart, her tears… his weakness.

"I humbly beg your pardon. You are correct. I did not think about all the changes this year brings. The changes in my life and yours" He paused and inhaled deeply. "But surely you must have c-considered…" The words caught in his throat.

It felt as if someone was squeezing the very life from him. God almighty, his thoughts flashed to the note she had left him, the one he had carried for ten years. It seemed at three and twenty he still did not possess the words to answer and now had no propensity to say them, but knew he must…

"If you find someone suitable to marry, you will start your own life. It would change everything we have ever known."

Jack struggled with every word.

He stared at the wall above the chair as he attempted to regain his own composure. What the devil? But he knew his own thoughts. There was not another man he wanted to see with her. Not even his best friend, Sheffield, who could make her a duchess. But that was as unreasonable as hers had been. He looked back at her tear-stained countenance.

Olivia blinked back the tears, and she had a bewildered look on her face.

"I suppose I never considered what would happen if I were to marry. I never thought I would ever leave Birkshire House," she paused, "and you. It is my home; it is my heart."

Olivia was stricken, and the tears began again. "I cannot. Oh, I cannot do it." She sobbed.

Jack pulled her to him and stroked her hair. "Oh, my pet, you are truly caught somewhere between a young lady and my seven-year-old little princess?"

He could feel her head nodding against his chest. He slowly pushed her away from him, pulled his handkerchief from his pocket and dried her tears. She took it from him and wiped her face and, indelicately, blew her drippy nose. She glanced up at him and let out a deep sigh.

"I suppose I am truly a spoiled brat. I should be sorry, but I am not. I never considered that you would be doing something other than coming with us, and just, just, well, I guess, always being with me, and – and – being my, my very dearest…friend," she folded the handkerchief and wiped her face.

"*Merde*… you know, growing up is hard." She tried to give him a smile.

Jack laughed aloud. If she only knew how he really felt. There was nothing he wanted more in the world than to stop time and keep things as they had always been between them.

"Oh, Olivia, I have missed that unrestrained tongue of yours. But do remember, French is not so foreign in London, more especially within the Ton. It is as important as dancing, almost." He kissed her on the forehead and lifted her chin. "I am glad you are going away. Maybe you can put some of those refined manners away for a few days. Brighton is not as onerous, and there are fewer Ton mamas searching for rumours. You must be mindful still, of course. It is not that far away, you know."

Olivia giggled and agreed. She was so tired of having to consider every word before she spoke. "It is exhausting," she chortled.

"I'll tell you what I will do." His mind as muddled as hers.

He pulled her up and away from the chair. Holding her shoulders, he turned, sat, and peered up at her. She was the most beautiful creature he had ever seen, his angel from the day she was born, and he would be damned if he would not find a way to keep her.

She smiled, wiping the tears from her eyes with the back of her glove.

"Sheff, Worth and I were planning to do a bit of shooting in late summer, preparing for the fall hunt. You and mother will be leaving for the country in July. Would you like to come with us? We could take the horses, ride out to the lake, make a day of it," Jack could see her eyes brighten.

"Oh yes!" She slung her arms about his neck.

Any mention of home, horses, shooting and the lake

brought a smile.

"You know, Sheffield is quite taken with you. He said you were not that same little girl he remembered."

By God, if he must watch her court someone else until he could figure this out. It would damn sure be someone with which he approved. But even the thought of James making his Olivia a duchess made his stomach uneasy.

"Really? You think so?" she could not help but giggle. "I do like him very much."

"Yes, he loves dancing with you, the walks, and the rides at Richmond Park and even the stuffy visits here. He seems to like your hoydenishness," Jack was trying to seek a reaction, but if there was one, he did not see it. Then again, he did not care to do so.

"And I suppose, if he is truly interested, he needs to understand you will never be a typical young lady," Jack smirked, "and although I cannot imagine you as a duchess, apparently, he can. One never knows."

Olivia made a fist and smacked him on his shoulder. He winced, then laughed. "Not very duchessy of you."

"I do not believe he is interested in me for a wife. But we do enjoy one another's company. He is the dearest friend."

"That's my girl! Now, let us get you on your way, and I promise I will see you as soon as you return. Take a stroll by Prinny's residence, you might see him there, and if I know the prince, he will remember your introduction at the Carlton House ball."

He stood and took her hand. As they walked through the front doors and he helped her into the carriage, he could not help but think there was an ocean between the two of them now. His mind was on where his future lay, while Olivia was still clinging to the childhood she missed.

He knew that would soon change, but it seemed a deeper chasm than ever before. His only thought… he would be glad when she caught up with him. Still thinking of the letter written so many years ago but had been read more times than he wanted to admit. She had promised to grow up someday. As the coach pulled away and disappeared in the distance, he felt an ache in his heart… wishing she would hurry.

CHAPTER 14

The viscount returned to the foyer and headed toward his father's study. The sound of a carriage stopping in front caught his attention, and he paused in the hallway.

Struck by the intrusive nature of a young man presenting his card and the appearance of a disagreeable encounter with the butler, he waited in shadowed silence to note the exchange.

"I must see Lady Olivia." The young man insisted. "I know she is here. I saw her only yesterday."

Gray was patient yet stern, and the viscount was beginning to question the supposed gentleman's lack of propriety. He watched as he started to push his way inside. Gray's arm flew up to block his entrance, and the caller, devoid of decorum, pressed passed him. At that instant, the six-foot-two figure stepped from the shadows and aggressively approached the discourse.

"Can I be of service, sir?" Came the gruff voice from the darkness. The young man taking notice of the tall, Corinthian wearing a scowl, determination, and a look of authority, abruptly stopped, but still undeterred in his mission.

"I have come to see Lady Olivia, and I must be permitted to see her." Halting his paces in front of the receiving room door, Jack addressed the stranger.

"I believe the butler has explained to you she is not in residence."

Lord Andovir was quickly losing his patience with the young man's insolent behaviour.

"She must be here. She is not at the park, nor at Gunter's. At this time of day, she would only be there or here."

He had now pushed his way further into the hallway and was standing directly in front of Andovir, who had become excessively annoyed and glared down at what he now considered an insolent fool.

"There are two particularly disturbing items within your speech, sir. First, and most worrisome is your familiarity with Lady Olivia's habits. Secondly, you are presumptuous to think our butler is giving you a hum. I like neither of them. What is your name?" He growled.

"I have no business with you." The young man was being presumptuous and arrogant.

Pushed too far, the viscount remained calm. "That is where you are seriously much mistaken. At present, I am the lord of this house, and everything that goes on within its walls is inordinately my business. Now, I will ask you once more, what is your name?"

"I beg pardon. I am a bit overwrought. I am Lord Ralph Barrymore. I have been calling on Lady Olivia quite regularly."

"I've heard the name." Attempting to compose his address, as he had heard of him, but was neither pleased nor impressed. "Lady Olivia is not at home. Leave your card and be off."

Lord Andovir was no longer in the mood to be welcoming or civil. He had heard this young man was bold, brash, and pushy, insisting on occasion for two dances with Olivia. Andovir was beginning to imagine, she may have misinterpreted his overzealous nature after witnessing his improprieties first-hand.

"No, this cannot be. I must speak with her before…" he stopped abruptly then continued, "my father has sent for me, and I am to return to Aberdeenshire immediately. I will not return to London for weeks. Where can I find her?"

"You cannot." The viscount, having had enough of the insolence, was ready to physically remove the bloke. "It is time for you to leave, either on your own or with my assistance. Since you seem to know so very much regarding Lady Olivia, then you are bound to know I am her guardian and will take whatever necessary to ensure her privacy. You will get no more answers from this house. Goodbye, sir!"

With a firm look and the sheer height and weight difference, Lord Ralph Barrymore took his leave. Gray closed the door behind the chap and turned to his lordship.

"Thank you, my lord. I have not liked that one since the first time he passed these doors."

"Gray?" He looked at the butler curiously. "Why have you not said so?"

"It is not my place, my lord."

"I have no quarrel with that, but you have served this house longer than my years, and your considerations are respected." Jack's sincerity was apparent, and the butler obliged.

"Thank you, sir. I hope I have served this house respectfully and with much dignity and prudence. Therefore, I will tell you now, I do not like Ralph Barrymore. He overstays well-bred manners and takes advantage of the naive kindness of Lady Olivia." He stated with the utmost indignation. "If that is all, my lord, I will take my leave and return to my duties."

Lord Andovir nodded, and the faithful servant ambled down the hallway. Jack wanted to snicker from the butler's rise to anger in defence of this house and the family that resides within it, but he knew Gray meant every word. If the butler had an adverse opinion, he had better do some investigating regarding this young man. His actions today were quite unnatural, and there was something troubling about him.

***

When the viscount arrived at White's later that evening, he found Sheffield, Worthington, and Hawthorn seated near the bow window. As he pulled out the chair and sunk into it, his irritation was obvious.

"What has you in a dudgeon?" Sheffield asked.

"Humph!" The viscount grumbled. "One Ralph Barrymore, I doubt any of you have crossed paths with him?" Andovir glanced around the table and immediately knew his assumption was wrong.

"Him again?" The marquess leaned back in his chair, balancing on two legs, "cannot make out if he is buffle-headed or is here to cut a sham."

Andovir leaned forward and placed both arms on the flat surface, "So, you have run across the impertinent little bastard."

"I have… at Birkshire Place," Shef answered.

"Interesting, same here. Just today."

"There to drive Olivia to distraction, I imagine." Sheffield sat his chair down on all fours.

"Is that your impression?" He asked, curious at the reaction.

"I think, he is a cursed rum touch. Something else though, not yet sure about it. Odd one. But clearly, he wishes to make an offer for Olivia, but she has held him off. She is too kind to be rude, but he is persistent."

Worthington and Hawthorn remained silent, taking in the conversation. Hawthorn, the more serious and distrusting of the lot, interjected another reason.

"Or…not besotted or a bufflehead at all, but a pure and simple fortune hunter. What do you know of him?"

This put the other three uprights. They leaned into the table. It seemed the initial search for fortune hunters had found nothing and been forgotten.

"I know nothing," Andovir admitted. He had spent little time at Birkshire Place. His father had left him duties to attend in London, and after the first fortnight of escorting Olivia around London, he had made himself scarce. He had not cared to watch fools make cakes of themselves. Sheffield had called on Olivia, with his blessing, many times, but they had agreed not to discuss it.

"Shef may know more than any of us."

The marquess pulled on his cravat, feeling a bit uneasy regarding his afternoons spent with Olivia. His own feelings regarding the reformed hoyden had become more involved than he had planned or admitted.

"I have been present when he came calling. He is pushy and rude, as you say. He attempts to claim an inordinate amount of her time and, if not challenged, remains much longer than propriety allows."

Sheffield looked to his friend for permission to continue. Andovir waved his hand to proceed. "Olivia's lack of ability to be unkind or rude, aids his propensity to be unpleasant. I do not think she likes or dislikes him. However, I do think his overindulgence fascinates her. She believes him to be a harmless toadeater, sees no harm in him, but her inexperience clearly shows."

"He is a Marquess' son?"

"Whose?" Andovir broke in.

"Not English," His lordship stated flatly, "Scotland."

"What?" Jack groaned. "Is he the heir apparent?"

"No, if I remember correctly, a second, maybe third son."

Worthington pitched his farthing into the fray. "Appears to me, the young bloke needs some looking after. Speaking young, do we know how old? Does he attend university, or is he out?"

The two looked at him dumbfounded. "You know, I cannot say. His open infatuation for Olivia illustrates his immature youth, but the reality of it, I do not know."

Andovir looked to Lord Gillford, considered the most level-headed among them. He had not been born to a title, the son of a second son. A lofty military title had been bought and was quickly recognised for his skills, placing him in the clandestine service to the crown through the War Department. The sudden accidental death of his uncle and cousin, elevated his father to the title of a prestigious earldom, and within a year, the 4th Earl succumbed to an illness of the lungs.

"Let me see what I can find out about the Marquess. I am taking my mother to stay with her sister, who lives in Aberdeenshire."

"Thank you, Haw...Gill, damn, need to grow accustomed to the new title. I know I speak for myself and Sheffield. Anything you can find will be helpful."

The matter of Olivia was left to Hawthorn, and the conversation turned to boxing matches. There were exhibitions in two days at the Fives Court, and word was Tom Cribb had a youthful bruiser to exhibit. The wagers were too slight to keep any of the four from laying blunt on the enticing odds. The betting books at White's were busy. Many tankards and wagers kept them entertained until near daybreak.

Andovir and Sheffield found themselves walking together, making their way from #37 James St. towards Ryder, around five in the morning. Neither was foxed, but both had dipped a bit too deep.

"I want to say, it was quite considerate including me in gratuitous to Hawth. I do mean it, you know." Sheffield placed a hand on his friend's shoulder as they moseyed down the street. The viscount nodded.

"No need. I know you have an affection for her. Just not certain to what extent, and I can tell you, if I must, after calling you out...and deloping, a 'course, I can only see giving her up to you if it is her wish."

"That means a great deal, you know. But I also know you ain't figured yourself out. Until you do, my position is only interference for you. As far as Olivia, she compares each to you. She does not know her own thoughts, but that she does plain enough." Sheffield pulled a flask from his pocket and took a swig, staggering a bit and passed it to his friend.

Andovir took a drink and felt the burn all the way down to his Hessians. "Good God, man, where did you get that stuff?" He handed it back to his friend and wiped his mouth on the sleeve of his topcoat. "Not rightly certain, but if we weren't already half-sprung, we might shoot the cat."

"I might still." Andovir staggered and coughed, then cleared his throat, "By and by, just want you to know while we are in this fix, I am grateful for your attention to her. She will be waiting for us this summer, promised her fishing and hunting."

"She is a good sport, you know, never minded her competitive nature either. Not a bad companion and easier to look at than you." Sheffield laughed so hard at his own joke he nearly stumbled off the walk into the street, not that it signified at five in the morning, but Andovir reached out and pulled him upright just the same.

"Just know this, if you decide she ain't the one, I will see her as a duchess before I let anything less decide her fate. I know I am top-heavy, but my brain is clear on that. Course, I wouldn't be sayin' it if I wasn't a bit lit up. Don't want a facer, and I would surely get one."

Andovir knew Sheffield meant every word he said, even if they were jug-bitten. They meandered their way down the street. A hackney pulled up, and both men fell into it, thanking the driver profusely for noticing their need for one.

***

The next day Jack woke with a horrid headache and did not rise until noon. He made his way to Birkshire Place, and Emma prepared one of her concoctions she was quite famous for in the Birkshire household. Even so, he remained doubtful much would be accomplished this day.

In his father's study, he rummaged through paperwork left for Henry Standish. If he could manage to make sense of it, he would at least try to see him this afternoon.

He could not dismiss the frustration of the Barrymore situation. Recounting the strange interchange in the foyer, Sheffield's opinion, along with Gray's dislike of him, Andovir was certain there needed to be quick action taken. The more he thought on it, he hoped Olivia was having a time of it in Brighton. A missive to his mother was one thing he felt he could accomplish in his condition. He suggested she keep Olivia in Brighton as long as possible without going into detail, only suggesting something indeed had surfaced.

CHAPTER 15

Lady Birkshire easily kept Olivia in Brighton. The sea breeze was restful, and even without knowing the reason, she was enjoying her own respite.

Prince Regent did indeed venture to the Pavilion. Upon seeing Lady Birkshire on the street, had sent invitations to a small affair. Wishing to attend the lavish dinner party, Olivia was easily convinced to extend her stay in Brighton. There had been dancing after dinner and she was honoured when the prince requested her to stand up with him for a waltz.

Olivia was further delighted to learn the prince had known her maternal grandfather and had been quite fond of him and was thrilled when he shared some stories about the duke and her mother. She decided maybe the regent wasn't as bad as she had heard.

The salt baths were splendid, and she enjoyed her time on the beach until the sticky sand and salt air became intolerable. She attended the local assemblies, spending time with a small group of young ladies she had become acquainted with at the lending library. She received invitations to their homes on several occasions and reciprocated. Olivia was indeed having an enjoyable time in Brighton.

The countess, having a close friend living there, had secured a rental overlooking the sea, and the two spent many afternoons there reading. A delightful book, a light breeze, and fresh salt air was perfection.

After three weeks, Olivia and Lady Birkshire returned to London. The countess had sent word to her son; there were several balls planned over the final two weeks, and she had gone to great lengths to secure invitations before leaving for Brighton, and she dared not miss those already accepted.

Olivia, too, was beginning to miss a few of her London friends. She had never known many females her own age and discovered that when the young ladies were left unchaperoned, some of the most inappropriate conversations occurred. The young ladies she had met in Brighton had been less rigid with their openness and were extremely informative about what was expected of a well-bred young lady. Now a bit enlightened, she was anxious to rejoin the discussions with her Town friends regarding expectations and proper behaviour, now that she had a better understanding of what happened to those who did not abide by the strictest of rules.

The gossip, of which she had little interest prior to her trip to Brighton, now caught her ear. The girls secretly spoke of the patronesses and leading women of the *haut ton* and how merciless they could be, some being their own mamas. She now understood the tragic tales of those girls who had been ruined by sadly placing trust in a supposed gentleman who turned out to be no gentleman at all. Even a duke's daughter or granddaughter could not be saved from downfall, even in the name of love.

It was becoming very apparent to Olivia that love was not something of interest to her anytime in the near future.

But her time away from London brought answers to many questions. The small group of young ladies she met in Brighton seemed to be far more knowledgeable about men and freely shared their experiences, whispering, shooshing, and giggling throughout their visits. She was not certain if it was The Season nearly at its end or the better understanding of what was expected of her, but whichever, the trip to the seashore had given her a confidence she had never possessed.

At the first ball upon returning, Olivia was pleasantly surprised to see Jack in attendance. Not only was he present, but he was quite attentive. She was not sure what had changed, but he danced with her twice, along with Sheffield and Worthington requesting sets. He and his friends were mingling with her during the entire event; she was never more pleased. She was certain being surrounded by three of the Ton's most eligible and sought-after bachelors could not harm her reputation.

However, the little entourage seemed to be a bit too interested in some of her suitors. A few of them seemed to lose interest after looks were cast in their direction by what appeared now to be her guards. Lords Andovir and Sheffield seemed always to be at her side, and she was very often bookended by them. Not that she wanted potential suitors, but dance partners were altogether another matter. The one thing London had taught her was she loved dancing.

Barrymore was the only one of her prior suitors to remain steadfast. Others had made offers and were now betrothed or married. She had made a conscious effort to form a less friendly relationship with him, but he was overly persistent as usual, and the apparent tension between him and Lord Andovir had not gone unnoticed.

She also noticed there was resistance to him by Sheffield, who blocked his attempt to request a second dance as he took her elbow and gently passed her to Lord Worthington, who quickly claimed it as his.

At that point, it became abundantly clear that Jack and his friends were interfering. She surmised they were not only meddling, but it was orchestrated between them.

The following Wednesday at Almack's, once again Lords Andovir, Sheffield, and Worthington were at her side. When

Lord Ralph requested a second dance, he was cut out by the Earl of Gillford, to whom she had just been introduced. He informed Barrymore that he had claimed the dance, which she knew he had not, but she would not think of offending the earl.

She found him charming, immensely handsome, and an extraordinary dance partner. He indeed had a great deal to offer. He looked a bit older than Sheffield and Worthington. At the end of the set, Olivia began innocently flirting as he escorted her back to her aunt. She glanced up at him several times, even placing her free hand on her own, which had been tucked into the crook of his elbow. It was almost scandalous she knew, but she was growing tired of the three guardians constantly dictating her card.

However, the effort was fleeting when she was deposited back to her chaperones. He kissed her hand, acknowledged the lovely time, and then her elation vanished as quickly as it had appeared.

"How have you been, my good man?" She heard Lord Andovir ask the very person she thought, for one moment, might be her knight in shining armour.

"Very well," the earl nodded. "And you, Andovir?"

But even before the viscount could answer, Lady Birkshire stepped forward. There was a small pause, the earl bowed, and all Olivia's thoughts were crushed.

"And how is the fairest maiden in the Birkshire countryside?"

No! Olivia thought and scowled. They all knew one another, and by all appearances, very well.

"Perfectly well," the countess responded, smiling, "and you as handsome as ever. We missed you at the country party, but your note of regret was gracious and kind. How is your dear mother?"

"Very well considering. She misses London, but father's passing unsettled her nerves. She is visiting her sister in Scotland; I've only just returned."

Olivia suddenly recalled; he had been expected but sent regrets. She should have known; she really should. But she had no idea, even then, he was more than an acquaintance.

"John was quite distressed upon hearing the sad news," said Lady Birkshire.

"My father thought well of Lord Birkshire. I will give my mother your regards when I see her again."

"Oh, please do, and include his lordship as well. He and your father traded many hounds and horses, years ago. He was a dear friend."

Wonderful, Olivia miffed, not only was Gillford a friend, but so were his parents. Lovely!

Lord Gillford turned away, but she noticed he leaned toward the viscount and whispered in a lowered voice. She couldn't hear, but she could see the look on the viscount's face; he was not pleased. Hawthorn and Sheffield, without bidding their goodbyes, swiftly took their leave. Curious, she thought, everyone seemed to be acting strangely. But the music began, and she quickly directed her attention back to her dance card.

Olivia was far more relaxed after her time in Brighton; she loved dancing, admitting it was the one thing she missed in the country. Of course, she noticed Jack and James had claimed her waltzes, knowing it was no accident, suggested they might want to leave at least one for someone else. When she issued her complaints, they reacted as she expected, complete denial by both. They assured her to be an exceptional waltz partner and a shelter from the overzealous mamas. She questioned the first excuse but could not fault the second, and again tried to excuse them. Olivia's youthful obstinance was being encroached upon by self-awareness.

The viscount watched as she floated around the room with such elegance and remembered the first time, he saw her sweeping across the floor of Almack's; she had been breathtaking, but with a sense of wonder and uncertainty. He was watching a graceful, blooming, enticing young lady. The tiny little innocent girl had indeed become a woman. He knew it from the depth of his soul to the unexplained tremors the very sight of her conjured within him. As he watched, his thoughts betrayed him; she held her body so straight and tall, and that dress, it hugged her body in the most— in the most— Jack choked. My God, he was standing in the middle of three hundred members of the ton, lusting after Olivia. Lord Sheffield's sudden emergence to the pair interrupted his thoughts.

"I beg your pardon?" Andovir turned to face his friends.

The Marquess of Worthington eyed his friend curiously, "I say, would you like to share the delightful morsel who has you drooling all over your neckcloth?"

"No!" Jack snapped. "I mean," catching his abruptness, "I, I was not, I mean…"

Worthington shrugged, "Fine, fine, not wanting to share, I see." He retorted amusingly.

Sheffield grinned at them both and joined the banter. "No, Worthington, would not want to convey any little chit I set my eye on with you or Andovir. But I think, in his case, it is his attempt to avoid the mamas fishing for him, rather than the other way around. And as usual, it seems our dear friend is once again the catch of The Season, whether he likes it or not."

The viscount growled at both his friends in total confusion. "What the devil are you talking about Sheffield?"

The marquess laughed, "Same old Andovir, unaware that the mamas of the ton fall at your feet, year after year, attempting to turn your head with one of their daughters."

"Oh, good God, they just include me on the list of every male still breathing in London, including the two of you."

Sheffield raised an eyebrow, "You actually believe that do you not?"

The viscount looked at his friend with curiosity. "What's the bloody difference between me and the two of you? Except you both are better prizes, heirs to dukedoms."

His friend grinned at the viscount. "True enough, but the difference is you, my friend, are redeemable."

He gave both friends a smirk and turned back to the dance floor. The song had ended, and he was trying to find Olivia… again. She was getting damn hard to keep up with these days and had become far too comfortable at these large balls. She had taken it upon herself to identify the rakes and was a bit too at ease with them, no longer seeking her chaperones' confirmation for a partner. She was known for turning down many a hand, which she could do without offense. But her dowry alone kept her the prize of The Season, and this newfound innocent act of seduction kept him agitated and concerned. If he could keep her in sight, it would be difficult for most to navigate the labyrinth of her entourage.

She needed watching over now more than ever but seemed

more determined to escape her gaggle of guardians. He was getting frustrated with his chaperone position; it was beginning to feel more like a game of cat and mouse. Between keeping the undesirables away from Olivia and avoiding the ambitious and desperate mamas who were convinced he had decided to marry, he wasn't sure which was more difficult, but it was becoming quite tiresome.

The time in Brighton had done wonders for Olivia, but the recent changes had both amazed and perplexed him. She was maturing into a graceful, captivating, and quite radiant woman. The difference after the trip to the seaside was astounding. What happened there? Jack continued his search around the room. Where the devil was that girl? She was surely going to be the death of him.

***

The next morning, he rode to Birkshire Place and strode into the breakfast room and slouched into a chair, glancing over at Olivia's plate.

"Mmm, coddled eggs," he said.

Still irritated with his interference, she ignored him but could not help but watch him rise and make his way to the sideboard, piling his plate with eggs and bacon. How could any one person eat that much food, she thought. She turned her head to one side, staring at his backside as he went about adding butter and jam and moving down the buffet. The tall figure obviously spent much of his time at the boxing and fencing salons. Noticing his shirt and jacket bulging at his upper sleeve and chest, she acknowledged he had always been muscular. It fascinated her to watch his muscles flex against movement through the years. She raised and flexed her arm, sniffing at the lack of muscles in them. His brute strength had always astonished her growing up, especially in the stables with the horses. She tried but never could gain the strength he seemed to come by naturally.

Her eyes slipped to his slender waist, down to the breeches that curved over his hips and thighs and... she felt something catch in her throat; she couldn't swallow. She gasped under her breath; she could feel the sweat beading on her brow. What the devil? Oh my, what was happening? Goodness gracious, her brow was covered with beads of sweat.

Dear me, were these the risqué thoughts of the forbidden subjects the girls spoke of, and told were not appropriate for a young lady? She grabbed her serviette from her lap and quickly wiped her forehead. She looked down at her plate and began to spread more jam onto her toast.

"I beg your pardon, did you say something?" turning his head just a bit, still focused on his plate.

"Oh no," she said, quickly stuffing her mouth with toast and jam. For heaven's sake, had a moan slipped from her lips. No, no, it could not have.

"I thought I heard you say something," He took his seat but paid little notice of her unsettled demeanour. They both were eating in silence.

Olivia glanced up at him, just as he was about to take a bite of bacon, her own lips slightly parting, as his opened for the strip of pork, how luscious they appeared. What a lucky piece of bac...snap...crunch, she nearly jumped from the chair, her thoughts taking her completely by surprise. Good Lord, she was making a complete cake of herself.

Attempting to regain her composure only to find the mere act of raising his hand from plate to mouth was sensual. His sun- kissed hands were large and powerful, fingers long, nails neatly trimmed and manicured. She gulped, trying to shake the scandalous thoughts from her head. Why had she noticed his hands? How irritating, of course, they were strong; she had witnessed his strength many times. The memory of the stables flashed, not the angry words, not the tears, but my God, that embrace, that kiss...my Lord, that kiss, strong and unyielding passion.

She cast a glance his way, observing him reading the paper in one hand, as he raised a bite of egg with the other. She managed to stifle her gasp just in time, snapping her mouth shut. What was wrong with her this morning? She had been staring at his lips, thinking how soft they appeared. Her mind was so confused; she couldn't remember but was certain they were soft. She slid her tongue across her dry lips. What in heaven's name had come over her? She had to get out of this room. Grabbing a piece of bacon, shoving it in her mouth, she pushed her chair from the table, nearly tumbling backward. Jack flinched at the speed and determination of her exit.

"Are you quite all right this morning?" He asked startled.

Olivia nearly choked on the bacon. She hadn't thought he was even aware of her. She coughed and coughed again, raising her serviette to her mouth.

"Yes," she coughed again, "Yes, I, I am fine," she struggled to clear her airway.

Jack looked at her curiously. "The way you devoured that bacon, you might think to eat a late supper before retiring," he said flatly, watching her now attempt to free herself from the table.

She tried to think of something witty to say, but couldn't catch her breath, much less form words.

Finally, she cleared her throat enough to mutter in a strained, scratched voice. "Yes, yes, of course."

Olivia found her feet and quickly quit the room, informing him she would see him later. With a nod and a wave of his hand, Jack returned to his newspaper, shaking his head.

"Silly little chit," he murmured and returned to his eggs.

Slipping through the doorway, she promptly leaned against the wall, breathless. She inhaled deeply and felt her shoulders stiffen; what had just happened? Her serviette still in her hand, she began fanning the sweat beading up on her neck, her insides jerking right down to her – oh my? She had no idea, but whatever it was, she knew it had been something. Thank goodness, Jack was unaware of it. He would surely have thought she had gone mad, and she had the very same notion.

She began to wonder, could these be normal thoughts when you were…were becoming a woman? She closed her eyes and tried to relax; she was shaken by the unrecognisable desires. Whatever could have caused those thoughts, and of Jack. He was like her brother. Well, he was not, not her real brother, she thought about that. No indeed, he was not her brother, no relation at all.

But he considered her a little sister, did he not? She shrugged, frustrated. Then disappointment swept over her; indeed, he had always thought of her that way, and even if he had not, in his mind, she was a child and probably always would be. Feelings she could not understand overwhelmed her as she slowly trudged her way up the stairs, trying to unravel her newfound emotions. Each step caused another thought… step… why could she not have these same feelings for Lord Sheffield? Step… why did Jack have to think of her as a child? She sighed as she reached the landing; there seemed to be books on every subject in the world, except how to become a woman. No one with experience would speak of it, so someone should write it down. But then again, where would one find such a book? She blushed thinking of it. She entered her bedchamber with more questions and no answers.

***

Later that afternoon, Olivia joined the countess in the drawing room. Embroidery in hand, she focused her full attention, trying to maintain a row of straight stitching. Never much good at the task, it was not helping that her thoughts were continually wandering back to her new unexplained feelings.

She remembered a conversation with one of the young ladies she met in Brighton, who had been betrothed since birth; her life seemed complete, with no worries, and no London Season. Initially, she found it outrageous, the thought of babies being betrothed to strangers, based on their fathers' contracts, but she could not shake it from her thoughts. She supposed it was her dislike of the marriage mart, the constant line of suitors, the politeness, the nonsense of having to submit to one party after another trying to find a husband.

Why did one need a husband? Who wanted to go off and live with a complete stranger or very nearly one? She could find little sense in it. Worst of all, most of her suitors were only interested in her dowry. One had the audacity to ask how much it was and if it included land. How on earth was she to know, she had snapped, wishing to slap his face. It had become quite tiresome.

After her reaction to Jack, she decided there must be more to it than simply living with a stranger. But he was the only male she had ever dared look at. She had asked him once how his legs and arms had become so strong; he had only shrugged and said it was because he was a man; she had laughed. Now she not only realised those were questions which one should never ask but worse, the thoughts were vulgar and should never be thought of or spoken of by a lady. It was obvious she had missed a great deal in her youth.

She could not imagine her life without Jack in it, even if she had stayed angry with him for almost everything he did of late. But this was supposed to be different, was it not? These feelings, the talk of marriage, it was all bewildering. She wasn't completely ignorant, knowing the male and female bodies were different. She had seen the statues at the museums, but after that, she was quite clueless. Worse, no one ever spoke of it, and she learned long ago that questions were unacceptable.

She was becoming curious about this whole marriage, wife, children, and now this betrothal business. She might not get answers about marriage, a wife, and babies, but maybe the betrothal thing was safe enough.

Olivia decided the only way she was to know was to ask. Dropping her needlework to her lap, she abruptly turned in her aunt's direction. "Aunt Annabelle," she said, her tone sensible and sombre.

"Yes, dear?" The countess placed her embroidery in her lap facing her.

Olivia cleared her throat. The last thing she wanted to admit were the desires, unexplained emotions, and sensations, but she was curious as to why the four people, who supposedly loved her unconditionally, had not chosen to betroth their children. Why had they just not made the decision for her?

"Aunt Annabelle," she said again, a bit less sure of herself.

The countess turned her head to the side and raised an eyebrow. She knew this child; she was about to ask or say something uncomfortable. She sat silently as Olivia gathered her thoughts and took a deep breath.

"I cannot but wonder, you know, all this trying to find a husband, and at least so far, this season, finding no one," her brows furrowed as she hesitated, then continued.

"And you know, there is no one you and Jack," she paused,

"Nor... I can even consider."

"I must agree," her aunt interjected at the statement.

"I was thinking about our conversation, the other day."

"What conversation, dear?" Annabelle broke in, turning back to her needle. So far, she was thoroughly confused by the direction of this discourse, or if it even had a direction.

"The one regarding families betrothing their children." Olivia's throat felt dry and about to crack.

Lady Birkshire looked up in confused curiosity. Olivia lowered her eyes, took a deep breath, and began again.

"Why did Uncle John and my father not just betroth me," she paused.

Annabelle looked up in shock and froze, a deafening silence fell over the room until Olivia finally drew a long breath and continued, quickly...

"To Jack, of course... but I...."

Her words were cut short by the startling sound of Lady Birkshire's large, heavy embroidery hoop hitting the floor and rolling across the hardwood surface, banging to a halt as it slammed into the thick Aubusson rug. It was followed by a rather unladylike gasp, which was ensued by the rattle of a dropped teacup.

"I beg your pardon." The countess stammered; her face drained of colour.

She leapt to her feet, ignoring her embroidery hoop and the

roll of thread strung across half the room, left in the wake of the rolling ring. Lady Birkshire began to pace up and down the drawing-room floor, pausing occasionally, glancing towards Olivia, but not really looking at her, parting her lips, then clamping them shut, then starting the process over again. She tried to look at Olivia but could not. The only thing she seemed able to do was repeat her ambulating.

Olivia, not regretful in the least of her question but was beginning to wonder if she was to have an answer from her undeniably vexed aunt. Her ladyship was stunned, befuddled, bewildered, and rattled. For the first time in her entire life, Annabelle Norrys, Countess of Birkshire, was rendered speechless.

Walking and wringing her hands, trying to put her thoughts together, she had lost the ability to use her God-given sensibilities. She began to slow her pace, needing more time to resolve this in her mind, she motioned to Olivia to pick up her embroidery hoop and thread. What was this child thinking? She did not know what she was saying, she could not. Pure and chaste, she knew nothing, Annabelle had made sure of it. She stopped and drew in a long breath.

The crystal blue eyes of the little girl of six stared at her patiently, waiting for a response, appearing to hold her breath. Her aunt looked at her, really looked at her, she was not six, oh, dear lord, she was a woman, a fully developed woman. Annabelle choked back tears. When did this happen?

She had been so busy ensuring Olivia was everything Marian had hoped, she hadn't stopped to see past the perfect dresses, the perfect hair, the perfect lessons, the perfect... well, the perfect everything. Her aunt had completely overlooked the simple fact, Olivia had turned into a young woman. One with more grace than she had ever dreamed possible, but still a young lady, not a little girl.

When Annabelle thought of her childhood and the mischief, she and Jack had so easily made a part of their lives... Jack? What in the world? What had-- she shook her head, this is ridiculous, they had been friends since childhood, since the day she was born. They had always been together. But Olivia was an innocent, she knew nothing of the intimacies of that question, only knowing of pure love. Olivia already had more love in her heart for Jack than anyone could possibly understand, why wouldn't it make sense to this child when she couldn't find the same affection with anyone else?

Finally making sense of things, and her nerves coming under control, she thought how little Olivia knew about the act of love. Well, at least she thought she knew nothing of it. And only a small part regarding the meaning of marriage, it meant you lived with your husband, he protected you, he looked after your every need, and you were satisfied in one another's company. That is all she had seen or been told. The two marriages she had known were built on love and respect, and that she had with Jack and knew nothing more.

At least she certainly hoped she did not! Not the responsibilities of the marriage bed, she was confident, she did not! Oh, dear Lord, what was she going to say, it certainly was not the time to discuss marriage responsibilities. Goodness, the thought of it turned her face red. She had to choose her words carefully. The countess drew in a long, deep breath.

"First of all, your parents' death took us all by surprise."

Olivia whispered softly, "I know," and lowered her eyes, unable to meet her gaze.

The countess retook her seat and reached for Olivia's hand. "It was very sudden, and the contracts were only to take care of one another's children. It was all done with the hearts and minds of four very young parents, our only concern, being two young children," Annabelle sighed, "The thought of either of you as an adult, I dare say, never entered our minds."

Lady Birkshire looked toward the ceiling. "Now, in hindsight, I wonder just what were we thinking? Your father, God rest his soul, did have the foresight to think about your financial security. It was as though he had a premonition, though he never said so." She paused, "He took care and pride in the thought of your financial well-being, but Olivia," She dwelled on that a moment.

"The fact is, neither thought we would be fulfilling the other's promise. It was such a distant thought for two young couples who were healthy and vibrant. If your mother and I had not had such a time bringing you two into this world, I dare say we probably would not have thought of such things at all."

She let out a long sigh. Olivia could see tears in her aunt's eyes as she spoke. "And, above all things, in every interaction, we shared our hopes and dreams for the two of you. We loved you both dearly. The only thing we wanted was for you to be happy. We wanted you, especially, to find love. Now that I think of it, we did have a laugh once, would it not be wonderful if you did discover one another? But you both were babies, and thinking of marriage for either of you was beyond our years."

"'I mean, I wanted Jack to attain love, of course. But for men, it is different, of that you know. For men, there is no rush to marry, there is not the overwhelming challenge to be chosen for marriage. They decide one season they are ready for such a union, no matter their age, literally go out and acquire one."

Her aunt let out an even bigger sigh. "Is any of this making sense, Olivia?" She paused, then continued. "I know it sounds horrid, but it is a fact. I knew Jack would do fine for himself, whereas you, we had to ensure everything was perfect to attract the right gentleman. There would be absolutely no settling for you.'"

Olivia looked up and let out a little laugh. "I – I think - maybe I understand.'"

They didn't want her to settle. Well, of one thing, she was certain, living her life without Jack would be settling. Her heart felt just as it had when she was thirteen. She looked at her aunt with more questions but noticed her weary face. She had caused enough suffering for one day, so she changed the subject, lifted her shoulders, and patted her aunt's hand.

"'Enough of that, we should go shopping. I fancy I may need a new bonnet. The wind caught mine, and it's now a bit floppy.'" Olivia giggled, trying to lift her aunt's spirits.

Lady Birkshire was relieved she had altered the conversation, but she hadn't the strength to go shopping after this interview. An afternoon nap sounded like what she needed. She looked up with weary eyes.

"Why don't you take Sarah, dear? I think I need to rest for a bit," she said. Olivia smiled, bent down, and kissed her aunt on the cheek. As she walked out, she gave her a little wave. Annabelle gave a slight lift to her wrist and slumped in her chair, exhausted.

CHAPTER 16

Lady Birkshire sat in her library, the sun shining through the side window, and she could catch a glimpse of the ladies and gentlemen strolling along Park Lane. She sighed as she remembered the days when she and Marian walked arm in arm, giggling, laughing, and discussing their dreams. They were wonderful memories. But now, she tapped her fingers on her desk, her chin balanced on the other hand as she pondered.

What had Olivia really been thinking yesterday? If only she knew. The lack of suitable gentlemen callers weighed heavily on her. Could that be it? Was she only curious about contracts and betrothals? Aristocratic families found it a customary practice, especially in the highest ranks. Many of the older generations would never allow their sons or daughters to marry beneath their station. An earl's daughter, a duke's granddaughter— it never occurred to Annabelle to speak with her regarding her ranks of privilege. There were many things she had not discussed with this child.

Olivia had mentioned an acquaintance in Brighton, but she thought it was purely curiosity. Or... Annabelle gasped and pitched forward in her chair... she could not... he would not. No, she would not ask such a thing of him. But Olivia was maturing, becoming... no, she shook her head... not becoming, she was a young woman. Oh, dear Lord, what had she discovered over the past few months?

What about the recent young ladies and young gentlemen in her acquaintance? What did these young people speak of these days? All the places she had been in London and Brighton, what had she seen, and for God's sake, what had she been told? London was becoming a city without question, quite scandalous, and a lady's virtue was always in question. Olivia had always had a chaperone, well, at the very least, left the house with one, and she had always been in the parlour during her afternoon calls from gentlemen, but had she always paid full attention? Goodness, she had tried to be discreet, working on her embroidery, reading, and other distractions. Oh dear, what might she have missed? What had these gentlemen said beyond her hearing? Several had certainly wanted to marry her, a couple desperate to do so. What could they have proposed in whispered conversation? Surely no! Annabelle's imagination had completely run away with her. She grabbed her quill and paper. In a barely legible script, she posted a missive to John. She needed him, she needed his wisdom.

Only if, in that innocuous child's mind, it was consequential, and she could not seek counsel with Jack— Jack? What if, what if... why hadn't she thought of it before? What if Olivia had sought his prudence? Lord, those two pontificated of... of... dear me, of all things outrageous. She had chastised him for years to mind his intercourse with her. They had been far too, too at ease with one another. Had he heeded? Had Olivia heeded? Of course not. The countess was categorically discomposed; what in Heaven's name?

Annabelle finished the letter and rang for the butler. When Gray entered, he found the mistress dashing around, snatching her gloves and handkerchief, and searching for something more—her distress quite evident.

"Can I be of service, milady?" Annabelle seized the missive from the desk and shoved it into his hand.

"Yes, Gray," her quickness and urgency startled the devoted butler.

"Have a footman, or groom, oh, oh, anyone who is convenient, convey this to Lord Birkshire today." Gray, alarmed by his mistress' befuddlement and obvious anxiety, was duly concerned.

"What is amiss, milady?" Gray, the butler for many years, knew that if her ladyship sought his lordship by way of their fastest horse, something was terribly wrong.

Glancing at Gray's countenance, she guessed her behaviour must seem odd and tried to calm herself.

"I need John, I mean, Lord Birkshire immediately. Nothing urgent, well yes, it is urgent, but not a matter of life or death."

She discovered her bonnet, and placed it without regard on her head, hastening the ribbon into a bow. "Well, it could be, depending on… goodness," she murmured to herself.

"Just get our best rider away," pulling on her gloves.

Gray nodded and with haste, left the room.

***

The large brass lion's head in hand, Lady Birkshire was nearing its release when the door of her son's townhouse flew open, and Lord Andovir came to an abrupt halt, catching his mother stumbling across the threshold.

"Mother?" he said, surprised at the figure in his arms.

"Good gracious!" she said, catching her son's outstretched arm.

Finding her balance, while pushing her bonnet from her face, she barged past her son. "We must speak."

The viscount, recovering from his mother's unannounced invasion into his house, glanced outside to find no one else.

Confused, he closed the door and turned on his parent.

"What could possibly be the urgency, Mother?" he said surprised and agitated, "I have appointments this afternoon."

She glared at him. "Cancel them," she snapped, searching the hallway as the vertiginous bobbing up and around of her ladyship's bonnet with flowing satin ribbon ensued. Endlessly meandering the spacious foyer and in need of a chair, she demanded...

"Where the devil is your drawing room? My goodness, do you have tea? I need a cup of tea," clearly agitated, she was in a rather unsightly tither.

The viscount, quite busy all morning, failed to recognise the obvious despair of this whirlwind of a lady who had entered his home.

"Mother, I need to take care of some business this afternoon. And how the devil did you get here anyway?"

It Suddenly occurred to him there hadn't been a coach or carriage in front.

"I walked," she scoffed, still looking for the drawing room and showing clear signs of exasperation.

"You what!" he gasped.

Now appreciating the seriousness of the situation, he pointed to his parlour. He noticed his butler sedately and surreptitiously awaiting his master's requirements but not wishing to be caught in the fray of the flying female bonnet seizure. Jack acknowledged him with a roll of his eyes.

"Would you please have tea and cakes brought into the parlour? It appears I shan't be leaving after all, and by all appearances, my mother will be staying for tea." He heaved a sigh, "Also, send a note to Hawthorn of my delay."

His master's frustration was obvious. The butler nodded and quickly left the hallway, murmuring something that sounded very much like, "And this is the reason I choose to work for bachelors."

Grimacing at his butler, the viscount turned back to his intruder. Jack found his mother indiscriminately censuring his oversized leather wingback chairs, which were meant to accommodate the male gender, not feminine, petite ladies. It was a bachelor's townhouse, after all, and ladies were frowned upon calling in these buildings. She settled into the sofa, which appeared as near a normal size availed, then promptly placed a kerchief to her nose.

Mulling over the last few minutes, Jack was perplexed. His mother had never come to the townhouse, wouldn't think of doing so, had walked from Park Lane around Grosvenor's Square, barged into his house, and demanded conversation and tea. One of these actions was not a good sign, but together - Jack had the sudden urge to follow his butler.

"Whatever has disturbed you so, and how can I help?"

His mother snapped, "Help? Help?" she shouted, again placing the handkerchief to her nose. Jack's head jerked backwards in retreat from this violent retort.

"You, more than likely, are the very cause of it," she said brusquely, straightening the ruffled cuffs of her sleeves, more from nerves than need.

He raised an eyebrow, his mind wandering over the past few days, what could he have done to upset her so and for her demonstrative morning visit. Most disturbingly, she had walked, his mother, from Park Lane. Granted, she was a healthy woman, but even a quiet promenade in the park to be seen, she just did not do. Jack heaved a heavy breath and sat across from her, out of arms reach, of course.

"What have I done?" he asked condescendingly.

"I don't know."

The viscount sneered with dual raised eyebrows, "What? You don't know!" The absurdity would have been endearing if she had not been so disruptive.

"You walk here, barge into my home, disrupt my afternoon, have me cancel my appointments, and you don't know?"

His mother had clearly gone mad! Knowing better than this, he declared, she was having one of those lady's days, his father spoke of. His father had said, "Come along, boy, and for God's sake, don't ask why." Oh, how he wished to hear those words now. Why had he waited until the last minute to leave for his appointment?

"Well, I am not certain exactly what it is you have done, but I bound you've done it," she retorted, "it is why I am here, to learn what it is you have done, of which, if I did know, I would have no need of coming, now would I?"

Jack let out a long breath, suspiciously eyeing his mother. He might as well relax and attempt some instructive conversation, as this delusional, confused sparring match was getting him nowhere.

"Let us start again, shall we?"

His mother straightened in her chair, moved forward to the edge, gave him a menacing stare, and blurted out, "What have you said to Olivia?"

Jack sat back in the chair, "I beg your pardon?"

Of course, it would involve Olivia. Everything involved Olivia – the damnable little chit, his appointment, his waking hours, his dreams, his every thought. For God's sake, even one of his courtesans told him a few weeks ago in a fit of passion that her name was not Olivia. Good God... breathe Jack, one distraction at a time. This is your mother; pay attention, he thought, rubbing his forehead.

"I haven't addressed Olivia since, since…" he considered this, "since yesterday morning at breakfast. I cannot recall the conversation, the usual bantering, nothing of importance – nothing at all."

He wanted to help, but he had no recollection of the exchange. It was rather odd, now that he thought of it.

"She did without warning spring from the table, nearly tumbling out of her chair, grabbed a piece of bacon, damn near choked on it, and left abruptly, muttering something about engagements to attend. I did find that odd, but she's always been a little clumsy, you know. She has been a bit off; I suspected our close mindfulness of her, has her back up."

She removed the handkerchief from her face, observing his curious expression.

"Yes, I am sure of it, but necessary. What do you mean odd? She said nothing; I thought you two talked of everything."

Jack studied that for a moment. Everyone had seemed a little strange of late, including his mother. What was she really wanting to know? What did she want him to say? He had no idea. Bloody hell, he was entirely vexed.

"If Olivia has said as much, are you going to tell me? Or do we need to continue this ridiculous game of charades?"

She scowled at him. "She asked some peculiar questions yesterday afternoon, and I began to think, maybe you…" she cut herself off.

With a look of smug indignation, Jack leaned forward.

"You naturally thought I said something inappropriate to her," he placed his arms on his knees, "I assure you, Mother, I have no idea what you could be referring to. On that matter, I have done little else but strive to keep her manners and propriety at the highest level. To the point of near exhaustion. So, I doubt I can be of any help at all."

Jack leaned back again in his chair and crossed one ankle over his knee. "I might ask you, are you certain something did not happen in Brighton? I have found her quite different since her return. I meant to speak of it with you."

"It was wonderful. She befriended several young ladies; they enjoyed the beach and sea baths, and after you encouraged us to remain, we were invited to the Pavilion. The Prince Regent knew she was the granddaughter of the Duke of Norton, from her presentation, and when he learned of her being in Brighton, we received invitations to a dinner party. The prince was enchanted with her. There was dancing afterwards, of course, and he asked her to stand up with him. Oh yes, she was introduced to the Duke of York and the Duke of Clarence. She was impeccable, gracious, and elegant, reminded me of her mother. I suppose the weeks in Brighton catapulted her into maturity. I was pleased, are you not?"

Annabelle felt it best not to mention her friend and the betrothal question. She let out a sigh and apologized to her son, who obviously knew nothing.

"I am sorry; I am only vexed and distracted. I worked myself up to the point I wrote and asked for your father to come."

At that, Jack swung his leg to the floor and leaned forward. "You sent for father?"

"I didn't know what else to do." She nodded, "I need him here to discuss... things."

Jack had not fully appreciated the position he had been asked to fill, chaperoning his mother and Olivia, and his own fervent behaviour had been a difficulty of itself, without being forced into her companionship every night. An uncontrollable smile crept across his countenance. He had savoured the time, the laughter, the talks, reminisces of their childhood. Conversing? They prattled on so, but about what? Nothing important, yet everything, and it was relaxing and comfortable. Well, it had been until... until he recently waltzed with her, until the touch of her hand sent lightning through him.

There had been something different after her return from Brighton, and he no longer viewed her as a child. He saw the woman; the appeal and felt the desires he knew he should not.

He could no more control those thoughts and desires than he could breathe. It occurred to him that she had caught up with him. "Stop," Jack murmured under his breath.

"Stop what?" his mother asked indignantly. "If you are referring to your father..."

"No, no mother, I completely understand. I wasn't talking about father. I am pleased to hear he is coming."

"Oh," Annabelle said flatly as she looked at him curiously, her thoughts still filled with unanswered questions. Then she remembered his quick departure from the country party and Olivia's melancholy reaction the next day. Oh dear, had the two been connected somehow?

"Jack?" His mother began more controlled and quieter.

The viscount looked at her wryly. "What?"

Straightening again, poised in her most graceful position. "Dear," she started again, pausing yet again.

He eyed her with suspicion, his throat beginning to tighten in alarm. Whatever it was, she was undoubtedly struggling with it.

"Jack," Annabelle said again. "Did something" she paused, "- or rather did... I mean you," she paused again.

His patience waning, he grimaced at her. What the devil was going on in her brain? He knew she had one, and normally used it quite well. But this afternoon...

He looked up as she cleared her throat. This was getting old; old and irritating, but he remained silent.

Finally, she stammered and softly whispered, "Nothing happened between you and Olivia at the country party this spring?"

"What!" he roared and sprang to his feet, immediately catching himself and grasping the back of the wingback.

What the devil? Who was this woman? Surely Olivia hadn't shared the stable incident. No, she wouldn't be asking.

His mother quickly leaned back within the safety of the sofa, clearly startled, and then stood, "I beg your pardon, I think I should go. I am not at all certain I am being sensible." She retrieved her gloves.

He stepped from the chair and seized them from her; he placed her hand in his. "I assure you Mother; I have done nothing to shame Olivia or to give you concern. I promised you I would not, and I have not."

Annabelle's eyes softened. He could see there were still many questions. He knew his untimely departure from the country had left her confused. Now Olivia's disagreeable countenance, maybe it was time to speak of the inexpressible.

"Mother, can you remain a few more minutes? I need to speak with you."

Annabelle drew an uneasy breath and wondered…gracious, what next? She watched her son pacing, stumbling over words, and not quite knowing how to put together a sentence.

"Mother, what if I told you…" he trailed off, closed his eyes, gathering his courage.

While in his head, he controlled the past, present, and future, once in the light of day… however. He returned to the chair across from her.

Lowering his head nearly to his knees and raking both hands through his hair. His mother made a move to stop the habit, but withdrew her hand and the motherly response. Placing his face in his hands, he quietly murmured, "Mother, what if I told you I think I have feelings for Olivia?"

Annabelle's immediate reaction was, well of course, you have feelings for Olivia, you love her. But as the words formed, she understood that was not what he meant and remained quiet.

He was revealing a sentiment that quickly made sense to her. The last time he arrived from school, Olivia was sitting in the drawing room. Upon her entry, she recalled the way he was watching her, thinking nothing of it at the time, but the reflection of it; then when he came home the last spring… Olivia was no longer a child, and he had witnessed the altered state. Probably not certain of it, did not want to accept it, but now could not deny it. She could see without a doubt; he no longer saw her as a child or a sibling.

"Oh, Jack, I am sorry. I should have seen this; I should have…" She reached across the space between them and placed her hand on the back of his head, twirling the chestnut curls through her fingers.

His head buried in his hands, he moved his forefingers to his temples and pressed them in deep to ease the stabbing pain.

"I don't understand it, or when, or how it happened. How could you possibly know what I am saying? I tell myself it will pass. I shouldn't look at her that way. I was trying so very hard to find her a good husband…" he stopped and jerked his head upright, staring at his mother, "wasn't I?"

His mother quickly withdrew her hand, placing it in her lap, and gazed at him. "What do you mean?"

"I have made excuses, sought reasons to dislike every suitor.

Good God, Mother, am I responsible for Olivia not finding a suitable husband? Am I keeping her from happiness?" He stood, staring out the window. "You know she accused me of it, said I was intimidating her suitors. She thought I would never approve of any of them." He turned and faced his mother. "Was she right? Was I purposely finding things wrong with them, someone who would love her and take care of her?"

Annabelle stood, and moved to her son, placing her hands on his crossed arms. "I don't know, were you?" she asked softly.

His eyes were closed, he bent his head, and slowly opened them, meeting her gaze as he dropped his arms. "I don't know, I just do not know."

Annabelle could see his anguish and torment. My God, he was in love with Olivia! She had watched him protect her from the time she was old enough to walk... no, from the day she was born. He had taught her so many things; if he loved it, he wanted to share it with her. And Olivia had worshipped the ground he walked upon. She had cried rivers of tears when he left for school, and waited by the window, peering down the long driveway, in anticipation of his return.

Tears began to fill Annabelle's eyes; she was beginning to understand, it had never been a love between a brother and sister. She had been his princess; he her knight, her protector. Oh God, but what now?

She embraced her son, withdrew and reached up and ran her fingers through his mussed hair.

"Don't bother, I think I have pulled half of it out over the past few weeks." She had no answers, he knew, but it felt good to share his turmoil.

She smiled at him, taking his chin in her hand. She could not stand the hurt in his eyes. He was blaming himself for Olivia's failure to secure a husband, but at the same time trying to figure out his own feelings. She released his chin, taking his hands into hers.

"Truthfully, I do not think Olivia is interested in finding a match. I am not certain what is going on in that head of hers. But as for you, your father should be here tomorrow, speak with him. He is very wise and a reformed rake himself." She winked at her son with a wry grin.

Jack laughed out loud. She smiled, managing, she hoped, to chase a bit of sadness from him. "I really must go. Speak with your father the day after. We will have breakfast at eleven?"

"Let me have my carriage brought around to take you home." The viscount motioned for his butler.

Taking her arm, he escorted his mother into the foyer. She stopped and placed her hand on his face. "I love you; you know." Smiling and squeezing his chin, then lightly tapped his cheek.

He was tired but managed to smile. He had fought these demons alone for so long, unleashing them was a welcome release. He escorted his mother to the equipage. The footman let down the step and assisted her into her seat. She bent forward and waved goodbye out the small window. Standing in silence, he watched them pull away.

CHAPTER 17

Lord Birkshire, the 7th Earl of Birkshire, disliked London, due more to the dirty streets and the stench, especially in summer, preferring the fresh clean air of the countryside. Even the rain was tolerable in the country; at least it was clean. John peered out the window as the carriage moved through the west London streets. Hyde Park came into view, and he relaxed at the thought of soon seeing his Annabelle, which always brought a smile.

Her missive held no explanation, except urgency, indicating everyone was well. She only needed his wisdom and guidance. But insisting he come as quickly as possible and would be expected the following evening.

Changing quickly for dinner, he was straightening his sleeve as he entered the parlour, the tall, distinguished gentleman gave pause, as he was captivated by the two lovely ladies engrossed in conversation near the window. His dark chestnut hair, touched by shimmers of silver at the temples, complimented his distinguished, handsome appearance and the air of confidence with which he cleared his throat.

The ladies snapped their heads toward the doorway and the intrusion was met with keen differences. Annabelle, expecting to see her husband, leapt from the duvet, running to his side. Olivia, unaware her uncle was expected, managed to withhold a gasp of delight as she recognised the familiar face.

"Oh, John," her aunt exclaimed as she threw her arms around his neck.

"I must come to London more often," He winked at Olivia and smiled, "I daresay I don't receive these greetings in the country."

Olivia extended her hand, which he accepted, pulling her towards him and placing a light kiss on her cheek. John turned back toward the hall and extended elbows.

"Shall I escort the two loveliest ladies I've ever set my eyes upon to dinner?"

The threesome laughed and joked throughout the meal. Their family dinners had been missed by all. On several occasions, the earl glanced at Annabelle, waiting for her to relay what prompted the urgent request. He was perplexed by the silence; they had always spoken openly in front of Olivia. It wasn't like his wife having urgent business, then to leave it unattended.

After supper, the three retired to the parlour. "John dear, if you would like a glass of port, I can have one of the footmen retrieve it from your study."

"Nonsense Annie," he retorted, patting her hand. "I will have brandy, and that will suit."

He made his way to the sideboard, removing two snifters, holding the decanter, he glanced over his shoulder and raised an eyebrow to his wife.

Annabelle considered it for a moment; she needed a bit of courage for their conversation. She smiled and nodded wearily.

John poured a splash, then on second thought, filled the glass to a third.

Shocked by the level of amber liquid, she looked up at him and cleared her throat. "Uh, yes, just right," she choked, and he chuckled.

Olivia made a bit of small talk, enough to be polite, and announced she had a busy day ahead. Her aunt nodded, confirming she had everything ready for the Pendergrass ball the following evening and she took her leave.

Annabelle waited a few minutes to ensure Olivia was down the hallway and up the stairs. She peeked out the door, then quietly closed it, making her way to her husband. John grinned a sheepish grin.

"Miss, it is highly improper to find yourself behind closed doors with a questionable gentleman," he said teasingly.

She cut him off, "Do stop," she said. "Don't tease me, I am much too – too – oh, John."

He took her hand and pulled her to the sofa to face him. "All right, Annabelle, what is this urgent matter, which has you so disagreeable?"

"John," frustratingly so, she was having as much difficulty speaking of it with him. For goodness' sake, they could speak of anything.

He looked at her, seeing she was struggling; he grasped her hand. "Annabelle Catherine, you are distressed indeed. It has you completely vexed; tell me and let us get it over."

She placed her free hand on top of his. "I think, no I fear - no I do not fear it, but I am afraid for him," she stuttered.

John's eyes narrowed, "Afraid? My love for whom?"

"Our son," she murmured.

"Our son!" he barked, a little surprised.

His son was old enough to get himself into a lot of things, but he also knew he needed no help from his father to get out of them.

"I am afraid he has fallen in love," she blurted out, lowering her head, and sniffling a bit. She pulled her handkerchief and blotted her nose gently.

John wrenched his mouth. "And that is a problem?" He was beginning to understand how one of those horrid teeth- pulling doctors must feel.

Annabelle stammered again. "Well, yes - no - not exactly, well, maybe… Oh, I don't know." Again, dabbing her nose with her handkerchief, as moisture filled her eyes.

The earl tilted his head and in a stern voice. "Annabelle! "She looked up and he saw the pooling in her eyes. "What is wrong? Tell me this instant."

His lordship knew his son and he knew he hadn't compromised a young lady, nor did he think he had fallen in love with an unsuitable one. A rake he was, but not a stupid one.

She blinked back the teardrops. "I think he is in love with Olivia," she blurted it out without pause. Burying her face in her handkerchief as the tears were released without warning.

Putting his arms around her shoulders, John began to laugh. "Oh, Annabelle."

She snapped her head to his, "I am not being ridiculous, so do not even say so." Suddenly she felt as though he wasn't taking her seriously.

He wiped the salty drops trickling down her cheeks, released his hold, and moved to refill her brandy. "John Jacob, this is serious."

The earl turned and smiled as he poured another glass of the amber liquid. "I suppose it could be or would be if you are only just now learning of it," he said quietly.

"What do you mean? It is only just so; he hasn't resolved it himself." Irritated by her husband's lack of concern.

He walked over to her and clutched her hand in his. "Is this what has you upset?"

"Yes, of course, Olivia keeps asking me why we didn't betroth the two of them because she has not found a suitable match and I am not certain she is taking any of it seriously. She sees it all as ridiculous. I go to see my tormented son, who believes himself in love with her. Good Lor..." she stopped herself. "Good heavens John. Our children are miserable, and I don't know what to do."

John put his arms around her and pressed her head to his shoulder, pulling her to him. "Nothing, my love, we are to do nothing at all."

Annabelle tried to pull away and look at him, shocked by his reaction. She had called him to London to do something, now he was saying they were to do nothing. He held her tightly in place. "My dear, I know I am only a stupid man. I know I do not notice what goes on right under my nose. But I must tell you, your son has been in love with Olivia for at least the past five years. The fact is, I am impressed he has finally come to the realisation himself. There must be some serious suitors coming up to scratch."

Annabelle jerked away and looked at him, "what?"

John smiled, "the only way a man will ever admit he is in love with a woman is when another man tries to claim her."

She looked at him suspiciously. He nodded in assurance. "But what of Olivia? She doesn't care for suitors, dislikes afternoon callers, and says they are dead bores, dead bores? Well, except Lord Sheffield, and I fear that is more of a friendship, at least that is what she calls it. She is growing weary. I am fearful she may settle for someone, anyone, just to stop what she considers all sixes and sevens. I believe it to be the reason she wishes we had betrothed them."

John took her face in his hands, "My dear," he brushed a lock of hair that had fallen on her forehead. "Smart girl, by the way. It is what we should have done in hindsight. Why do you really think she asked about a betrothal between her and our son?"

Annabelle stopped, and turned her head toward him, confused and overwhelmed. "I suppose I hadn't thought why, other than she dislikes making decisions. All I know is they were both admitting things to me, looking for answers and I have none, not one. I only pace in front of them and appear a silly goose."

John pulled her to him and let out a small laugh. "You, a silly goose, I dare think not. Only a mother searching for a way to make the pain go away."

"Pray, what does a father do?"

"We hope the pain will not destroy their faith in mankind and they will find the answers before the cut is too deep." He respired. "I will remain in London. It is nearly time to return to the assemblies. I can, if nothing more, pull you from the abyss when things get untidy. Which they will, Annabelle. Olivia is young and you have protected her so, she has much growing still to do to understand her own heart. But I can tell you. I know my son, and he is in love with her. I am not sure he wants a wife, just yet. I have known he was in love with her for some time, and rumour is, she compares all to him."

"Rumours? What do you know of rumours?"

"You are not the only one with prattling friends." Laughing at her, "And what of it, can you perceive a more perfect union? Is it not what you and Marian dreamed of when they were only babes? You may consider me a fool when it comes to such things, but I do not forget what you tell me. True, there is nothing we can do, except reassure them their love is a respectable, suitable, and acceptable one. I can see where they may question it. It would be difficult to untangle, especially for our innocent Olivia. But we can assure them it is quite agreeable." John stared at his wife, waiting for agreement and calm resolution.

She stood, "I suppose I must agree, but?" Standing and clasping one arm and placing his finger to her lips, wiped the remaining tears from her face and smiled down at her. "I think, my lady, it is time we found your bedchamber."

CHAPTER 18

Jack's appointment that afternoon was with the Earl of Gillford. He had returned the night of their brief meeting at Almack's. Indicating he had news and believed the information had uncovered Barrymore's true motives.

Initially, Hawthorn found nothing. It appeared the Marquess of Hatton was either beyond reproach or very private with a loyal staff, and he had found no more regarding his third son, Lord Ralph Barrymore. Usually, if something is amiss, someone in the ranks of servants is a chinwag. The secret then, if damaging, finds its way to a local pub; followed by an intoxicated bloke arriving home; sharing the scuttlebutt with his wife; to awaken the following morning with it forgotten.

The Earl of Gillford had been quite enthusiastic about his aunt and forwarded a letter informing her of their early arrival. The Countess of Gillford and her sister were quite the tattlers, and Hawthorn assured Andovir that if they hadn't heard about it, knew of it, or together were unable to find it, there was nothing to be found.

After the cancelled meeting, Gillford penned a missive to Andovir to be at White's that evening at eleven. When the viscount arrived, he found the earl and Sheffield. He pulled out the chair between them, with a clear view of the room.

"Hawth," Andovir nodded, then turned to Sheffield and nodded. Sheffield raised his tankard. "Let's have it, am I to kill the bastard?"

Straight to the point, Jack was deadly serious. The earl chugged his ale and rested his tankard on the table. "It is possible, but I'd rather not see you at Newgate or, truthfully, having to deliver you personally to the continent." then lowered his voice. "After a sennight, I found nothing. It was as though the Marquess didn't exist. There was nothing good or bad to say about him by anyone. In my line of business, that is both peculiar and alarming. My gut told me everyone was doing it a bit too brown. No doubt, I'd have to travel to Aberdeen for a few days and find a tavern or gaming house. Luck on my side, I found one, not far from Huntley Castle.

It was a high-stakes one, and there was plenty of brass and ale flowing, but these men were there for the sport and not the drink. There were several games of chance, cards and ivories being played, with several ivory turners, besters, and bonnets looking for a dupe to swindle. After about an hour, guess who walks in? None other than Barrymore himself."

Jack grunted disgustedly.

Hawthorn ignored the interruption. "He walked over to a familiar lot, pulled out a chair telling them to deal him in. There was resistance and a bit of disgruntled discourse. The table runner inquired if he was alone or if the Marquess was joining them, showing clear displeasure at him being alone. I was even and decided to continue. I could not hear all the exchanges, but I heard enough. Father and son found regular excitement in the cards; the son bad at it. The Marquess had grown tired of covering his mark. It was clear those at the table welcomed the Hatton money, but not markers, especially from the third son. There was an apparent concern about future payments of vowels, and all were privy to the Marquess' displeasure in the mounting debts. I gathered, being near the castle, the Marquess picked up most of them."

"So, the bastard came to London this season for one reason – a hefty dowry. Damme, how the devil did the word get out about hers? God help me, I will kill the tattler, along with the

Marquess' son. If one is to be exiled, it might as well be for the whole of it." Andovir was seething.

"Is he still calling on Olivia, with no encouragement?" Hawthorn found this curious as well.

"Daily, until they were off to Brighton. I assure you, his attitude the day of their departure was repugnant." Jack growled, his jaw clenched, "And bloody hell, the worst of it, I think Olivia likes him."

"No, she don't!" Sheffield interjected flatly.

"What makes you so sure?" Jack snapped.

"I have seen their exchanges. He is overbearing, but she only tolerates him and is kind. The same treatment, I have seen her give a stray cat." Sheffield uttered gently.

Jack snarled, "She couldn't be mean to a snake. Too trusting, too naive, and too damn friendly," Jack slammed his fist on the table, shaking the steins.

"Now what?" Sheffield peered at them both.

Richard Hawthorn was calm, calculative, and spoke without emotion. He was a seasoned special agent of the crown, who had seen enough enemies to recognise one when he saw one. "The Season ends soon; he will try something before then if he believes Olivia to be his only choice."

"After my nearly tossing him out, he will be more cunning, I fear." Jack raked his hand through his hair. Then with elbows on the table, pressed his fingertips into his temples.

"If she is only tolerating him, he will be desperate, and if Sheffield is correct, he knows she has no intentions of accepting him. He will compromise her or worse, kidnap her and remove her to Scotland. I figure his father's castle. Nothing or no one to fear and there is sure to be a vicar in the pocket of the marquess? If we do not stop him before he reaches Scotland," Hawthorn was trying not to provoke Andovir, but they all had to know what they faced.

Jack let out a heavy breath. "I will kill him," his voice low, almost silent as he thought of Olivia being taken by force.

"He would have to drug our little wildcat." Sheffield allowed more of his own feelings to show than intended.

"Damn it to hell, worst of all, I don't know how to manage Olivia. She is so angry for the interference; it would not do to put the damn little chit into one of her pets. She would use him to give us the slip, too naïve to know the danger. I sure as hell don't want to fight her obstinance. Should she tell me, I am mad..." Jack swallowed hard, leaning back into the chair.

"And, if he should sense her contempt towards us, he will use it to gain the advantage," Sheffield interjected, agitated, and concerned.

"What do you mean?" The earl looked at Sheffield.

"Her breeding and manners will keep her from blatancy, but she may use him to avoid us." Sheffield looked ill. He and Olivia had become confidants, but she was angry with his interference too. The only difference was, she was not in love with him and didn't care to see him miserable; she wanted nothing more than to torment Andovir.

"We will have to double down tomorrow night at the Pendergrass ball. It is one of the last balls and is certain to be a crush. Keeping Barrymore in our sights will be more important than Olivia." Hawthorn's brows still furrowed.

"Then you will attend tomorrow night?" Andovir appreciated Gillford's involvement. He was still in mourning and had already done more than expected.

"Wouldn't be anywhere else! Listening to that weasel and the rest for several hours, I have no doubt he is to the point of non-plus. It's doubtful he knows the actual size of her inheritance, but her naivety makes her an easy target, and he figures the dowry enough never to be on the rocks again and good enough to back his debts from year to year. It is a gamble; if he knew just how much, he might just hold her for ransom, but either way, I have no doubt she is his target, that much was obvious. My own table referred to him as the Nine of Diamonds; in Scotland that is not a good portrayal and speaks volumes regarding their lack of character. I hesitate to share the cant language."

"Out with it, we need to know." Andovir bristled.

"One called him a hell-born royster, another… a blackguard," Hawthorn added.

"I can see it in your eyes, Hawth, there's more. Out with the worst of it." Andovir demanded.

Hawthorn hesitated. "One said all in his altitudes, but he's cleaned out, playing on vowels with no sure betrothal. But the worst and what brought me quick like, was the one who said, the marquess has turned him out, so if he must, bit her, *nolens volens*, he will, desperate fool and all. Someone ought to warn that chit's family. They never mentioned Olivia by name. But Barrymore said himself, it wouldn't be long he would be a tenant for life, and this wench would ensure he remained at the table for years." He paused, seeing the rage in his friend's countenance. "I am sorry, Andovir, I didn't want to tell you the whole of it, but I got little help from Bow Street, he has done nothing, they said."

"He talks a lot about her dowry; you think he knows how much it is?" Sheffield couldn't believe this was happening. This whole night had found them outside of propriety. Rakes they may be, but they played within high societal rules and honour.

"I doubt my father knows; she could be the wealthiest chit in England for all we know. A great deal at the Exchange, Nathan Rothschild handles it. Barrymore believes her wealth to be enough. But the bastard will never live to see a farthing of it!"

Even in the dim light, Hawthorn and Sheffield could see the onyx eyes of a madman. "Is Worthington to come tonight?" The earl felt a turn of conversation was needed to calm his friend.

"I will contact him in the morning, he'll be there," Andovir said as another deep breath left him. The three men finished their drinks and parted ways, planning to orchestrate their plan before tomorrow evening. The viscount was furious when he left White's. Without notice, he ended up in Hyde Park before he realised it. He had to think. If only Olivia was not so damn irritated with him. She was sick of what she called her gaggle of guards. He was sure, if he told her Barrymore was a dangerous fortune hunter, she would be hell-bent on proving him wrong. *God help me.*

***

The next morning as the floor clock pounded out eleven strikes, the young viscount was pulling off his gloves and handing them, along with his top hat, to Gray, with an unfamiliar serious countenance.

"Father in his study?"

"No, my Lord, the breakfast room." The old butler recognised the frustration.

"Thank you, Gray."

The door to the small and quiet breakfast room was open.

"Good morning, Mother." He nodded. "Father, I expect your trip was a pleasant one?" He bowed slightly.

Jack made his way to the sideboard, filling his plate. He acknowledged Olivia with a smile and nod.

She returned a strained "My Lord" and returned to her toast.

"It was, until we got to Town, you know my keen affection for it." John grinned.

"How long do you intend to grace us?" His son asked.

"I am not certain, but with Parliament drawing to a close, and then there is your mother" He glanced at his wife, raised an eyebrow, and smiled. "I figure to stay until the end of the assembly. Much change is going on with all the industrial growth, you know. You must keep up, my boy. These are important times."

Annabelle raised her teacup in agreement. The viscount had other concerns and only nodded. The industrial growth, Napoleon's escape from Elba, the recent horrific battle at Waterloo, the war in the Americas, good God, the entire world was a mess, including his very own, but he could only manage one at a time presently.

"You will be attending the Pendergrass Ball tonight?" Jack asked with deliberation; useful information to add to his plans for the evening. His father's wisdom and experience would be a much-needed resource.

"Wouldn't miss it! Must see our lovely young lady adorned in her finery." John teasingly glanced toward Olivia, who blushed and gave him a prim smile.

Wanting to moan regarding the perplexity of the statement, the viscount only nodded. Breakfast conversation was filled with the theatre, readings, and balls Olivia attended. Jack tried to ignore the entire replay of the many functions and obligations, focusing on his eggs and ham. Twisting his fork over his coddled eggs, his only desire was to see the end of it all, with Olivia sitting in the town coach headed safely to the countryside.

"Jack – John Jacob Anthony Norrys!" Annabelle's voice was annoyed.

"I beg your pardon," He looked up at the empty table and his mother standing in the doorway.

"Are you coming? You have much on your mind this morning, have you not?"

He was sitting alone, still twirling his fork in the congealed coddled eggs. He laid his fork on his plate and pushed from the table. "I need to speak to Father if that is agreeable?"

"Understandable. Will I see you before you leave?"

"Of course." He bent and kissed her cheek as he took her arm.

Taking her son's hand pulled him to her and kissed his cheek. He nodded and followed his father into his study, who was already making his way to the liquor cabinet.

"I know it is a bit early, but you seem to need something a bit stronger than tea." John motioned to his son, holding up the brandy decanter.

"I don't think that would be in my best interest." The viscount slouched into a chair.

"So, we shall get straight to the matter." He watched his father take the leather high back behind his desk.

Jack sat up rubbing his forehead, before he spoke, "We have a problem." His jaw clenched painfully.

"I do believe that is why I was summoned post haste, is it not? And, unless I am mistaken, it is you who has the problem. I have had the pleasure of your mother's audience."

"For God's sake, that no longer signifies." Fuming, he stood and circled the chair, gripping the tall back with his hands. "And yes, WE have a problem, it involves us all."

His father leaned forward, placing his elbows on his desk. "Very well." Remaining content that the issue had not changed.

"His name is Ralph Barrymore, and his father is The Marquess of Hatton - Scotland." Jack snapped.

John could hear the anger in his son's response but remained unmoved. "The Marquess, with whom I am acquainted, but I gather we do not approve of his young son?"

"No, we bloody well do not," he roared. The viscount began pacing and running his hand through his hair. Finding his way again to the chair, he seized its leather back as if to strangle it. "He is a snaggy bastard!"

His father's eyebrows rose, "I thought you said he was the son of a Marquess?"

"He is, the second or third son, not the heir," Jack blurted out, realising that did not signify.

"It seems we may not have much with which to be concerned, it is Olivia's choice."

Frustrated, Jack raised his voice and then lowered it. His father's calm countenance was not new to him, and he understood his anger was no means to resolution.

"He is a fortune hunter, and he has his sights on Olivia's. I am certain he has absolutely no affection for her." Attempting to curb his fury, "He is a gamester, rolled up, with outstanding vowels; the money lenders are done with him, and the Marquess has cut him off. He is desperate for a dowry for his entire future, and according to some information from the local cronies, he is desperate enough to take her by force."

At this, John Norrys shoved his chair back and stood abruptly at the last words. "Damn it to hell, your mother spoke nothing of this. I am her guardian; it is most certainly we," John said, looking rather ill. "His name crossed her lips at breakfast."

The room stilled with the tension of both men. John Norrys was normally a man of calm and easy-going nature. However, it was another matter when it came to protecting the weaker sex and defending them from unscrupulous behaviour.

"What the bloody hell, I did not hear her mention him." Jack took a long breath. "What did she say?"

"That he seemed to be the only one interested in her, and everyone else was only friends of yours. She did have a rather curt tone as she mentioned you."

"Yes, she is bloody angry, but I will not allow her to be compromised or kidnapped," his voice caught, and he attempted to remain calm, "if possible. It is a game for her to evade us. The last time she found a corner, sat in a chair, and waited for me to come around. How the hell do you find someone who stands five feet and sits among five hundred or more? And with a haughty, supercilious countenance, when I finally found her." Jack ran his hands through his hair again.

"Son, you will not have a hair left on your head if you do not stop running your hands through it." His father could see his son was almost enraged.

"I - I don't know which way to turn. She is infuriated with me, if I say a word, she won't believe me, and I fear it will drive her to him, like defending a mangy dog. And without a doubt, he intends to compromise her, as she has made it clear, she has no affection towards him, save friendship." Jack rubbed his temples.

Now it was his father's turn to take a deep breath. "This was not expected. I fear if I speak with her, she will know my knowledge is through you. I would enlist the Marquess, but what I know of him, he cares little for his children, including his heir. I am only an acquaintance; he may approve of such behaviour. Lord knows the old ways have died hard with some."

Jack walked to the front of his chair and sat. His father took the opportunity to do the same. "Lord Hawthorn remains associated with the war department and has spoken to the magistrate at Bow Street. Their position, he has done nothing. But they have given Hawthorn authority to do what he must if Barrymore tries to take her.

"Well, it sounds as if you have done all you can do."

"No, what I would like to do is throw her in the damn town coach and haul her back to the country. But then I would be guilty of the same thing." John agreed, trying to calm his son, assuring him he would remain close to her at the ball. "Good luck with that."

"I assume your mother knows nothing of this latest?" "No." "Then let us keep it that way."

"I think that is wise."

As his son left the study, Lord Birkshire found himself finding agreement with Olivia. If only he and his best friend had betrothed these two at birth. Who would have ever conceived a caring father's last wish of security for his only child would ultimately have such dire consequences?

CHAPTER 19

The following afternoon passed quickly at Birkshire Place, final-minute details and fripperies delivered, maids rushing up and down stairs, laying out ball gowns for last-minute pressings and inspections. The house was in total, yet organised mayhem. By the end of The Season, every detail for preparation and readiness was quite routine, but to the unknowing, it appeared complete chaos.

There was still an uneasy feeling throughout the house. Olivia had been quiet for two days, leaving her aunt worried the little goosecap would do something half foolish. After their recent conversation, her ladyship wasn't at all certain, Olivia wasn't willing to settle or give up entirely on marriage. For such a kind, loving girl, when something got stuck in her head, she was the most stubborn, obstinate child, but recently, she had not been disagreeable, only quiet. That was far more distressing for Annabelle than when she was in one of her normal pets. She hated not knowing what was going on with her children. John had assured her to trust him and trust him she must.

Christina pinned the last curl in place and fastened Lady Birkshire's large emerald necklace, assuring it lay on her décolleté perfectly.

"I am certain we will be rather late this evening, so please do not wait up. I believe I can manage until morning." Christina nodded, curtsied, and watched her ladyship disappear.

Lady Birkshire found Olivia peering out the parlour window at the evening strollers on Park Lane. "Oh, my dear child, you look radiant."

Olivia's dress was mesmerising. The underskirt was of pale lavender satin with a lace overlay embedded with sequins and crystals. The ornate embroidery on the puff sleeves was covered with crystals, bringing a life of its own with her every movement. The entire presentation was captivated by her alabaster skin and light sapphire blue eyes. Olivia was as confident as ever in the magnificent dress, and the countess smiled and clasped her hands together in delight as she watched her gently swish the skirt about, and the crystals cast sparkles about the room in the bright candlelight.

The Earl entering the room was met with his wife's exuberance. "Wait until you see Olivia."

His lordship cast his eyes upon his ward, inspecting her up and down. "This cannot be that tiny babe swaddled in pink blankets, sucking her fist so long ago, it just cannot."

She didn't remember much about her own father, but her uncle had always made her feel like the daughter he had never had. "Thank you, my Lord," She whispered demurely and curtsied.

"You are captivating, my child. I am certain your dance card will be filled in quickly tonight. I hope you will save one for me." He kissed her cheek and gave her a mischievous wink.

Olivia could not hide her pink flush. "I would be honoured," she smiled in innocent childish wonder.

The three turned to the doorway as voices from the hallway drew closer. Lords Andovir and Sheffield strolled into the drawing room; their conversation was cut short by Lord Birkshire clearing his throat. Sheffield bowed and greeted Lord and Lady Birkshire.

Andovir's gaze immediately fell on Olivia, and he froze, no longer aware of anyone else's presence in the room. A rather large lump formed in his throat and his breath caught in his chest. His tanned face paled; his countenance empty of expression.

"Are you feeling well, my son?" His father was aware of his son's unrestrained adoration. Jack blinked and swallowed hard but was unable to remove his eyes from her. Olivia lowered her own, his regard having its effect.

"I am well," but his thoughts deceived him.

"She looks lovely, does she not?" His mother attempted to break the uncomfortable tension, directing her query to Lord Sheffield.

Lovely? Alluring, enchanting, and desirable were Jack's descriptions but settled on stunning and gave his brain a castigating speech. Sheffield was equally overwhelmed, but his masterful and easily found words announced she would be the most beautiful and charming in the ballroom, also contemplating what an exquisite and worthy duchess she would make.

***

The soaring, crescent-cast stairway into the ballroom made for a grand entry, and Olivia drew many looks and hushes upon her entry. Her slow and calculated descent provided the two escorts who followed an opportunity to survey the room. Gathering her demeanour with a slight hesitation at the lower landing allowed Andovir and Sheffield to grace each side. She beamed with pride at the immediate attention before remembering this was the very entourage she wished to escape. However, her petulance gave way to pomposity with the obvious attention of two of the Ton's most eligible bachelors.

The ballroom was soon filled with debutantes, ladies, matrons, and gentlemen. The Ton mamas congregated to critique the appropriate and inappropriate fashions worn by the remaining eligible young ladies competing for husbands.

The gentlemen gathered in small groups making their observations, shrewdly choosing the debutantes to place their designs and mercenary means to avoid others. The ambitious mamas dexterously hunted and schemed for suitable and expedient remaining bachelors, dragging their poor superfluous daughters along. The remaining male postulants darted into alcoves, behind tall plants, and out the exits to safer areas of the large manor.

The Season was ending, the mamas desperate, and the young ladies wishing to avoid the shame sure to befall their families and their dreaded prospects of being placed upon the shelf.

Olivia was enjoying herself, with no wish to seek or be sought. Gracing the ballroom floor with smooth and graceful partners was her only desire. She looked exquisite and garnered the attention of new and old suitors alike. Of course, Lords Andovir, Sheffield, Worthington, and Gillford were never far away.

Olivia confronted Jack and James, once again in disapproval. Jack made it abundantly clear that tonight her wishes did not signify. As the night passed, she grew irritable and contentious.

"Why are you doing this?" she demanded. "I really do not understand."

"It does not appear you are short of suitors," he flatly stated as he easily gazed over her head, scanning the room.

"But they know you are watching. It is irritating." She discreetly stomped his foot.

"Oww, stop that, you little wretch!" He gave her a stern look. "To whom is it irritating?" he quipped.

"To me." Said exasperated.

"Just as I imagined." Glancing down at her. "I beg of you, for once in your life, trust me," he said, lifting his eyes to look around the room once again.

"I do trust you. I only wish to understand your insistence." She glanced around the room, then turned back to him. "And who are you looking for? If I didn't know better, I'd think you are one of the magistrate's runners. Gracious!"

She followed his gaze again. "Oh, look, there is Lord Ralph.

I think he is coming this way. I hope he wishes to dance."

Jack stiffened, and the conversation by the nearby Sheffield, Worthington, and Hawthorn ceased. Olivia rolled her eyes and stepped closer to Lord Birkshire.

"Good evening, Lady Olivia." Noticing the older gentleman next to her, Lord Ralph extended a leg and gave a low bow. Offering her gloved hand, he brushed a light kiss across it.

"Good evening, Lord Ralph."

Hearing the name, Lord Birkshire wrapped his free hand around his quizzing glass and stared down his aristocratic nose at the young man greeting his niece. The countess stepped up accepted his greeting politely and introduced her husband.

Again, he stretched a long leg in a deep bow. However, his Lordship, without a word or movement, continued his stare, evaluating the young man slowly. Barrymore swallowed hard, knowing immediately that the Earl of Birkshire did not care for him. The earl gave a pompous nod and raised his quizzing glass to his piercing eye but offered nothing more—a subtle cut, not quite direct, but only for Olivia's sake.

Barrymore decided it was best to move along, removing himself from the critical eye of the earl. Before taking his leave, however, he ensured himself a dance, so as to judge Olivia's mood. Seeing no change in her countenance, he was satisfied. However, as he moved away, the watchful eyes of the four men did not elude him. When he reached one of the corner doors, he exited hastily.

Olivia, unaccustomed to her uncle's masterful cuts, looked at him curiously. "Did you not care for Lord Ralph, sir?" she asked.

Lord Birkshire, choosing his words carefully, smiled down at her. "I detest those who do it a bit too brown."

Olivia giggled, "He is quite the toadeater, but he dances well." She noticed the quick eyebrow raise of her uncle and assured him she knew him to be beneath her touch and for him not to worry himself.

The four bachelors were now close enough for clandestine conversation. "Where does that door lead?" Worthington whispered to the other three.

"I am not sure," Andovir being closest murmured.

The manor belonging to Sheffield's uncle informed them it was a short hallway with a lady's retiring room and exited into the garden. He had played here as a child and knew the layout well.

"I thought the garden exited on the south corner?" Worthington interjected.

"It does, but the exit from that hallway is further within the garden," Sheffield continued. "I wonder why he would exit there."

A moment later, all four were aware of Barrymore entering the ballroom again, but from the south entrance. Glances of concern moved between suspicious young men. They decided it would be best to disperse around the ballroom.

It appeared Barrymore was exploring the grounds. All four noticed his drinking had increased. A drink in both hands, they watched as he emptied one and retrieved yet another from a passing footman.

Hawthorn did not like what he saw, before the four dispersed he gave them a word of warning, "He is drinking heavily, I fear for courage. If he has decided to make a move, I believe it will be tonight." He gave each one a stern look, "do not lose him."

They nodded and spaced themselves around the crowded ballroom. It was indeed a crush, even with many families remaining in Belgium after the Waterloo Battle.

As they moved around the room, each remained near an exit to the gardens. All four, experienced and successful in the art of seduction, knew a lady was easily compromised there. Heavy landscaping and dim lighting made for cloistered and veiled rendezvous.

Olivia partnered on the floor for a cotillion, Jack took the opportunity to alert his father, who assured him he would remain near Olivia.

An hour passed with nothing more than Olivia's laughter and dancing to be monitored, which was excoriating Andovir. The supper dance was a waltz, and Lord Sheffield had secured it with Olivia. Jack remained in the card room too agitated to consider food or drink, but knowing she was safe with Sheffield, he attempted to relax. However, catching sight of Barrymore, weaving in and out of the ballroom's multiple French doors and still drinking heavily ended any chance of him finding a moment of peace. Jack sighed heavily and pawed his forehead praying for this night to end.

When the orchestra commenced, the four guards took up their posts around the room. Olivia was unaware of anything more than overbearing guardians and continued to dance, drink lemonade, and giggle with her friends. Elizabeth Jameson had come to London with her aunt, who was happy to release her into the chaperonage of Lady Birkshire and she and Olivia were inseparable.

Barrymore made no additional effort to approach Olivia. Andovir was relieved, but Hawthorn believed it was cause for alarm. Lord Ralph had made several strolls to and from the garden with partners and alone. Hawthorn found this most disturbing and, when he shared his opinions with Sheffield, he too found it troubling.

The ballroom was unbearably warm, and the guests were moving in and out all the doors seeking cooler, fresher air. The refreshment table was another frequent gathering area. After being graciously returned to her aunt's side after a quick-paced quadrille, she beckoned Elizabeth to accompany her to the ladies' retirement room.

She declared their direction to her aunt, assuring her there was no need to escort them, motioning toward the nearby door and hallway only a short distance. Her aunt nodded and watched them exit.

Lord Andovir noticed her leave and glanced at Sheffield, who was closest to the hallway. The marquess nodded, moving closer to a footman standing near the west door nearest the hallway, glancing occasionally at the outdoor area.

"Oh Olivia, what a remarkable evening. I dare say, we haven't missed a dance," Elizabeth giggled, as the girls made their way toward the exit. "It has been delightful and will be quite dull returning to the country."

"Faith, as for that, I look forward to it. I do love this manor though, the doors opening into the conservatory from the ballroom. You can smell the roses throughout the room, and those in the garden are sublime."

"Can you see them from the dancefloor?"

"Not really, they are outside the brick area with the tables and torches. We can return by way of them if you would like."

"Oh yes, above all things. I do love roses," Elizabeth smiled.

"They are my favourite. Have we never strolled through the orangery at Birkshire?"

"No, but I am usually in such a hurry, my errands, you know."

"They are beyond perfection." Olivia told her.

The ladies exited the corner and disappeared into the hallway. James motioned for Thomas to meet him at the south door. "Do you have an eye on Barrymore?"

"No, he was waltzing, but I lost sight on the opposite side. It is such a crush, and it is so warm, guests are moving in and out in clusters. It is quite impossible."

"At least he was dancing. Olivia and her friend exited for the retirement room some time ago. They should be returning soon. I will move closer to the west door. Good God, we must locate that damn bloke," James was suddenly becoming uncomfortable with Olivia out of sight.

Sheffield strolled to the southwest wall, snatching a champagne from a footman's tray, never taking his eyes off the south door. Normally quite calm and not easily alarmed, the marquess did not like the feeling afflicting him. Something was wrong, Olivia and Elizabeth should be back. Unless the allure of the roses had redirected them. He walked toward the viscount and earl.

Andovir, speaking to his father, was noticeably disquieted and agitated. The viscount saw Sheffield and met him halfway, neither amiable nor satisfied with the current situation. It was agreed that the ladies should have returned. Jack could only pray they were viewing the roses.

Worthington caught up with them. "Have you seen Olivia?"

"No, she and Elizabeth left for the retirement room too long ago. What of Barrymore?"

Worthington inhaled. "I have lost him."

"We are headed to the south hallway. Find Hawthorn and go to the garden," Sheffield urged, still fighting his apprehension.

"We will go to the south door." The viscount was already moving. Worthington turned to leave, but the marquess caught his sleeve.

"Meet us at the entrance nearest the hallway. Olivia loves roses; she could be showing them to Elizabeth." Sheffield motioned toward the terrace doors.

Worthington moved around the edge of the floor toward Lord Gillford. Noticing his aggressive approach, the earl met him near the south entrance, together they exited into the piazza.

Sheffield's movements were swift but calm, not wanting to draw attention. Andovir, however, had no such concern and was moving swiftly. But reaching the hallway was met with multiple closed doors and frustration overwhelmed him. Sheffield pointed to one as he reached his side.

Then they both stopped short, Elizabeth exited the doorway, brushing the front of her dress. "Oh, Olivia, I..." Aware of two large figures, she lifted her head. Startled, she peered at them curiously, recognising them, she glanced around. "Where is Olivia?"

"With you!" Jack hissed, instantly nauseated.

"She was," Elizabeth replied.

"Where is she now?" He demanded sternly.

Sheffield reached out and grabbed his arm to aid his restraint. The situation they both knew was now dangerous, but information was critical.

"I don't know. We were headed to the garden when Lord Ralph called to Olivia, wishing to speak with her."

Andovir's eyes closed; his head fell back in an agonising response of helplessness. He felt Sheffield's grip tighten on his shoulder as he coaxed the young girl to continue.

"We joined him, just past these doors. He was a bit intoxicated, I think, but seemed friendly enough, not rude, or vulgar. His champagne was full, so I suppose he was not drinking so much."

Sheffield could see Andovir growing agitated, but they must

know what happened without alarming Elizabeth. The little chit just kept talking; Sheffield too was growing weary of her loquacious behaviour, but neither wanted her aware of the situation. If no one were the wiser and they caught Barrymore trying to compromise Olivia, they could repair any damage.

Elizabeth was fidgeting with her dress, trying to explain... "He insisted on speaking with her in private, but she assured him anything he had to say could be said in my presence. As he turned to whisper to her, he spilt the entire glass of champagne on my new dress. I was mortified."

Jack was unravelling, but the information was essential.

Elizabeth continued. "Olivia took her handkerchief and attempted to assist me. Lord Ralph suggested I should seek additional serviettes in the retirement room. As you see, there was quite a lot of it. Olivia opened the door to assist me, and he caught her arm, pleading with her for only a moment, assuring me it would only be a second. Olivia nodded at me, saying, one minute. So, I excused myself. I had only just now observed how long it had been and sought her assistance, and you were here."

Sheffield could see Jack's fists and stepped between him and Elizabeth and motioned her to the ballroom, assuring her they probably returned there, and that she should join them.

"We were to admire the roses, but I supposed she tired of waiting for me. Yes, I should go, I should let my aunt know about my dress." Elizabeth, another innocent country mouse, sounded unconcerned. The marquess escorted her down the hallway to the ballroom entrance.

The viscount turned toward the exit and hastened toward the garden when he noticed the darkened corridor. Remembering word of a vestibule leading to a maze, he abruptly halted. Sheffield was nearing him from the ballroom, Worth and the earl coming in from the south garden exit.

CHAPTER 20

As the door closed behind Elizabeth, Olivia turned to Barrymore, "Pray, Lord Ralph, what is it? I need to assist Elizabeth. You have ruined her gown."

"Her gown is the least of my concern." Barrymore averred.

"Sir, I beg your pardon, that is her first ball gown!" She was appalled at the lack of concern.

"Oh, dispense with the formalities, Olivia."

"I dare you to use my Christian name. I did not give you leave to do so!" Olivia said appalled.

"Don't be absurd." Barrymore retorted.

"I beg your pardon, sir, what liberties you seem to be taking in your… your condition," Olivia said, scoldingly.

"My condition indeed. If I am in a condition, it is due to your dalliance." He accused.

"My what? Lord Ralph, you are foxed!" she said shocked.

"Oh, do stop. I have made my wishes obvious to you on many occasions, and the time has come to stop keeping me on the knob."

"On the what?" She was growing tired of his pretence.

"I have repeatedly requested your hand, and yet you give me no answer."

"I most certainly did so, on every occasion." She answered indignantly.

Voices were heard coming into the hall from the ballroom. Barrymore looked over Olivia's head, then with little regard, pulled her further down the hallway and into the darkened corridor.

"I dare you to drag me, remove your hand from me this instant." She screeched scathingly.

"Olivia, do not be disagreeable, you know you are going to marry me, so stop being so petulant." Barrymore asserted.

She stilled, "I am not going to marry you. I have given you no notion of it. I am sorry if being kind has made you believe such nonsense, but you are mistaken." She said astonished.

"I am the only one of your suitors who remains constant, and make no mistake, my dear Olivia, you will marry me." His callous tone caught her off guard.

"I will not! Stop being so nonsensical. Now let me go." Still not understanding her situation.

Olivia pulled her arm violently away from him, but he caught her quickly with his other. He yanked her to his side tightly and moved further into the darkened vestibule. His taller, heavy frame was no match for her flailing her limbs. She attempted in vain to gain leverage, as he carried her down the hall.

"Stop!" She cried out. "Let me go, you are hurting me."

Swiftly moving, Barrymore reached the end of the long-darkened hallway and thrust open a large wooden door onto a small area, lined with dense evergreens with a narrow trail leading away from the door. Kicking the door closed, he released her with such force that when her feet touched the ground, her teeth clattered. She clenched her jaw to ease the discomfort.

He tightened his grip on her shoulders and upper arms, drawing them together. Unfamiliar with this part of the estate, she pleaded with him, "Please, let me go."

Olivia tried to hide her alarm while attempting some sort of reasoning. The flight instinct was overwhelming.

"No, you damn little light-skirt. You listen to me." He shook her violently, causing additional pain in her shoulders and neck. Then he grabbed her around the throat, pushing her chin up with his thumb. "We will be married as soon as I get you to Scotland. There is a vicar on my father's estate."

"No, we will not! I will not marry you. I have no affection for you." Olivia's voice quaked, beginning to realise her peril.

She heard an ignoble laugh, his eyes were cloudy and dark, and the sneer at his mouth and the intense, cold stare found her vacilating from disbelief to betrayal.

"Your stupid wench, you've been reading too many novels. Affection? Affection does not cover accounts." He mocked.

Olivia's naive mind and breath caught; she was attempting to untangle a web of incomprehensibility. The rapid pulse from her initial attempts at freedom was careening into fear. Within a second, she understood, that Ralph Barrymore was a fortune hunter and one with no scruples. How she had not seen it before, enraged her. She must get away from this madman. Make no mistake, she heard in his voice, his intentions were real. If she did not free herself, she was to be abducted.

She began swinging her arms fiercely to break free. Between her ornate gown and soft slippers, she made no impact.

Barrymore only became angrier and more determined. He took her arm, twisting it to her back, pulling and trapping her against him. His hand slid to the side of her neck, and his fingers tightened on her throat.

"What are you doing?" her voice hoarse and strained.

He released her neck and turned her toward the path, with her arm still bent to her back, securing his hold with every step. Trying to slow their pace, tears were streaming down Olivia's face. He was hurting her, but she must ignore the pain; she could not allow this to happen. She twisted toward him to escape. When she felt the freedom to move away, he grabbed her just above the elbow and began moving faster. Stumbling and resisting, she tried to halt the forward motion.

He stopped long enough to seize her neck once more; Good God, he was going to choke her. Olivia's head was spinning as she continued to strive to free herself. He lost his hold on her throat, and the relief was immediate. She swallowed, her throat throbbing in pain. He viciously coiled her elbow again to her back, jerking her off her feet.

"Keep moving," He demanded in a wicked low growl. Olivia gasped at his tone, her tears stopped, and terror began to rise from the depth of her soul.

"No!" She screamed, but it was barely a whisper, her throat raw. She could not let him carry her away from this house.

Barrymore stopped abruptly and viciously yanked her to him.

"Stop resisting. I am not opposed to flogging an unobliging female, you might heed that with certainty after we are married."

Olivia could see his vile dark face, his mouth turned down, the crease of his brow furrowed, and his eyes narrowed. Panic filled her as she heard the words of this demon; his demeanour assured her; that his threats were real. How could she have misjudged this depraved human being?

"Why do you want me?" She managed to ask.

She tried to speak, but the words were raspy and rough. She had to remain aware of her surroundings. He had dragged her from the house, the bushes were thick, buffering the sound coming from the ballroom. The cold hard truth hit her; she must save herself.

"Your flush dowry, of course. According to my friend at the bank, it is quite large, and I need it. God, stop talking and come along."

"No. If it is money you want, I can give it to you. My uncle can have it tomorrow. You need not do this." She knew she had to keep him distracted, but she was already so weak.

"Have I appeared such a fool these past few months? I must have played my part well. I have a fondness for the gaming table and brothels now and then. A third son of title and wealth has nothing."

"I will give you however much you want, name it." She had not the strength to help herself, she had to use her wit, at least to delay. She knew she would be missed quickly.

"I had considered holding you for a hefty ransom, but why should I settle for a paltry handout when I can have the whole of it," Barrymore said haughtily.

"Your reputation will still be ruined, and your father may very well protect me." Olivia reasoned.

"What a stupid little fool you are. I knew you were a naïve, simple country bumpkin." He berated. "Nobility will conceal any scandal, and do not look to my father for protection. He will be glad to be rid of me."

"What of me?" She told herself to keep him talking to stop this nightmare.

"What is to become of you?" Barrymore laughed vilely, "I dare say, I don't care. You will find something to amuse yourself with. Lucky for you, I don't need an heir."

"You will be caught, my uncle, my brother..." discerned by his fallaciousness.

"What a little fool." He contrived. "I am a gamester, a betting man. You will be in Scotland before they know you are missing, we have only to reach my tiger and coach. I hold the power in Scotland. You will be safely stashed at Huntley Castle, no one dares to cross its threshold."

The wickedness of the monster's voice horrified her. She knew nothing of the person he had become in a moment's time. Her mind was racing to resolve her situation. Fight, Olivia, fight, you must fight. Her thoughts kept repeating inside her head.

He soon began tugging her again, as she continued to resist, grabbing anything within her reach. The tall hedges twisted and turned along the narrow path. The twelve-foot-tall bushes carried long branches, large and menacing.

He pulled her around one corner, and she grabbed a limb, jerking him off balance, but he snatched her free of it. Two fingers of her glove ripped and dangled from the branch, but not before the sharp spine of the evergreen tore through her soft skin. He heaved her toward him, slapping her across the cheek.

Olivia grimaced and grabbed her face; blood was immediate. Checking his hand, he wore a large signet ring. The cut was deep, the salt from tears mingled with the oozing blood, it was agonising. The painful sting jolted down both arms and legs, nauseating her.

"I told you to keep moving." He glowered. "As you see, I do not care of hurting you for compliance."

He growled and spitefully smiled down upon her. She staggered from the pain, her eyes blurred, and her skin burned.

Olivia dropped to her knees. He hoisted her up again, this time tearing her dress, ripping the sleeve off her shoulder. He backhanded her again, on the other side. Olivia let out a scream of pain, but he quickly bound both wrists to his chest.

"Go ahead, scream. No one can hear you above the noise of the frivolities." He mocked with a fiendish grin.

He thrust her around one last corner. It was a small open area, about ten-foot square. Olivia's eyes were blinded with tears, and she could feel the pressure of her face swelling. Through the tears and pain, she saw a small stone bench resting on two pillars.

"We are here. My Tiger will be here soon; he will not fail me and cannot be far behind."

Still holding her arm, he focused on the openings on the opposite side from where they had entered. "I suppose the coaches are jammed. But he will be here soon." He was rambling and seemed to be reasoning with himself about the unexpected delay.

He slammed her onto the bench, ordering her to sit. She darted back the way they came, but he quickly grabbed her around the waist, pulling her back into his grasp.

She slung both arms between them to prevent him from pulling her into him. She was not certain where the strength was coming from anymore. The cuts and bruises were stinging, bits of blood and clear- yellowish fluid oozing from the open wound on her cheek. But with tight fists, she kept pushing away from him.

He hurled her towards the bench, and as she fell, grabbing for it, the seat slipped off its braces, crashing to the ground. Olivia landed on the fragmented pieces and Barrymore stumbled on top of her. He was grabbing for her as she pulled herself under the leaning concrete seat. The broken slab gave her leverage, and she pulled herself under the collapsed bench.

He continued laughing wickedly, trying to drag her to him. "You are indeed feisty, for one so small. I dare say, it will not be a dull marriage, little wife."

Olivia felt her stomach churn with disgust and swallowed the urge to vomit. Rage was driving her now. Still digging for contact, her fingers touched a small stone, a rock, a shattered piece of bench, she wasn't sure, but it moved. A bit larger than her hand, she wrapped her fingers around it. She knew she had to gather her wits and all the remaining strength she could manage. She was exhausted, but this was her last hope of escape, and she would only get one chance.

He grabbed her around the waist, pulling her from under the broken slab. She allowed him to pull her toward him, keeping both her arms above her. He was astride her small frame, laughing as if it were a game, and he was about to win his prize. He leaned toward her, reaching for a better hold. Olivia raised the broken piece, grasping it with both hands and with all the strength she could muster, slammed it against his temple, her arms collapsing from the intensity of the blow. Barrymore collapsed. For a moment, she lay still, exhausted. His weight was too much for her to escape. She pushed against his shoulders to brace herself, but he would not budge. She bent her legs, working them between their bodies, and rolled him off with nothing more than willpower.

She dragged herself to the side of the broken bench, struggling to her knees, balancing on the one standing pillar. She pushed to her feet and felt an alarming pain in her arm. She held it against herself as she peered at the body next to her; blood was pouring from his head, and there was no movement. She tried to swallow, but her throat was on fire; sobbing and choking. She sat on a piece of the remaining pillar, her bodice torn from her gown. She reached for the shredded silk, her hands sore, filled with twigs and mud, the blood on her face now mixed with the dirt where she had wiped the tears. Barely able to breathe, she coughed and gagged, her throat swollen.

No longer able to hold back the repulsion of the attack, she fell to her knees, turning toward the shrubbery, losing the contents of her stomach. She spat, choked, and coughed, her throat burning from the bile. Reaching for her skirt to wipe her mouth, she saw it was drenched in blood. Crawling away from the horrid mess of her own making, her hair unpinned, and one of her shoes was missing. The lost slipper, she recovered from under the rubble and slipped it on her foot. Unable to breathe, dizzy, eyes nearly swollen shut, bruised, cut, and holding her arm against her, she passed out.

***

Entering from the south entrance, Worthington and Hawthorn saw Jack's clenched fists and sickened face; their worst fears had materialised.

"He has her." The viscount's voice filled with pain and anger.

Sheffield reached them at the same instance, knowing they had come through the garden, he knew they were in the maze.

"There is another entrance down the hallway, but God help me, how he knew of it, I do not know."

The four started down the dark corridor when Jack suddenly halted; a broken champagne glass lay in their path. He ground the remainder under his boot as James passed him and swung open the heavy door.

"I know this maze well." Sheffield began running along the path. The remaining three were keeping pace, horrified! So many options, left then right, then right again, but Sheffield knew every turn. Who would design such a monstrosity? As fast as they were moving, each noticed signs of broken limbs, twigs, and pieces of lace and satin. Not one of them doubted that Olivia was fighting for her life.

For the viscount, each step was in slow motion. He was a man obsessed, demanding his feet to move faster, the rage growing with every step. He had now become the madman.

They rounded what was to be the final left. Three of them abruptly stopped at the horrible scene before them. Jack ran straight to Olivia.

The scene held no secrets. As he raced to her side, the torn dress, the blood, the dirt, he was trembling uncontrollably. As he lifted her into his arms, he whispered, "My God, what has he done to you?"

Feeling the moisture plaguing his eyes, but with strength and conviction, he willed her to open hers. "Olivia." He pleaded.

Attempting awareness, her whimpers became sobs, coughing and choking, but unable to speak. Strength catching him by surprise, she managed to pull herself further into the safety of his arms. "You came for me." Her voice was scratchy, hoarse, and barely audible. He tightened his arms around her. Falling against his chest, she fell unconscious.

He slipped his arm underneath her, tucking her into his embrace. What violence she had been dealt. He could see the black fingerprints of the large hand on her face, filled with dirt, blood, and sweat. There were scratches and a large bruise on her bare shoulder.

Helplessly, the three walked up without a word. It was gut-wrenching for James; he had grown so close to her over the past few months, and he loved her too. When he saw the torn dress and the bare shoulder, he slipped off his coat and wrapped it around her, then placed his hand on Jack's shoulder and squeezed it. He turned first to Worthington and Hawthorn, then toward Barrymore lying motionless in his own blood and watched as the earl knelt over him, reaching for his pulse.

"He's alive," he announced, dropping his arm, and standing to survey the scene.

Worthington noticed the bloody sconce, lifting it and holding it away from him. "This appears to be the weapon."

Lord Gillford nodded, still deciphering how to proceed. He had authority from the magistrate to do whatever was necessary. But he wanted and needed more than anything to avoid a scandal for Olivia. "Looks as though she hit him on the side of his head with that broken piece."

James turned his head toward Olivia and whispered. "Good job, my sweet."

Gillford continued to walk about the area and turned back to Sheffield and Worthington to discuss the next action.

Jack was whispering to Olivia and stroking her hair, his head bent over her. They could not see his face, nor hers, but he held her like one holds a precious child; she seemed to be floating in and out of consciousness, making no motion to leave the safety of his arms.

"He reeks of alcohol and is obviously drunk, and there is too much blood here to move him without suspicion." The earl was still building his story for Bow Street.

"Probably the only way he had the guts to do this." It took everything inside of James not to kick him in the side while he lay unconscious.

"Don't!" Hawthorn held up his hand to Sheffield. "We must make this appear as if he fell in a drunken state and hit his head on the bench. I think that would be best. We need only find a way to remove Olivia to safety and remove every piece of cloth along the path." He was working out the details. "We must remove Andovir and Olivia as quickly as possible, without being seen." The agent of the Crown had learned a great deal while working in the war department and knew what the Bow Street Runners would need to find.

"There is a gazebo, two rights and one left out of the maze. It is next to a carriage path, which leads to the stables. My uncle uses it when he goes hunting. There is another outlet past the stables. It exits to the main road, bypassing the main drive." James informed him.

"That will do!" Hawthorn replied. "Since you can tell Lord Birkshire how to get to the gazebo, go to him and tell him to meet Andovir there. Worthington and I will finish here and help Andovir and Olivia to the meeting place. Tell them they will be in the shadows until the carriage stops. Tell the earl to move as quickly as they can, without drawing attention. No time for anything else. Someone must have been meeting him. I dare say, we scared them off."

Worthington informed Jack of the plans; he only nodded. Standing, still holding Olivia in his arms, he turned to the three men.

"Thank you," he murmured. They could see the rage had been replaced with torment.

"Afterward, we will go back to the ballroom and take our leave. We should meet at Claire's on St. James Street, just to make an appearance," Hawthorn's suggestion was met with no argument.

Sheffield left for the ballroom, Hawthorn dealt with Barrymore, and Worthington assisted Jack through the remainder of the maze.

"Stop at the edge," Worthington instructed, seeing the gazebo ahead and the end of the tall evergreens. He placed his hand on his friend's shoulder, feeling the tremors, unable to determine if they were Olivia's or his friend's, maybe both.

Jack clutched Olivia to his chest, not uttering a word. Occasionally, he raised his head to the heavens, asking why, why this, why her? Then he heard Worthington giving more information.

"Stay in the shadows. The carriage will stop in front, then and only then leave the protection of the maze. I need to return and help Hawthorn. Good luck, my friend." With that, Worthington disappeared back into the maze.

Jack stood in the darkness, holding Olivia close to his heart. As he thought of all the damage he saw in the moonlight, he could only imagine all the ones unseen. He was numb; he had failed her.

Her head nestled into his chest, he could see her long blonde curls, draped across her shoulders were filled with blood, dirt, and twigs. He had failed her. Tears fell from his eyes onto Olivia's blood-stained, torn gown. Alone in the caliginosity, he could not hold back the sobs.

He heard the carriage wheels halt and stepped from the shrubs as his father stepped from the massive coach. The earl saw Olivia's limp body and turned back, opening the door fully.

"No, sit down," his lordship's voice stern. Annabelle had risen from her seat, intending to step out; hearing John's tone, she closed her eyes and waited.

Jack quickly entered the conveyance, holding tight to Olivia, not looking at either parent. He sat in the corner, adjusting and wrapping the coat and his arms tighter around her.

The earl jumped in the carriage, motioning the driver to make haste. The countess opened her eyes, the moonlight illuminating the interior, and looked over at them.

"Oh, my God," she wailed and reached for them. Lord Birkshire grabbed her.

"Wait, Annabelle, we will be home soon." He wrapped his arms around her, pulling her to him as she wept.

As the equipage swayed through the London streets, Lord Birkshire looked at Jack. "Son."

Jack raised his tear-filled eyes but said nothing.

"We will leave for the country house as soon as we can see the doctor and get Olivia ready."

The viscount nodded and fell back against the corner in darkness.

The coachman, noting the urgency, pushed the horses to their limit and arrived swiftly at Birkshire Place, pulling straight through to the mews. The whole party exited inside the building and entered the house through the servant's entrance.

Jack carried Olivia up the back staircase and into her bedchamber. His mother quickly followed, stopping long enough to wake Christina and Sarah.

Once in the bedchamber, Jack sat on the bed, still clutching Olivia to his chest. His face was ashen, his eyes empty, not looking at his mother. It was as if he was staring through every wall into an abyss. Annabelle quietly approached her son.

"You need to lay her on the bed. We must remove her stays and these clothes and wash her."

Jack lowered his head to Olivia's and kissed her hair, tipping her face to his, and cradling her into his neck. His mother could see his tears falling; it was as if his embrace held her together, and she would shatter if he released her.

"I'm sorry, my love, I am so sorry. I should have been there, I should have..." His voice broke.

He closed his eyes and slowly shook his head, kissing her forehead, and the bruised cheek, and placed the final one on the swollen lips.

Annabelle's tears fell at her son's voice, and she reached for the bedpost, shuddered woozily, and tried to hold back her own sobs. Christina clasped her shoulders for support.

Without a word, Jack stood and turned to settle Olivia on the bed. He clung to her and gently began to position each limb.

With the care of handling fine, fragile crystal, he placed one arm next to her and positioned the injured limb across her chest, lightly kissing her forehead once more. When he stood, exposing the front of the tattered gown, he heard his mother gasp in alarm at the sight.

"It isn't hers," Jack whispered emotionlessly. He drew his bloody sleeve across his wet face, streaking his face with the vital fluid. "But I think her arm may be broken."

Christina and Sarah burst into tears as they began carefully removing her clothing and cleaning her frail body. Her face was badly bruised and swollen from the gashes on her cheeks, the bruise on her neck showing two clear handprints. The one limb was swelling, and both hands had deep scratch marks filled with blood and dirt. The beautiful dress that had captured so much attention was shredded, filled with twigs, leaves, dirt, and covered in blood.

Nauseated, weaving slightly from held-back sobs, Annabelle watched the maids wash and clean Olivia's wounds and skin. Jack stood silently by the bed, staring into Olivia's face, unaware of the chaos around him.

His mother, seeing him there, turned and took his arm to pull him away. At first, he resisted, but she embraced him and walked him to the door. As they reached the threshold, he stopped but did not look at his mother. She glanced up at him; he kept his gaze in the hall.

"Will you go with us?" His mother whispered.

Jack shook his head. "No. I will send notice when I know what I am to do."

Annabelle lowered her head and whispered. "I understand."

She released her hold on him, her heart broken as she watched his slow walk to the front stairs.

When Jack reached the street in front of Birkshire Place, he turned and looked up at the window he knew to be Olivia's. Shame overwhelmed him; he had not been able to protect her. He should have been able to stop this, done more, should have told her, should have kept her from the ball, should have taken her home… He should have told her he loved her. Lowering his head, he began to walk. To where? He had no idea.

***

Jack kept walking, with no thought of direction or where he was going, only knowing he had to keep moving. He walked through the park, crossing this street, then that one, not paying heed to anything or anyone. Some streets well lit, some dark, it all went ignored. He heard the watchman cry out the hour but didn't know the time. He occasionally felt the bump of a pedestrian as he stepped from the cobbled streets, unaware of their path or his, nor rendering a response of apology. He just kept moving forward.

Suddenly, he felt his arms being restrained. He jerked free and spun around, like a caged animal. Two men, dressed in ragged clothing, had accosted him.

"Just give us ya' money an' we'll be on our way, nobody'll get 'urt," one man uttered.

"Not lookin' for no trouble, just your brass is all," said the other one.

He noticed each had a hand in a protruding pocket as if they had pistols. Already filled with so much rage and anger, he wasn't thinking, nor did he care whether he lived or died. He glared at them and in a voice even he didn't recognise, let out a vicious, unnatural, low, and deep growl.

"I am looking for something or someone to rip apart," he leaned his body toward the two men and stepped toward them. "It might feel good to kill someone with my bare hands; you two will do nicely."

The two men glanced at one another and took off running

into the shadows.

Jack brushed the sleeve of his coat where they had grabbed him, raked his hands through his hair, never giving the assault another thought, and continued his ambling. He found no satisfaction in the confrontation; his rage was too deep.

He was still walking as dawn broke. He looked up to find himself in front of his townhouse. He had no idea how he ended up there or where he had been. He stared up at his residence. He had to leave - this place – London – England.

If there was anything left of him to salvage, he had to go away, far away. He was of no use to anyone, especially not Olivia. He felt empty, his heart empty, but worst of all, his soul was empty.

CHAPTER 21

The doctor was summoned in the early morning hours and stayed for some time. His attempts to arouse Olivia were met with violent thrashing, which took the addition of Lady Birkshire and Sarah to hold her still. The doctor, concerned with her small frame, gave the Laudanum in such small doses that it wasn't until the third dose that she finally slept.

He left the bottle with Lady Birkshire with instructions, reminding her to be careful, and that the trauma may take days to pass. He also gave her a jar of Turlington's Balsam and Godbold's Vegetable Balsam for her facial gash, promising that if they alternated between the two, it would not leave a scar, but would take time. She was not to attempt to speak for several days; her throat was so badly bruised; he believed her vocal cords must be as well. He agreed that moving her immediately to the country, where she was most comfortable, would be best, and not to anticipate a physical recovery for weeks. He asked his lord and ladyship to escort him as he quit the room, leaving Sarah to sit with her.

In the foyer, he explained that the emotional recovery from such an assault takes time, and not to anticipate it too soon. Until her physical scars heal, do not expect the mental healing to begin. The doctor explained her treatment again and assured them that she should be fine in time. If there was anything he could do, they should send for him.

***

The journey from London to Birkshire had been long and silent. The hours passed slowly with the rocking of the coach. Nothing passed between his Lord and Ladyship except glances.

As they pulled into the drive, Olivia opened her eyes and stared out the window with no change of expression.

When the coach came to a stop and the footman opened the door, Olivia carefully and quietly stepped out of the equipage, refusing assistance. She tucked her free hand back inside her muff and silently walked up the steps and entered the house.

Graham greeted her at the door, holding back his countenance of dismay at the damage done to the little girl he had watched grow. She attempted to smile at him, but the light of the young girl was gone. No one perceived it as much as Graham. She lifted her skirt to clear her path and proceeded up the stairs to her bedchamber in silence.

Days passed, and Olivia never left her room. She would sit at her vanity as Sarah brushed her hair. Olivia stared at the unrecognisable image in the mirror. Touching the bruises and cuts on her cheeks and throat, she could not hold back tears. Sarah could barely hold her own when assisting her in and out of the tub to wash her battered and bruised body.

The cuts began to close, and the bruises turned a yellowish green. The doctor had placed a thick bandage around her arm, and it was to be kept still for several weeks, giving it a chance to heal. The gash on her cheek was becoming soft and pink. Sarah had alternated the balms religiously every day, and the scar began to disappear.

After her physical marks healed and her face returned to normal, a change was soon seen in Olivia. Every day, she came to the breakfast room, even greeted everyone with a smile. Not the vibrant one of old, but a genuine grateful smile. No one was certain they would ever see the childlike wonder and delightful young lady they all adored.

After breakfast, she made her way to the stables. After her arm was deemed restored, the bandages discarded, and her strength and mobility returned, she was quickly riding Spartan again. Birkshire's stable master accompanied her at first, but shortly, Olivia requested her old groom of ten years to escort her. At first, she travelled no further than the lake and back. She arrived each day for afternoon tea and dressed for dinner.

Elizabeth Jameson, the Vicar's daughter, who left her card daily, was finally received. She began regular visits three or four times a week.

Lord Sheffield contacted Lord Birkshire at regular intervals, sending numerous missives, flowers, and hard candies by courier. One missive indicated he would have sent Gunter ice but had found no way to do so. When he learned Olivia was riding again, he requested permission to come and escort her on the outings. Lady Birkshire invited him for a long weekend, and the results were so promising that the invitation became an open one. Lord Sheffield became a regular visitor, and Olivia was soon seen laughing and joking.

Unaware of how much he knew, the first visit was strained. They walked to the lake, and the footman spread a blanket and presented a basket with wine and bread. The day was chilly, but the sun was shining, and the autumn colours were exceptionally vibrant. The red, orange, and gold leaves were floating effortlessly to the ground around them.

"The leaves are falling like snowflakes," She commented as she knelt on the blanket.

James took pains not to make her uncomfortable, so he stood back until she asked him to join her. He took his seat across from the basket and picked up the wine bottle, motioning to ensure she wanted a glass. She nodded and reached for the loaf of bread, tearing away two slices, placing them on serviettes, and handing one to James.

"You are not chilled, I hope?" He asked.

"No, no, not at all, my cloak is quite warm. The sun is so comfortable, I was thinking of removing it."

He passed her a glass of wine, watching her face as she accepted it.

"Olivia, may I ask how you are doing?"

He noticed the wine begin to move in her glass; she quickly rested it on her knee. Her eyes peered down at the blanket, moving quickly from the basket to her glass and back again.

"Whatever do you mean?" she said blandly.

"Olivia, we have been confidants far too long to play games. You know very well what I mean." He avowed. "Please do not be coy with me; I care far too much for you."

Olivia could not meet his gaze, but their friendship had been too confidential and precious to her not to answer. She slowly released her breath.

"I am well. I - I am not ready to go out yet. I prefer to be in the company of friends and loved ones." She admitted.

"It would please me excessively to be considered among them."

Olivia felt a calm presence come over her and knew at once that she wanted and needed their confidence of old. There were tears in her eyes as she turned to him.

"It would also please me?" she paused, "James, I wish to know, and please - do not spare my feelings, as I must know the truth. How much do you know of - of it?"

Lord Sheffield moved closer and reached to place his hand over hers.

"I was present." He could feel her hand attempt to escape his grasp, but he held it steady. "Please, Olivia, do not withdraw. It is most important that you do not," he was determined to have this conversation. He needed to clear the air between them, almost as much as she did. He continued, "You must know how wicked the situation was. We knew you were in danger, and we had little time for rescue. Finding and protecting you was our only concern. We remember nothing more; it is all forgotten. Please do not upset yourself; we all care for you deeply. It would break our hearts to know we caused you one ounce of discomfort."

"All?" Olivia spoke very softly, but he could see the stricken look on her face. She lifted her eyes and met his and could see tenderness and worry in them. She knew if she wished to know more, he would tell her, whereas others may not. "Who else – who else saw?"

He deliberated on the matter for a quiet moment, exacting precisely how much she wanted to know. But he also believed she needed to know the truth. No matter her future choices, her life would be forever tangled with those who were there. The intense chivalry rising within, he carefully chose his words.

"Worthington and Richard Hawthorn, but we saw nothing. Andovir ran to you without ceasing his stride and covered you with his frame and coat." He searched her eyes through her tears. She was waiting for more. "Your dishevelled figure was hidden from view and Andovir hugged you to his heart and tucked you beneath the coat."

"Was he dead?"

"No, it was unfortunate. But you have nothing further to concern yourself. Hawthorn took care of it, and he is no longer in England." He watched as she drew a deep breath and released it.

"I am relieved and comforted by it." She lowered her head and wiped a tear that had dropped to her cheek. She glanced back at James, wishing him to continue.

"The story goes, he was heavily intoxicated, found himself lost in the maze with a large bottle of port and had drunk what he had not spilled on himself when he staggered and fell over the concrete bench, striking his head on its supporting stones. The bench was broken, and apparently, that is what caused the blow to be severe. He was found by a servant, who immediately reported it to my uncle. My father and I were with him when the news was given. My uncle was overset, so I assured him that my father and I would oversee it to avoid as much gossip as, pray tell, one can, you see. Sad story to tell, is it not?"

"Indeed, it is most shocking. And no one questioned it further?" She queried.

"Question His Grace, The Duke of Ratcliff?" He boasted loftily, "I dare say, not a one."

"Your father doesn't know the truth, does he?" she asked.

James could tell that was very disturbing to her. "No, but he knows his only son. I think he drew it upon himself; the lad must have tried to take on the Eaton Four in the maze." James chuckled, "Who was I to correct him?"

"Thank you," Olivia said softly.

James could see the relief in her eyes as her tears began to dry. "Hawthorn was authorised by Bow Street to manage him as necessary. He was dropped in the entryway of his father's home, and the Marquess was informed of the shame to the Hatton name. Lord Hatton forced him into His Majesty's service, and he was sent somewhere in the West Indies. Of course, it was that or hauled off to a debtor's prison. Which, according to Hawthorn, the Marquess wouldn't have cared, except of course for the disgrace of it."

"Thank goodness. But James..." Olivia hesitated, "are there not so very many more like him?"

James slid closer to her, picked up her hand and kissed it. "Not so very many. I fear the gossips were to blame for exposing you."

"What do you mean, the gossips?" Olivia looked at him perplexed.

"I speak out of turn, but I suppose it no longer signifies.

Early in The Season, a gossip sheet reported on your dowry."

"But how did they know of it?" she quipped.

"No one knows. There are countless questions unanswered."

Olivia began to understand a number of things with the slip of James' tongue. "Oh, James, I wish I had known. How dreadful I was. I would never have given you all so much trouble. What a horrid creature I am, and you were only trying to protect me. I now understand why Jack has not come. Why, oh, why did he not tell me? I thought – well, it does not signify. I was wrong, profoundly wrong, and it cost me so very much."

"It cost you nothing, my love. You will return to the sweet, beautiful young miss we all know and love, in time."

"I must believe it, James. But I must also feel myself worthy, which I do not."

"I know your heart; we have spoken of it many times."

Her cheeks turned a bright pink, and she stared into his eyes. "I am no longer worthy of that love, and I dare say I must forget it. He never felt the same. Now, I am sure, he never will. He saw everything, knows everything, and chooses not to come home." She faltered.

"You are wrong. You must know it and keep that close to your heart. The mere thought of him no longer caring for you as before is foolish. If I did not care for you both and want your complete happiness, you would tire of my begging for your hand, and I would not accept anything but that you would do so."

Olivia's lashes slowly brushed her cheeks, and the blush returned. "Thank you. You know, if my affections had not already been given to another, I would hold you to that offer. You know I love you dearly." She sighed. "You are my dearest friend and confidant. You will always be close to my heart, James. You give me strength and hope, but you deserve more than I can offer."

"My heart does not signify, only yours, my love. Together, we will find the feisty young hoyden we love to challenge." James was not sure he should tell her anymore. It seemed no one told her Jack had left the country that very night, with no direction. But she should know he left for the same reason, thinking himself unworthy of her love. Maybe another day.

"Speaking of such things, I see the sun telling us to make haste. I know Emma has laboured about, and we must reap the benefit. Then tomorrow, I race you to the heath and back, riding astride, like when we were youthful and wild." He began to laugh and pulled her to her feet. She hugged him tightly. He took her chin and lifted her face to his, and before his mind could think better of it, he kissed her. She tightened her embrace, and he deepened his kiss. He released her, stared into the blue eyes, and shuddered. She smiled up at him. "I will always love you, James Sheffield."

***

Christmas passed quietly, and in early January, Lady Birkshire was sitting near the fire in the front drawing room when she received a letter. She read it quickly, then dashed to the door, calling for her niece. When Olivia entered the room, she noticed tears streaming down the countess's face, both smiling and crying.

"Oh, my goodness, whatever is wrong?" She made her way across the parlour.

"Come, sit beside me," She pulled her niece to the settee and held the letter. It was a single piece of parchment, written on one side only, single-lined. She could see the joy in her aunt's eyes.

"It is a letter," she said excitedly, "from Jack."

Olivia stopped short, the smile left her face, "Jack," she said anxiously.

"Yes, yes, sit, sit," Annabelle patted the seat, "I will read it to you."

"Is he well?" Olivia asked, uncertain of the emotions swirling within.

"Yes, he is at Eustace Hall, having no word of where he had gone, I am relieved."

"You didn't know where he was? Why did no one tell me?"

Olivia was shocked. She was sure his parents had known.

"No, we heard nothing from him after we left London. We received a note from Lord Sheffield a week after we arrived, only divulging he was gone. Not even he knew where, but he promised to write. Well, he did not, until now." Annabelle's excitement was overwhelming.

"He was missing, and no one told me of it, he was missing?" Olivia cried frustrated.

"And this is the reason we did not," Annabelle opened her hand towards her. "I knew you would be distraught. Besides, he wasn't missing. When one doesn't wish to be found, they are not really missing," Her aunt concluded. "Do you want to hear the letter?"

"Yes, yes, of course." Olivia scooted where she could read along. Tears had filled her eyes, but no longer of pain, but joy.

"Let me see," Annabelle cleared her throat, trying to focus her ageing eyes.

"Dearest Mother,

I hope this letter finds you well. I've been renovating Eustace Hall for nearly a month. I caught a boat from Ramsgate working as a shipman until I grew sick of the sea. Reaching Lisbon, wishing to be lost, I wandered without direction. But the Norrys ethics began to wear on me. I required accomplishments or I would go mad. Eustace Hall was left to my account last year, and there was much to be done. I decided to return and complete the work necessary."

"What does he mean, Eustace Hall?" Olivia broke in.

"Eustace Hall is the title estate of Viscount Andovir. I believe John gave him the responsibility of it when he returned last year. He had talked of living there until he inherits the earldom," Annabelle said emotionlessly.

"I beg your pardon?" Olivia said capriciously.

"His father believed it would do him good to have the responsibilities to gain the respect of the peerage, until John," She paused, stuttered a little, "Until John dies… and Jack takes his place as the Earl of Birkshire." Annabelle turned back to the letter.

"Oh," Olivia said quietly. It was becoming obvious to her she knew very little of Jack's adult life. "Pray, let us continue…

"I have accomplished a great deal. The tenant farmers are satisfied with their new deals. I believe the farms will continue to be profitable for some time to come. The families are happy, and the small community here seems to get on with your son. I am sorry I caused you grief upon my untimely departure. I never meant to inflict pain on anyone, save myself. I know I have been the cause of much. I will never forgive myself for it. I only hope to live with my failures. I pray my penance of dedicated labour will bring relief. Please write. I am desperate for news from Birkshire House. I miss you all. Most of all, I miss my beloved Olivia. Please let me hear from you soon; I must know the state of things. Your devoted servant and son, Jack"

Annabelle folded the letter. "Eustace Hall, I am so glad he is at Eustace Hall," she said as she dropped the letter into her lap.

"Why? I wish he were here," She said, "but he probably doesn't…"

"Doesn't what," Annabelle snapped indignantly, "Just what do you mean, Olivia Catherine?"

"I only meant…" she stammered.

"I will hear none of this absurd nonsense. You must stop thinking this way. Did you not hear what he said in this letter? If you have any doubts about how he feels about you, you…" Annabelle stopped herself; it was not her place to share Jack's feelings with anyone, especially Olivia.

But she knew how much her son loved her, hurt for her, and blamed himself. She also knew somewhere between their childhood and that horrid night; he had fallen in love with her. Never could she forget the look on his face, never could she forget the way both of her children looked that evening. Olivia's innocence was taken by that madman, and Jack's faith in himself, gone. Ralph Barrymore tried to destroy her children, and God as her witness, she would not let him.

"I beg your pardon, I did not mean to anger you, pray, forgive me," She answered timidly.

"No Olivia, forgive me, I am not angry with you. I must learn to hold my peace. We all have our demons; I am no exception. My anger is not with you, but above all things, you must not think Jack does not want to be here and does not want to see you. That is all I can say, but we have letters to write, today."

"We…?" Olivia queried, "but he did not address a letter to me."

"Nor would he, but he will expect one from both of us," Annabelle stood and went to her escritoire, "I know my son, and he wants to hear from you directly."

Olivia wasn't sure Jack wanted her letter, but Annabelle insisted. She had no idea what to say. The countess took Olivia's hand and told her to write what was in her heart; that is what Jack wanted to hear. She went to her room and sat at her secretaire, dipping the freshly sharpened quill into the ink, her hand trembling. Write what was in her heart, could she, but most of all, she wondered if she had the right to do so.

CHAPTER 22

"God, you are beautiful. Jack could not remove his eyes from her. The light flaxen blonde locks flowed down her back. Facing the window and silhouetted by the moonlight, the thinly veiled chemise revealed every curve of her petite frame. Jack's hungry eyes followed her figure from her long neck, down the roundness and firmness of the divine creature.

As she turned to face him in the darkness, he placed his hands on each side of her tiny waist, then slowly eased them to her hips; she flinched. As his hands moved down her legs, she trembled. Jack knelt on the floor, reaching for the hem of the sheer undergarment. Gathering and layering it as he began sliding upwards, caressing the outer sides of each leg until he reached her thighs, then upwards until he reached her lower torso. He suddenly noticed there was nothing covering her except the gown. Aching with carnal passion, he caught the first glimpse of her femininity.

He slid the chemise up onto her shoulders as he began to stand. He kissed and fondled her with his tongue, exploring every part of her. He covered her right breast and swirled his tongue around the firm, erect nipple, his own body tightening as he tried to devour her. He sucked and pulled, flicking his tongue in every direction. She groaned. He jerked the chemise over her flaxen hair, allowing it to float to the floor. He released the imprisoned breast, straightened, and watched her hair fall gently against the bare skin of her back. She was now completely naked in front of him. She shivered, arms wanting to cover herself, but she held them still. Her head lowered, and Jack tenderly placed his hands on each side of her face and kissed her forehead.

Wrapping his arms around her, he took her delicate, but luscious wet lips into his. His kiss was soft, yet firm. He pressed the kiss passionately, crushing her against his own. Her lips parted slightly, allowing his tongue to drift from side to side, forcing them wider. One of his arms reached the curve of her bottom, pulling her hips closer.

In one brisk motion, he gathered her into his arms. She instinctively wrapped her own around his neck, holding her against his bare chest. He carried her to the bed and eased her onto the soft mattress, holding her breasts against his chest. He took her shoulders into his hands and began to push her away; he wanted to see her face, her eyes, her lips. His eyes moved from the figure he had gently laid in his bed, lifting his eyes to look upon her face..."

Jack awoke! He was covered in sweat, along with the sheet and pillow beneath him. He could feel the pain of his cock. It was stiff and straight. He groaned at the hardness of it. Without opening his eyes, he pulled the wet pillow from under his head and threw it angrily to the floor and rolled over to free his body from the wet sheets.

What was happening? The dream always felt real, and it always ended the same. Never revealing the face of the woman who was tearing his heart out every night. His torment was unbearable. He knew who was haunting his dreams, but why could he not see her face? He desperately wanted to see her, even if it was only in a dream.

***

His days were filled with the arduous task of restoring the estate back to its splendour, but he was miserable. The restoration needed included the house and the tenant farms. The house, closed by the prior estate manager, required minor repairs, but the farms were in dire need of a considerable number of renovations.

Redemption seemed to come with the long hours and manual labour he was contributing to rebuilding the place. Up with the sun, then dragging himself back at dusk, exhausted, he rarely partook of dinner or supper, instead throwing back two to three glasses of brandy. His valet had his daily return impeccably timed. When Jack managed the strength to reach his bedchamber, there was always a hot bath waiting. He was sure Finley wanted to kill him on several occasions. He would watch from the steaming tub as his valet attempted to remove his dirty clothes. It was the rare times he found humour. Watching Finley take his mud and sweat-filled breeches and shirts with only his thumb and forefinger, turning and pinching his nose with the other, Jack could not withhold a laugh.

The first few days at Eustace Hall, he was sure he would be forced to hire a new valet. But to Finley's credit, he managed to find a tolerance for the filth and smell, at least until he could pass them along to one of the chambermaids.

It was the only amusement Jack found here. He was lonely, missed his family, his friends, but most of all, he missed Olivia. How did things go so terribly wrong?

For the first few weeks, he relived that night over and over, in nightmares. Some nights he would reach her in time; others, the maggot was still standing over her when he turned the last hedge. But the worst were the ones he could not control. The ones where he pummelled the bastard to death. Those dreams seemed to never end. When he would awaken, his hands were still clenched, his muscles tensed from the fight. Thank God those had ended.

The ephialtes finally ceased after he received word from Sheffield that Olivia was better. The Marquess had travelled to the country house on many occasions to see her. They had gone riding, had picnics at the lake, had even tried some fishing while there. Sheffield had included in the letter that Olivia had told him he had no idea how to catch a fish and should take lessons from Jack. *You were never far from her lips.* He thought of those lines often.

God, how he missed her. He remembered the first vision after the letter from James. It was the first night he had a dream, rather than a nightmare. It was more of a memory, and it was comforting.

It was a long-ago fishing trip with Olivia to the pond. She could not have been more than five, Jack was nearly eleven. The dream had seemed so real...

***

"Please, Jack, I can do it. Let me try?" Olivia's tiny voice pleaded.

"No, Olivia, you will stick yourself with the hook." He warned.

"Will not," she pouted.

"You will." Jack turned to her sternly, showing her the barb at the end of it. "It is sharper than mama's needles and pins," he said.

"Oh," she said as she reached for the barb, quickly jerking her finger back at his words. "I was stuck with a pin once when nanny was trying to fix my dress. It did not feel particularly good," she blinked.

"I am certain it did not. This would feel worse," he said with much authority.

Olivia allowed him to bait her hook and then tossed it into the water. She was standing on the edge of the pond, watching her line and bait. "This is so very much fun. Thank you for bringing me," she giggled.

He mussed her hair and told her to be still. "A fish will not come close enough unless you hold still."

"Very well, I will hold my breath." She assured him.

The tiny little girl was determined she was going to catch a fish today. Jack was baiting his hook and saw her standing like a statue. He grinned to himself and turned to his hook. He heard her gasp, water splashing, a yelp, and turned in time to see a rather large one take her bait. He dropped his pole and ran to grab her line, but it was too late. The quarry grabbed the bait and quickly turned back to the centre of the pond, taking the bait, line, pole, along with Olivia into the water.

"Jack, Jack," she screamed not turning loose of the prized fish.

"Drop the pole, Olivia," he yelled.

Reaching the water's edge, he noticed she had dropped it, or the wily fish had jerked it from her.

Knowing Olivia as he did, he assumed the latter. He bent over and snatched her from the pond. "I've got you, Olivia," Jack stammered as he splashed into the ankle-deep water.

"But my fish, my fish, it is getting away," she shouted kicking her feet.

He was hauling her to the bank, all the while she was more concerned about the lost fish. "We lost my fish," she cried.

"Are you all right?" he was trying to get her to stand up

straight so he could inspect the damage. For a ten-year-old boy, this was not an easy task, especially when the child in question was determined to see what happened to her fish.

"Olivia!" He yelled, shaking her shoulders.

She stopped and stared up at him. That is when he saw the tears in her eyes, and he panicked. "Are you hurt? What is wrong?" Jack knelt on the ground, looking into her sad little eyes with tears streaming down her face. "Please, Olivia, tell me what hurts." Jack tried again.

She looked at him completely devastated or at least as much as any five-year-old can be. "I do not hurt anywhere, but my dress is wet, my shoes are wet, even my petticoat is wet, but…" she whimpered, "my fish."

"Yes, I know, your fish is gone," interrupting the pet, she was determined to pitch.

He picked her up and laid her head on his shoulder, carrying her home. He could feel her sobbing. "It will be all right, Olivia. Your mama will change your dress, and I promise we will catch your fish next time," he told her as he headed up the hill to the house.

"Promise?" She raised her head to peer into his eyes, sniffled, then dried them on his shirt.

"I promise," Jack said, chuckling.

***

The viscount was smiling at the memory. He would dream of other days spent with Olivia throughout their entire lifetime of memories. The dreams he would recall as if they were yesterday. She had always been stubborn and tough as nails, for a little girl. He awakened one morning, conscious of

Olivia's stubbornness, toughness, and determination. She tried everything he did. She was stronger than most girls and learned resources to accomplish whatever was necessary to compete. The more he thought of it, he was certain it had saved her that night. After one specific recollection, he was sure of it...

***

He was fourteen, Olivia eight or nine. They had gone riding but dismounted to investigate something; he no longer remembered what. They only intended to be a minute; the horses were ground-tied, dropping the reins where they stood.

Suddenly, a lightning bolt struck remarkably close, even closer to their steeds; both bolted and headed straight to the stables, leaving the two explorers afoot.

"The horses!" she screamed.

"Olivia are you all right?" He ran to her. "I'm fine, but the horses," she said.

"Are halfway home," he retorted, disgusted.

She turned her palm toward the sky and watched raindrops begin to fall into it, a bit too rapidly. "And it's raining," she smirked.

"Great," he blurted. "Well, we might as well start walking."

Olivia shrugged and headed homeward. The rain was coming down in sheets, and they were both quickly soaked. Jack noticed her wrapping her arms around herself.

"Are you cold?" he asked as he walked over, rubbing her arms.

"Just a little, but my boots are sucking into the ground, and I can hardly pick up my feet."

Jack was beginning to feel the same suction. It was also getting very slippery in spots where old fallen trees were covered in moss.

"Step carefully, Olivia. Some places are very slippery; take my hand."

He extended his arm, she latched on. The woods were thick, and there were downed branches and trunks everywhere. As he stepped over branches, he would lift her over them.

One was a large tree, and as he started to lift her, he slipped, sliding under it. Olivia's weight caused it to roll toward Jack, burying his foot.

She quickly jumped off it. "Jack, are you hurt?" she cried.

"No, just stuck in the mud. I will get my foot out. Just keep still."

He was tugging his foot when he noticed something moving along the tree. He cursed under his fourteen-year-old breath. It was a snake crawling up the dead trunk towards him. He tried not to panic. He knew there were adders in the area but had not seen one. He looked around but found nothing big enough to kill it.

"Olivia," He called, attempting to keep his voice steady and calm.

"Yes," she answered from some distance, unconcerned, her attention gathered elsewhere.

"This is very serious, come here."

She walked over as he pointed to the snake.

"NO!" she screamed.

"Calm down," he demanded. She immediately hushed and stood still.

"What can I do?" she asked quietly.

"I need something large and sturdy enough to kill him if he keeps coming." He was desperately trying to get his leg free.

"Like a big rock?" She asked, bending over at the varied sizes of hard items.

"Yes, do you see one?"

"I do. What will you do with it?" She was heading toward the rocks.

"I will bash its head in."

"Oh," she said. "Can you do that? You seem to be facing wrong."

"A little perhaps, but I have no choice. I must try."

His foot seemed to be hung on something else in the mud. He looked over at Olivia; she was trying to dislodge a rather large stone.

"That one is too big, try to find a smaller one."

"I don't think it will work; you aren't facing right."

He rolled his eyes in frustration. Why must this little nymph always argue with him at the worst moments?

"Olivia, just find me a manageable size one. I must try. If it is poison, I have to kill it."

"You only wish to bash his head in?"

"God, yes, Olivia, only hurry and bring me a damn rock, one of any size will do."

Jack was getting a little worried. The viper obviously disliking the intrusion to his house was determined to inspect the disturbance. The viscount continued to look down at what could be trapping his foot.

Just as he turned to see if Olivia had retrieved some sort of stone, the entire tree vibrated. Jack jerked around to find Olivia standing beside the tree where the snake had been, with her hands in the air, holding a huge rock. At that instant, he was trying to fathom how she was even holding it.

"Like that?" she asked candidly.

Jack was astounded. He peered over the side of the tree to see the snake lying on the other side with a very smashed head and the body wiggling in its dance of death.

"Well, uh, yes, just like that."

***

He laughed aloud. He thought about that last day. It could have been so much worse. She could have been kidnapped; she could have been compromised beyond comprehension, but her own tenacity, resolve, and determination had been what saved her.

It was the first time he had thought of that day without loathing it. The little girl, the young lady, and the woman Olivia became was strong and enduring.

He was in love with her, and if she had the same love, it could conquer every adversity. Somehow, he had to fix this. He had to make things right, finish this damn house. If there was any way he could convince her to have him, he had a wife to bring here and raise a family. Jack was more dedicated and determined to finish Eustace Hall.

***

The viscount was inspecting the ledgers of his tenant farms, very pleased with the numbers. He glanced up from his desk in the library to see Stinson standing quietly in the doorway, his white glove holding several letters, but he returned to his books.

"Beg your pardon, my lord," he said flatly. "I know you wanted privacy this morning, but you received several personal letters. I thought you might want to see them immediately."

"Just lay them on the corner in the tray." Jack never looked up.

The butler, aware of the relationship between Eustace Hall and Birkshire House, knew his lordship would not wish them carelessly lain on the desk. He cleared his throat.

"They are from Birkshire House," Stinson said, interrupting again.

The viscount's head jerked to attention, "Birkshire House?" he said, pushing his chair back, standing to retrieve the letters.

"Yes, my lord," Stinson stated, handing them directly to his lordship.

"Thank you, you are correct, as usual."

He dismissed his butler, requesting he close the door. He

leaned back in the chair, gazing at the missives. There were two from Birkshire House and one from Lord Sheffield in London. He laid the one from Sheffield on the desk and then stared at the other two. He recognised his mother's handwriting and laid it aside.

The last one he held in his hand for a moment, then brought it to his nose, sniffed, quickly identifying the aromatic flower. He closed his eyes; an eager smile crossed his face. He knew the scent… her scent.

Her maid would pick fresh roses, boil the petals, and squeeze the oil from them, just for Olivia. He held it to his nose, taking in the light rose fragrance, then regarded it at arm's length. He tapped it on the edge of the desk. What did it say? He wondered. He wanted to know, but then again, maybe he did not.

He knew Sheffield spent a great deal of time at Birkshire House. He had received many letters describing Olivia's mental and physical condition. Each visit, believing she was dealing admirably with the horrid experience. Had James and Olivia formed an attachment? Why else, these letters on the same day?

Oh, God, this could not be happening. Not now. He had the house finished. He was ready to bring Olivia home… Home. Now these three letters arrived together. A coincidence? Probably not.

He dropped the correspondence on the desk and shuffled them, retrieving his mother's. No, he thought, not Mother's. He retrieved Sheffield's. Yes, he would open it first.

Sheffield would never ask for Olivia's hand before he told him of it. Lord James Sheffield was a noble and loyal friend, but Andovir was also aware of the future duke's affection for Olivia. What the bloody hell was wrong with him leaving Olivia when she was at her most vulnerable? When she needed to be cared for and loved? He might as well have delivered her to Sheffield's bed. What a damnable fool he was. But wait, if Olivia didn't know, maybe he could still get there in time. But would he interfere? If she loved James.

"Open the bloody letter, you idiot, before you go mad," Jack thought to himself. He ripped open the seal and, with a flick of the wrist, began to read.

"My dear and loyal friend,

I have just come from Birkshire House. I was there for the weekend."

Jack's heart stopped, and his breath caught. "The weekend? No!"

"Olivia is back to herself again and more beautiful than ever. I know how much you have been worried about her. We rode out to the lake for another picnic on Saturday. She was laughing and joking. My God, it was good to see her truly laugh. It had been so exceedingly long."

"Good God, man, you are writing like a girl, what the devil? You have never written a letter this long. Get to the point." Jack, talking aloud to himself, scanned the page, frustrated. The last thing he wanted to hear was all the lovemaking between his best friend and Olivia.

"Now that you've passed over the lovemaking stories. I only have one thing to say, it is time for you to go home. I have no doubt whatsoever, does she not only love you, old boy, she is madly in love with you. She did not say it, but she doesn't need to say the words. I can also say without a doubt, if I did not believe her heart only belonged to you, I would have already asked your father for her hand. You are one lucky bloke, my friend. Go home and lay claim to what is yours, or I will.

Your humble servant, friend, etc. Lord James Sheffield"

Jack tossed the letter on the desk and grabbed his mother's letter, tearing it open. It was one page, only one page.

"My Darling son,

It is time for you to come home. We are all waiting. Your father insists and demands propriety regarding this matter.

Your loving mother."

"What the deuce is she talking about? She's gone mad. My mother has gone mad." He mumbled. He retrieved Olivia's missive, his hand shaking. This would be his destiny. His future happiness was within the contents of the small thin parchment. He broke the wax seal.

"My Dearest Jack,

I wish for you to return home soon. I have so very much to say, too much to place in a letter. I am told Eustace Hall is your new home. Your mother says you are responsible for the land and its tenants; it sounds beautiful. She says I would like it there. If you are there, I know it to be so. My heart aches, I miss you so, please hurry home. Always your humble servant, Olivia"

"Stinson, Stinson," Jack called impatiently, folding the letter, and tucking it into his jacket pocket. "Stinson!" Jack was out of his chair and headed toward the door.

"Yes, my lord." Stinson, out of breath from his lordship's panicked tone, met him in the doorway.

"Have my carriage, no wait. Have my horse readied for travel immediately." Jack started out the door.

"Yes sir…" Stinson began to inquire specifics but was interrupted yet again.

"No wait, I cannot do that." Jack stopped in the hallway. He had to think; he could not take his horse. He had no intentions of returning alone.

"I need the coach readied. Yes, the town coach." Jack mumbled.

"Yes, sir." Stinson turned and headed down the hallway.

"Stinson," Jack called again. "Once you have done so, please come to my chambers. I have instructions for you while I am away."

"You're going away, sir? For how long, my lord?" Stinson looked confused.

"Go, go, ready the coach. I will explain all when you return." Jack flew up the stairs to his bedchamber. He stopped two doors short of his own. He turned and faced the double mahogany slabs in front of him, took the handles, and walked into a room he had never entered before. He viewed its restored grandeur and new furnishings. It was perfect. The entire family wing had been restored, but he had never inspected the finished work. He was smiling as he touched the wall covering ordered from France. He had selected the fabric and colours, but the long-time housekeeper, Mrs. Berkley, had overseen the final schemes. Jack had confided in her on many occasions regarding Olivia, and the final décor reflected that she had known all along who was to occupy it.

Jack ambled to the double doors to his right and flung them open. This room he knew well, the sitting room between the lord and lady's bedchambers. He saw Finley looking quite surprised sitting at the desk. He did not know what to think of his master entering through those doors; he had assumed them to be locked. He immediately stood but said nothing. Lord Andovir was acting strangely. He was smiling, genuinely smiling, frankly, he was startled. He had not seen him happy in, well over seven months.

"Finley, we are leaving; we need to pack," Jack announced.

"When sir?" The valet asked quite surprised and dumbfounded but made no change in countenance. If anything, he had learned flexibility over the past months.

"Now! Well, as soon as you can pack. The coach is being readied." He declared and entered his bedchamber.

The valet's jaw dropped. His master never ceased to amaze him. He walked around the desk following his lordship into the bedchamber. "But, my lord, my lord… please a moment."

Jack kept hurrying about and Finley kept pace, trying to keep up with his burbling. "Where are we going? What will you require? Please, my lord, I need to know what to pack."

The valet was quite agitated, as his lordship was pulling out drawers and tossing things about. Finally, the poor valet stopped in the middle of the room, crossed his arms, and watched as Jack moved swiftly about.

Perceiving Finley had ceased keeping pace, he halted and turned to him. "What are you doing, man? Get moving?"

The valet dropped his arms and quietly addressed his lordship.

"My lord, I have no idea where we are going or what you will be doing, so I have no notion as to what to pack. Will you be attending a ball, going hunting, or will you be crawling about in the mud like you have been doing for the past months?" Sarcasm dripped from his tongue.

"Yes, maybe, and definitely not." Jack postulated.

"What?" Finley threw up his hands, headed into the dressing room, and pulled down the portmanteaus.

When he returned to the bedchamber, he found the master whistling.

"Oh, my God, he's finally gone round the bend, touched in the head, he is. Knew it was coming, should have expected it after the last several months." Finley was in shock.

His valet and a long-time friend stopped and faced him, "Andovir!" hoping that would get his attention, "I have no notion whatsoever to pack for Bedlam… my lord."

"What?" He gave Finley an odd look, "We aren't going to Bedlam. We are going to Birkshire House. I am going home. There will be parties, balls, riding, and maybe a bit of hunting—the snow geese this time of year, you know. And my father is always up for shooting. Finley, I am going to be married."

"Married, sir?" the valet stared at him dumbfounded.

"You heard me. Get moving."

"But sir, who?" The valet asked seriously.

"Who?" Jack turned to the valet as if he had fallen from a tree… on his head. "What kind of damn fool question is that? I am marrying the most beautiful, most obstinate, most gracious, most petulant, most wonderful woman in the world." He paused, "That is, if she will have me."

"Lady Olivia?" he asked surprised.

"Is there another?"

"No, sir." With that, the interchange ceased, and Finley

went straight to the task. He too was thinking of quiet, peaceful, and clean days ahead.

Jack had received the letters at 10:00 in the morning, and by 1:00 that afternoon, the coach was packed and ready. The black lacquer town coach was a stately equipage, drawn by four horses, with the red and gold Andovir coat of arms gracing the sides. The viscount sent word to the stables to have the four matched blacks hitched. It made for quite the sight. After all, he was fetching a bride home. It must be perfect.

The coachman's livery was black and red, trimmed in gold, impeccable and extremely regal. The viscount requested two extra grooms and additional outriders as well. There was no time to send horses ahead for changes, so there would be stops to feed, water, and rest the horses, but he intended to be at Birkshire House tomorrow evening.

It was late winter, not quite spring, the weather was cool, and if they took a steady pace, there should be no issue making the trip in a timely fashion. The coach was ready and only awaited Lord Andovir.

Jack was in the foyer discussing last-minute details with Stinson and Mrs. Berkley. They both wished to know of his return.

"I am not certain. I will send a message prior to our arrival." He was rambling but caught the look on Mrs. Berkley's face.

"I am sorry, I have been so busy I forgot to tell you. I inspected the viscountess' bedchamber, exquisite, simply exquisite."

The housekeeper blushed and smiled, still curious.

"I hope to be returning a married man, Mrs. Berkley." Jack was smiling.

"If I may be so bold," Mrs. Berkley asked. "Lady Olivia?"

Her heart swelled, and she felt a shudder in her chest.

He nodded with happiness. "The very one."

"Oh, my lord, I am so happy for you." His housekeeper beamed.

The viscount swore he saw tears in her eyes. She had been worried about the master since his arrival. He had told her enough about Olivia, and her heart was full knowing the time had finally come for his lordship's happiness.

"Ensure everything is in order, Stinson. Oh, and Mrs. Berkley, when I send notice of our return, fill her bedchamber with roses. She adores roses, as you well know. The orangery is filled with them, and the gardener assures me they will be ready." He was rambling again. He bid them goodbye and headed to the coach. Stinson and Mrs. Berkley stood on the steps and watched the coach pull away.

"I didn't know Lord Andovir could be so happy or loquacious," The butler said, looking a bit surprised.

"He obviously never spoke with you regarding Lady Olivia." She said smugly, with a raised eyebrow and a haughty tilt to her head.

"Uh… no, he did not." Stinson was caught a bit off guard. After all, the butler was to be aware of all things. He turned to her with many questions.

As they turned back to the house, Mrs. Berkley kept explicating. "No worries, I will fill you in. He has been in love with her since the day she was born, he says. He didn't know it, of course, he was only six or almost six at the time, but…" She was still talking, and Stinson leaned his ear, listening intently as he closed the doors behind them.

CHAPTER 23

Jack flipped open his pocket watch, half past nine and dark. Considering the quick departure and no change of horses, it could have been far worse. There had been no issues; no highwaymen; no broken wheels or axles. The horses were paced well, the trip made in good order. They would get a long rest in the Birkshire stables. He closed the cover of the watch with a click and stuffed it back into his waistcoat.

Peering out the window as the coach passed through the stately gate onto the long drive, the clip-clop of the horses making their way along the stone path to the front entry, he became keenly aware of just how much he had missed the place.

He had thought of going straight to the stables, but without notice of his arrival, he feared he might be met with a blunderbuss or, worse, a well-placed horse pistol. He had the coachmen halt at the front entry and, not waiting for a footman to let down the step, Jack opened the door, leapt out, and touched the ground of Birkshire for the first time in months. The valet on his heels, believing himself to have returned to civilization.

"You remember the direction and workings of the stable?"

"Of course, my Lord," Finley nodded.

"Very well, I will notify the staff to ensure none of us gets ourselves shot since our arrival will be a complete surprise." He gave the valet a grin.

Returning a weak grin of his own, Finley gulped, agreeing to wait for notice. He had hunted with some of the stable hands and did not want to catch them unaware, all were crack shots.

The viscount headed up the steps, two at a time, but just as he was about to take hold of the knocker, the door swung open. A stern-faced older gentleman, with a cold, expressionless, and irritated look, stared him down. Jack raised his eyebrows and gave the older gentleman a familiar smile.

"Graham. I should have known you would hear us coming up the stone path." Jack said, laughing. The old man blinked a few times, cleared his throat, and squinted his strained eyes.

"Lord Andovir?" the old butler's shocked voice was quaking and quite bewildered, "we weren't expec... I mean, this is indeed a surprise."

"Just so," Jack said, removing his hat and coat and smothering the butler with them. "Are my parents still about?"

"Uh, yes milord, they are, uh, well, let me..."

Graham was stunned; he was never one to stammer and stutter under normal circumstances, but this was clearly not normal. He had not seen Lord Andovir in over seven months and with no notice of his arrival, an unacceptable position for him.

"I believe they are in the drawing room next to your father's office," Graham replied from beneath the multi-caped driving coat, somewhat recovered from the shock. "Shall I announce you?"

"No, no, pray where would the surprise be? Oh, send word to the stablemaster, not to shoot my valet and horses." Jack laughed as he made his way past the butler down the hallway.

"Surprise them? I hope the surprise doesn't kill them." Graham grumbled under his breath as he shook out the coat and placed it in the closet. "It damn near killed me."

The viscount, with long strides, dashed up the stairs and with quickened pace, strolled down the hallway. If they were in the small parlour, it would only be his parents. Once he reached the double doors, he turned the knobs gently, not wanting to alert its occupants. They were sitting in two high-back leather chairs facing the fireplace. Excellent! He slowly crept inside the door, closing it quietly. They were both silently reading, his father the newspaper and mother a novel of some sort.

"This is the saddest thing I've ever seen," Jack said, just loud enough to gain attention.

John Birkshire snapped his head around and Annabelle was trying to scoot forward in her chair to do the same. The two shocked faces could only stare at the stranger.

"What the devil?" He heard his father say as he rose from his chair, folding the paper.

"Oh, my God! Oh, my gracious heavenly father." He heard his mother shriek as she grabbed her chest and dropped the book to the floor. Annabelle jumped to her feet and with the speed only a mother possessed at the sight of her long-lost child, converged on him with open arms. "You're home! John, my... our son is home!" She said as she pulled him to her. "Why didn't you notify us? You could have given us an apoplexy showing up in such a way. You know that is very unkind." Babbling as she pushed him away.

"Let me look at you. My word, what have you been doing?" She stated as she pushed him away from her again, surveying him up and down.

"I beg your pardon?" He scowled. "A great deal of manual labour and I will have you know I have been quite busy."

"Yes," she said, "as she examined him, the darkened skin, the heavily sun-streaked hair. "It appears a great deal of it has been out of doors, quite a bit of it."

He glanced at his father, who was shaking his head, giving him the 'just agree with her' look. It was quite apparent until his wife completed her lectures and reprimands; the conversation would go no further.

When his mother was finally exhausted, his father looked at him and inquired. "Why the surprise? Not that it isn't wonderful. Believe me, no one is any happier about you being here than I." He glanced toward his wife.

"It was a moment's decision, the blame lying partially with my mother." He said, frankly.

"Really, why?" She asked, with a bit of mischief in her tone.

"Your letter, of course." He answered wryly.

"My letter?" trying to sound surprised.

"Well, I did say partially. It was yours, Sheffield's, and Olivia's. If you must know." Jack said.

"I didn't know Lord Sheffield wrote you." She stuttered.

"Clearly. But that one 'bout gave me a damn bloody heart attack. I know what he's been up to, can't help but write me about it, constantly. He's worse than a girl writing a letter, you know. Wouldn't take up a correspondence with him, if you know what is good for you… Wait, you say you didn't know about Sheffield's, which must mean you knew about Olivia's?" he eyed her suspiciously.

"Well, not precisely." She hesitated, smiling. Jack raised an eyebrow, but before he could say anything, she continued. "I only suggested she might." She concluded.

"Well, she did. You did. Sheffield did. And here I am."

Lord Birkshire was shaking his head, laughing under his breath at both.

Lady Birkshire snapped her head toward her husband. "Why might you be laughing?" she demanded.

"Oh, nothing. But now that I can speak, I must know, and specifically, why you are here?" Jack's father was suddenly quite serious.

"What do you mean?" he asked with a grin.

His father stared at him. "Do not be covert with me. I know why you are here."

"You do?"

His father raised both eyebrows, drew in his breath, said nothing, and only glared at his son.

"Yes, I am sure you do." Relenting and directing his attention to his father. "And I suppose you have much to say about it."

"Indeed, I do. There will be changes that must be adhered to whilst you are under my roof. And take heed of it, as I am deadly serious, my boy. If you have your way, at least two weeks, but I can assure you, your mother will say no less than four and expect six?" Jack and his father were discussing the terms of an agreement.

The countess turned her head to one and then the other, unsure of what they were agreeing to or about. "What are you two talking about?" She was suddenly aware she was being ignored. She stood her ground, crossed her arms, and watched the proceedings.

"I will not have it any other way. You may very well be my son, but you are a grown man with your obligations, and - I," he paused, "have mine, which have little to do with you. Mine will not be compromised; do we understand one another?"

"We do." Lord Andovir extended his hand to his father.

"Very well, I will get my part in order, and the papers will be signed first thing in the morning." Lord Birkshire shook his hand with a smile.

"Thank you." With gratifying expressions on their faces, they walked to his father's liquor cabinet, poured two glasses of the finest cognac, and clinked glasses, acknowledging the success of their first contract.

Annabelle stood facing them and demanded to know what they had contracted. Her husband informed her it was none of her affair, and when she turned to her son, he tilted his head in agreement. She accepted the loss of this round bid them goodnight and left the room. The two men sat by the fire and had a long father and son visit, one which had been long in coming.

***

The following morning Jack hurried through an early breakfast and made his way to the front parlour. He had planned this day a thousand times over the past several months. Now, facing the actual task, he was nervous as a cat. He had no idea why, but his hands were sweating, and he kept pulling at his cravat and clearing his throat as though he was choking and unable to breathe.

He was staring out at the front lawn when he heard shuffling in the hallway. He turned and waited patiently for whoever it was to make their way into the blue parlour, where everyone passed through each day for tea and coffee. He was delighted traditions were not easily altered in his old home.

"I cannot believe this." The small blonde mumbled as she entered the drawing room. Her riding habit unbuttoned, exposing the muslin blouse beneath. She had a linen cloth attempting to remove a stain from the bodice. "Where is Sarah when I need her? I do not believe this…"

"I will be happy to assist." She heard a voice from across the room.

She abruptly stilled, dropped her arm, and the cleaning cloth floated softly to the floor, staring at the stranger in shock without so much as a flutter from her lashes.

She bobbed forward a touch, finally blinking at the figure. Her breathing erratic, legs unbalanced, and she was barely able to hold her slight weight. The queasiness building within caused her to grab the arm of the closest chair, never taking her eyes off the figure across the room, she eased into the chair. She gazed at the tall, broad shape with heavily streaked chestnut hair, a muslin shirt stretched tight by bulging muscles, face, and hands darkened from too much time in the sun; he was the image of the Greek God, Apollo.

"Oh." She murmured as her body went limp in the chair.

"Olivia, are you all right?" He said, moving quickly across the room towards her.

"I – I-I wasn't expecting… I was startled…. no, I suppose, I was shocked." She had dreamt of his homecoming but hadn't expected to be jolted by the sight of him, but she had also figured to have some warning.

"I should have sent word I was here, but I wished to surprise you... it was thoughtless and careless; it has been too long." He said apologetically.

He thought he was past the self-loathing, but it came rushing back, feeling rude, pompous, and selfish. Her letter had caused him so much joy; that he forgot there had been nearly eight months and a world of devastation between them. Each had rebuilt their emotional lives from what had felt like total annihilation at the time. He assumed she had reached the same place and time. Clearly, as their entire life had been, she had not.

What had he been thinking? He had expected her to rush to him as she had as a little girl, throwing her arms around his neck, kissing his cheeks, and... What a fool he was?

He found himself apologising again and moved to a chair across from her in the small arrangement, leaving a small tea table between them. She was still collecting herself, leaning to recover the linen cloth and fidgeting with it in her lap, but said nothing. As he watched her uneasiness, he feared it was a moment they would never pass.

"Should I go?" He struggled to ask.

"No," she said quietly, "I beg you, please do not. I am glad you are here; it was only unexpected." Olivia breathed deeply and released a sigh.

He had heard so often from Sheffield that he hadn't stopped to think that not one person at Birkshire House had heard from him in months and was not even aware of where he had been.

He sat straight in his chair gazing at her; she was different and, if possible, more beautiful than he remembered. Her blonde hair was a bit darker, the alabaster skin still perfection, the colour of her crystal blue eyes the same, but there was something else.

Startled, his insides wrenched, and a sense of loss shot through him; yes, something was missing... the innocence. The light that sparkled, the gleam in the eyes, the one only a child possesses and once you've passed its borders, you can never return. He choked back the lump in his throat and fought the moisture building in his eyes.

Of course, she had changed; she had witnessed the ugly side of life and the inhumanity of it. Sheffield imparted the return to herself, laughing, and joking. Indeed, maybe she had largely, but it was short-sighted to believe that in varying degrees, it would not remain. God, what an idiot, what a callous, insensitive fool he was. Jack stood and crossed the floor to leave.

"Do not go," she whispered, barely audible.

But he heard her; he always heard her. It was like a sixth sense between them, always knowing the other's thoughts and words, long before they were spoken. It was what had made the last year so difficult, the struggle of redefining the bond between them.

He closed his eyes and froze in place. He had intended to walk away. In his mind, his mere presence had hurt her.

"Please sit." Olivia motioned him closer. "Jack," she pleaded, "Please look at me."

He crossed the floor and lowered his eyes to hers. She saw the pain; her rejection had hurt him deeply.

"I am sorry," she said softly. "I only wish I had known you were coming. I could have prepared myself."

Jack knelt and slowly extended his hand toward her but stopped short, opening his palm instead. She looked up at him, then placed her hand in his. Her touch burned through him like a blacksmith's hot tongs. It had been so long since he had felt the softness of her skin, the mere touch of her fingers melted him.

"I have missed you." She sighed, squeezing his hand.

"Have you?" He queried.

"Of course, how could you ask such a terrible thing?" She looked at him confused.

"If I were you, I would not have missed me at all." He scoffed.

"Pray, do not say such things. I've thought of you every day and never understood why you… ," she stopped short. She no longer knew his feelings; he had a new life, a new home, another world entirely, which appeared to have no place for her. It had been far too long. "Why you left," she lowered her head.

"You want the truth?" Jack's eyes grew serious and were piercing through her.

Olivia watched as his expression changed; she saw a hollowness in his eyes that frightened her. She wasn't sure she wanted the truth. But she had to know. He had not written. His mother's letter gave no indication he wished to see her. No evidence of anything other than the same concern he had given all her life. He had asked about her, the same as he had asked of everyone else here. But she had to know what was in his heart. He held her future in his hands, whether agreeable or dreadful; she must know.

"Yes," was all she managed to say.

Jack let go of her hand. He stood and walked away from her, unable to watch her face as he finally admitted he had been a coward. He could not stand to see her in so much pain, and he was filled with uncontrollable rage. He had never wanted to hurt anyone in his life, yet all he wanted to do that night was kill, destroy, tear another human being to pieces.

"I was ashamed," he said quietly.

"Of me," she whimpered.

Jack spun on heels to face her.

"Of course not, not ever." He roared, then softened.

"Never, ever, what would make you say such a thing, Olivia."

"It is what has haunted me every day of my life for months. I was no longer the innocent young girl."

She lowered her eyes and he moved to her, bent down on one knee, and wrapped his arms around her, holding her tightly.

"No Olivia, I could never be ashamed of you. I was ashamed of myself. I hated myself, everything inside of me died that night because I had not shielded you from harm. I managed the entire situation badly. I-I could not forgive myself, and I was afraid you would hate me for it. I was supposed to protect you, always. The one promises I made to you so long ago. It seemed so easy until the night it truly mattered, and I failed. I can never forgive myself for it."

Tears fell from his eyes. Olivia slid from the chair onto her knees in front of him. Jack dropped his other knee. They were almost touching, their bodies too close, he took her hands in his, and they shed the long-needed tears of fear, anger, hatred, shame, affection, and love.

She threw her arms around his broad shoulders and buried her head into the crook of his neck. He wrapped his arms around her, pulling her to him and holding her head there.

In one swift move, he pulled her head from his and lifted her to her feet, taking her face in his hands. Lowering his lips to hers, first gently, then he deepened the kiss.

At first, she was afraid to move, unsure of what was happening. Then, he felt her hands slowly reach his hair, pulling him to her, lips parting, meeting his intensity. He pressed harder, parting them further with his tongue, searching her, her inexperience dancing to the intrusion. She was taking him in with more passion than he ever imagined. His body began to stiffen with desire; he wanted to take her, he wanted to engulf her entirely within his. He could feel himself growing harder, and he pulled her body to his, pressing her hips into him. He withdrew his lips from hers and moved down her cheeks to her neck.

Olivia gasped, the tingles and shimmers she hadn't felt in nearly a year along with the emotions overwhelmed her. She had no idea her body could respond this way. She could feel a need from within, not understanding what was happening; she only knew she did not want it to end. She wanted him, needed him.

There was an energy she could not understand or control; it was thrusting her hips into him without conscious effort. She could feel the prominence between them. Not understanding the significance but an uncontrollable desire pushed her body.

She did not know what it was, only wanting and needing more. She pulled at his hair, pulling him to her.

As he gently stroked her neck with his tongue, he slid to the hollow of her shoulder, dipping into the small crevice, licking, and stroking, his tongue reaching the precipice and sliding over the edge, falling to her breasts.

Jack knew he could not do this, not now, not yet. He withdrew her arms from around his neck and placed them at her side. He stood and sat her again in the chair. He needed to make up for a year of confusion, which he now understood.

She was perplexed by his sudden movement. She didn't understand why he had stopped. She had been waiting for him for so long, and she suddenly understood so much - his tenderness, the thrill of his touch, it all seemed so right to her. Why had he pulled away?

"We can't do this, Olivia."

Her eyes searched his for understanding and found none.

He brushed a wisp of hair from her face, she slightly turned toward the large hand and leaned into it.

Jack held it for a moment against her face.

"Go for your ride. I have some business with Father, and I will meet you back here afterwards, shall we say 2:00? It will give you a chance to get over my abrupt entry back into your life, and we can speak then. So many things have changed, and I have much to tell you. Some you may not wish to hear, things that may displease you, but I must tell you."

Her tender eyes met his, and when she smiled, he could see remnants of the old Olivia.

"I would like that exceedingly. I have much to say. I believe if I attempted at present, it would come out wrong."

"I feel the same." He lifted her to her feet.

"I will drink a hot chocolate, then Spartan should be saddled, my groom will be waiting."

"Father should be in his study. I must oversee business matters, and it will allow you to return to your normal morning. I am sorry, Olivia, I was only… it does not signify." He squeezed her hand, and she nodded. He placed a light kiss on her forehead and quit the room.

She watched him walk down the hallway toward his father's study. She rubbed her forehead, then wrapped her arms around her waist, attempting to hold the warmth building inside, as she made her way to the small mahogany sideboard for the hot chocolate and cakes.

Recalling his words, not certain she completely understood. Why on earth would he think there could be anything he had to say that she might not wish to hear, and what had really changed? Certainly, some had, but not between them. But she brushed the thoughts aside. She was far too happy to see him, to be worried about things not spoken.

As the beverage trickled down her throat warming her, she replayed their interlude and smiled. She had never been so happy, only wishing she had been prepared; her overreaction had hurt him terribly.

She finished her cake, removed her cup and saucer to the small table, then reached for her riding gloves, slipping into them. She inhaled a deep breath and headed toward the side exit to the stables. She would pass her uncle's study and hoped the door would be ajar, she desired another glance of him as she passed. She wouldn't interrupt, she only wished for a glimpse; their time had been too short. She sought to reassure herself it had been real and not a dream... another one of those dreams where she woke up and he was gone. She would pass quickly and take little notice. Jack's business was of no concern of hers and she would not be seen.

As she approached, she noticed the doors closing as if someone had only just entered and failed to shut them completely. There were three voices. She did not recognise the third, but easily identified the earl and the viscount, both addressing the newcomer in unison.

"Standish."

Where was Graham? It appeared whoever it was, needed no introduction or announcement.

"Well, Jack my boy, I understand felicitations are in order," the stranger hailed.

Felicitations? Whatever for? Returning home? But that sounded silly. Olivia paused in the hallway for a moment.

She knew she should not be there; knew she should not listen; but she could not help herself. Maybe that is why Jack wanted to speak with her. She stepped to the side of the hallway near the door.

"I suppose so, thank you," she heard the viscount reply.

"How is the countess taking the news?" Standish asked.

"Well, the first time I told her of it, she was stunned, and I believed shocked at the idea, but she has had time to think of it further and is pleased. She's always said her children's' happiness is her priority," she heard her uncle say.

Then the three men were laughing. But what were they speaking of? Then she heard Lord Birkshire's tone turn serious.

"Did you bring all the documents and contracts?"

"Of course. Can't have a proper marriage without them."

Olivia's heart stopped, and she instantly became ill. She could not breathe. Oh, my God, that is why Jack was home so quickly without notice. He was getting… no, no it cannot be. She felt faint. She sank into the chair outside her uncle's study. Her face was warm and stinging. She had to get out, out of this house. No, this could not be happening.

She found her feet and rushed to the side entry, stopping outside in the garden, leaning against the iron fence. She felt as though she was about to empty the contents of her stomach. How could this be happening? Jack getting married? Why had she stopped to listen? She grabbed the sides of her head with her hands, covering her ears. She took a deep breath; no, it was good that she had heard. Now she could think before she had to face him. How foolish of her, falling again for her childish hopes and dreams. She rubbed her temples then took off running like a scared and confused rabbit to her only place of comfort… the stables.

She made her way to the back entry and slammed the door shut, leaned her back against the large wooden door, and slid to the stone floor. She wrapped her arms around her bent knees, buried her head into them, and sobbed.

After she managed to cry tears, thought to be exhausted, she dried her face, stood, and made her way to the front. Her groom was making last-minute adjustments to Spartan's saddle.

"Th're ya 're. I'z about ta give up on ya."

"I was a bit delayed."

He set the steps next to Spartan and helped Olivia into the saddle. "I'll git me on an' be rite be'ind ya."

"No!" Olivia commanded. "I can manage on my own today. I won't be out long, and I had rather be alone." She took the reins from her groom and began to move Spartan out of the saddling area.

"Not sure the 'ead 'ill like 'it, mum."

"I don't care. I want to be alone. Tell anyone who asks I demanded it." She called back as she exited the stables.

"es mum." He walked off mumbling and shaking his head.

Olivia turned Spartan away from the main house. There was a seldom-used gate at the back of the property where the entry to the road would go unnoticed. She had to be away… from this place, these people, everyone; she wanted to be lost.

The latch was high and easily reached from the back of a horse or carriage, making it easy to manoeuvre for a quick escape. Once reaching the dirt road, Spartan took up a quick trot, then a fast canter; she released the bit to allow a near-dead run.

There was no thought given to a destination; she only wished to move, to flee the pain in her heart, and that meant putting distance between herself and Birkshire House. The tears streamed down her face, the wind drying it as quickly as the drops fell to her cheeks, sticky and salty. The flying wisps of hair sticking to her features, she reached to wipe them away with her forearm.

She pulled up the reins and brought Spartan to a halt. Without notice, Olivia found herself at the entry to her old home. Her cousin, Kit, lived there, he was always welcoming, and encouraging her visits anytime.

At this moment, she needed more than anything to be welcomed here. She longed to walk through the stables where she and her father walked, checking his fine hunters, each morning and evening. It was foaling time, and there would be new young colts throughout the barn. Spartan was born here; she remembered the day as she leaned forward, patting his thick neck. She wanted to visit her parents' grave, unable to remember the last time she had been there. Oh, how she wished they were here. None of this would be happening if they were. Oh, God, why had her parents been taken from her?

As she turned up the drive, she prayed her cousin was home. She had not seen him in well over a year. But if not, the servants all knew her, and she could walk through the stables and visit the small family cemetery.

She struggled to remember her childhood; the large house came into view, and more than anything, she wished to see her mother and father come running from it. God, how she needed them. The Norrys were her family now, but she had no desire to see them, and the grim reality was, she loved them dearly. Where would she go from here? Lost was all she could feel, but she could not think of it; it hurt far too much.

She tied Spartan to the post near the walkway and trudged up the steps. The butler opened the door before she reached the top step, and she glanced up at the creaking sound of the large door.

"Lady Olivia. How nice to see you?" The butler greeted.

"Hello Harris, is my cousin home?"

"I believe he is in his library. I will an…"

"Olivia!" A tall dark-haired gentleman was heading in their direction and interrupted the butler.

"Oh, Cousin Kit! How are you?"

The man looked to be in his early thirties but remained youthful in manner.

"I am well! You are looking beautiful as usual. I suppose you are here on that handsome steed of yours, Spartan?"

"Indeed I am. He is tied out front."

He took her outstretched hands in his and kissed them both.

"I was only thinking of you yesterday. I hope you are here to stroll through the stables?"

"If it is convenient."

"Of course, of course. I have told you, anytime. You are always welcome here. But I will escort you today because I have something to show you. I am quite excited about it. How long has it been since your last visit?"

"It's been some time. At least a year or so."

"I thought as much."

After donning his coat and hat, he took Olivia by the arm and led her out the door. He was talking about the foaling season and had so much he wanted her to see. It seemed this was to be a healthy season for the mares and their progenies. When they walked into the first stable, Olivia's heart leapt, and her spirits were immediately lifted. She adored this place, so many memories.

The activity was brisk, and there were more workers than she had ever remembered as a child. "How many foals are you expecting this year? My goodness, it is busy."

"We have 15 already, and we have 13 to go. But I must show you the special one. It is the reason I have been thinking of you."

As they turned down one of the aisles, Olivia saw an old friend. "Brindle!" she blurted, and her heart leapt with joy. "Oh, Brindle."

"Wait." Her cousin grabbed her arm, but he had a suspicious grin on his face.

"Do not tell me, she has a foal?"

"Yes, only yesterday. It is to be her last before we turn her to pasture."

"My goodness. I must see her."

"That you will and her foal. As soon as he was cleaned, I said, I must call on Birkshire House and Miss Olivia."

She grabbed Kit's forearm and hurried him to the mare's stall and gasped as she peered across the straw- covered box.

"Oh, my goodness." As the dark grey mare nickered, poking her head across the stall door, nuzzling the girl. Olivia wrapped her arms around the old mare's neck, as she stood mesmerized by the solid black colt asleep in the corner.

"Who is the stud?" She jerked her head toward Kit.

"Spartacus!"

"What?" Olivia's heart skipped, and she felt as if the wind had been knocked from her chest. She whirled around to face her cousin with tears building in her eyes. "Spartacus!"

"Yes, it will be the last one for the pair, and who does it look exactly like?"

"Spartan!" Her voice trembled from the catch in her heart and the lump in her throat. The name bursting forth with tearful joy as she lifted the latch and pulled at the stall door.

Brindle, meeting her old friend, wanting personally to show off her new baby. The mare lowered her large head to Olivia's back and nudged her to the corner. The tiny colt opened its eyes and threw its head up at the sight of the stranger. The young girl dropped to her knees and reached gently and softly to the newborn, then began rubbing all over the little one.

Her father had taught her to massage everywhere on a newborn foal, let them smell and feel the touch of a human early, the memories flooding through her. Even Kit was surprised when she bent over the foal's nose and sucked in the essence of the small creature, then blew her own breath into the foal's tiny nostrils.

It was exactly what Olivia needed. She stayed in the stables longer than originally intended. Kit introduced his new mares and the other 14 foals. When they reached the main house again, the butler announced nuncheon. Olivia was invited to stay, and in no hurry to return to Birkshire House, she partook of the light meal with her cousin. They talked of the new breeding program, which kept her mind occupied.

Afterwards, she graciously thanked Kit for his time, the visit in the stables, and the meal; mounted Spartan, reminding her cousin that she would be leaving by way of the family cemetery.

She pulled Spartan up at the gate and tied him to the wrought iron post. She made her way to the two graves that shared one large monument. She knelt in front and swept her fingers across the words at the base of the tall piece of stone, *'A loving husband and father, wife and mother who loved deeply,'* Olivia sniffled and choked back tears.

"Oh, mama, papa, I miss you so."

She knelt beside the stone, closed her eyes, and leaned against the cold statue.

Startled, she raised herself to her feet. She had fallen asleep against the monument and dreamt of happier days long ago. When her life had been simple and innocent… childhood.

The day had grown long, and she had no choice but to return to the one place she did not wish to go. In no hurry, she lulled Spartan into a slow rhythmic trot most of the way. As she entered the back gate, she noticed the sun had set, the day drifting into the crepuscle. She had stayed away longer than she had intended. When the stable came into view, she watched curiously as several of the stable boys began yelling.

"Spartan's 'ere, Spartan's 'ere and 'er ladyship!"

She dismounted Spartan, and her groomsmen came running up to her and grabbed Spartan.

"U'd better git up to tha 'ouse, my lady; everyone is lookin' fer ya."

"Oh, it is rather late, is it not? Thank you." She dropped her riding crop on the side table and dashed through the small garden that led to the kitchen door.

As soon as she entered the kitchen, she heard Emma gasp. "Oh, dear Lord, thank you, God!" The old woman glanced to the heavens, made the sign of the holy cross and grabbed Olivia hugging her to her breast.

"Emma, what is wrong?"

"You need to go straight to the library, quick like. Your aunt is 'aving a fit. No one knew where ya wuz." Emma pushed her through the door into the hallway and motioned her to hurry.

When she entered the library, she saw her aunt, uncle, and Jack standing at the desk, with their backs to the door. Her aunt had a handkerchief to her nose, and she was sniffling.

"Where could she have gone? She must be all right, or Spartan would have returned, do you not suppose so?"

"Unless Spartan was hurt as well." Her uncle replied.

"Oh, dear God, please, no, I could not bear it!" The countess was nearing hysteria. The earl placed his arm around her.

"Now, now Annabelle. We'll find her."

Olivia quickly made her presence known. "I am sorry. I did not mean to cause anyone distress. I lost track of the time."

Three heads whirled around, and Annabelle quickly closed the space between them. "Oh, Olivia!" She screeched and grabbed her shoulders, clutching her to her chest.

The two men stood frozen and silent, not quite knowing how to respond to her sudden appearance. Olivia was unable to move or speak from the tight grip of her aunt. She was trying to move, but it was of no use.

Finally, Annabelle relaxed and pushed Olivia back where she could look at her. "You naughty child, you frightened us to death. Where have you been all this time?"

"I was at my cousin's."

"Kit's? But why would you go there? And today? It never crossed my mind you might have gone there."

"I needed reflection, and I needed to visit…" She hesitated, "my parents. I was a bit nonplussed."

She glanced over at Jack. He was pale and appeared badly shaken. In fact, as she examined his face, he seemed to be about to cast up his accounts or had already done so. She directed her attention back to the countess.

"I wanted to see if there were foals, and there were 15 already, with 13 more to come. I suppose the excitement of the day overwhelmed me."

She shared with them about Spartacus and Brindle and that Spartan had a full brother who looked exactly like him.

"I should have known. You miss the little ones this time of the year, don't you, my dear?" Her uncle had made his way over to her and patted her shoulder. Olivia nodded in agreement.

"Kit has said for several years now, I was welcome to come anytime. I was so excited to see all the little ones and especially Spartan's baby brother. Kit has not mentioned him to anyone yet. He told his stablemaster I had the first option on him. I agreed to it. Spartan being Brindle and Spartacus' first colt, it was only right that I should have the last. He is only a day old, so it will be a while before I can keep him. I think I should consider retiring Spartan from jumping in the next year or so. Do you not?"

Her uncle was uncertain who the question was directed but took it upon himself to answer. "I think by the time this new one is trained and ready to jump, it would be a perfect time to retire Spartan."

Beginning to regain his colour, his worry and distress turning to irritation and annoyance Jack interjected, "Spartan isn't the only one who needs to think about retiring from jumping."

Olivia pulled away from her aunt, glaring at him indignantly. "What do you mean?"

"Mother, Father, would you give us some privacy, please?"

Although it sounded much like a request, his parents knew it was not. Lord Birkshire took his wife's hand and without another word hastily left, closing both doors behind them.

Her desecrations of the day forgotten; Olivia concentrated on the audacity of anyone... daring to question her relationship with a horse.

"I beg your pardon?" She proffered.

Jack made his way across the room and glared down at the small frame. Seeing she was not hurt, or dead, or God forbid kidnapped, and after listening to the details of her delightful day with Lord Kit Sinclair, he was over his fear, and nausea, and was headed for full-blown exasperation.

Stifling his alarm and anxiety, clutching to his relief, calmly drew a deep breath. "I understood we were to meet at 2:00 this afternoon."

When he didn't find her in the drawing room, Jack at first was only surprised at her tardiness. After a half hour, it turned to worry, then every minute afterwards turned to fear. Two hours later, the entire household was in total panic, and he in uncontrolled torment.

"I told you; I lost track of time with the babies." Recalling the real reason, she had lost track of time, attempted to walk past him. Jack snatched her upper arm, turning her to face him.

"You had us worried sick. After an hour, we were convinced something had happened to you. When interviewed, your groom admitted you seemed upset and insisted upon riding out alone. Of course, I knew why you were distressed. The entire stable was sent in search of you. Your personal groom and I covered the grounds, he travelled all your normal paths, and neither of us found any trace of you. You had said you were anxious to speak, then you vanished. We were all wracked with worry."

Olivia was no longer upset; she was hurt and angry. Her world had collapsed around her without warning, and he had the nerve to chastise her? She would have none of his arrogance. She jerked her arm from his tight grip. "I know why you came home. I overheard you and your father in the library as I headed to the stables. That is why I was upset."

"What?" Jack was staggered and confused, but also disappointed. "I – I – I don't know what to say. I didn't mean for you to learn of it that way."

"I am certain you did not. I assume it is the reason you wished to speak with me, and I could not bear it. I did not want to hear it." The little pint-sized kraken was unleashed.

Jack was stunned. He raked his hand through his hair and brushed past her to the window. They both stood in silence for what seemed like an eternity. Trying to regain his composure and his ability to speak, softly turned to her.

"Is it James?"

"What?" she almost shouted in surprise and confusion.

She had no idea what he was asking, she could only continue to stare at him indignantly.

"Is it Sheffield? Is that the reason?"

"What are you talking about? What has James to do with this?"

"I know he loves you, Olivia. He told me so. But do you love him?"

They had both turned to face one another across the room with hurt and confusion.

"Of course, I love him, he is my dearest friend and my confidant. But — but what does that have to do with you marrying?" She was perplexed at the direction of the conversation.

Jack looked at her strangely and with a quick shake of his head, looked at her in confusion. If she didn't want to marry James, then... wait... "If you don't want to marry James, then why don't you want to marry me?"

"You!" Olivia was still too agitated to understand his words, then her breath caught.

What did he just say? Oh, good lord, what was happening? She stumbled to the nearest chair and grabbed the arm of it. Jack watched her stagger and in three strides was by her side.

He went down on one knee. She placed her fingers to her temples pressing as if her head was about to explode. He tried to take her wrists, but she placed them on the chair.

"Olivia, what is wrong? What have I done?" He tried to withdraw her hands from the death grip she had on the chair, but she held them firmly.

Lifting her eyes to meet his, "I am so confused. Why did you kiss me this morning?" No longer angry, plainly muddle-brained, she slowly allowed him to take her hands, as she melted into the chair. Lowering them to her lap, he held them there. His eyes were lost in the depths of her crystal blue ones and without hesitation. "Because I love you!"

Startled, she lowered her eyes to her hands and placed one over his. He loved her… he had always loved her… like a brother. He was her heart and if he had found someone to make him happy, she would learn to live with that decision. It was the hardest thing she'd ever done, but she raised her eyes to his and quietly asked.

"Jack, who are you going to marry?"

He could see she was totally and genuinely vexed. What had she discerned from the library door? As he thought about the morning conversation, he began to understand she must have only caught bits and pieces. She had heard them discussing the betrothal documents, but he couldn't remember anyone saying her name or anyone else's.

"Olivia, what did you overhear this morning?" Amused at what appeared to be a total misunderstanding, he attempted not to sound happy. He had discovered at least one of her childish habits had not been lost to the tragedies of the past year.

"You discussing marriage contracts with someone, and they offered you felicitations, and your mother was shocked and – and – and…"

"And then you ran away. Hmmm? Does that about cover it?"

"Well, when I heard you receiving and accepting felicitations, due to your impending marriage, the contracts being delivered and you had not asked me, what was I to think? Besides, you haven't yet told me who you intend to marry."

Jack started to laugh but Olivia was still frowning. Still down on his knee, he reached into his pocket and pulled from it a small box. She didn't breathe as he opened it. A small filigree ring with a ruby, a sapphire, and an emerald encircled by diamonds, peered back at her. Her lashes fluttered... as tears filled her eyes, she met his.

"That's – that's," she gasped, her throat tightened her voice into forced silence.

"Oh, Olivia, you are such a silly goose, and I love every inch of you. I love your clumsiness, I love your obstinance, I love your petulance..." She furrowed her brow and frowned. He laughed again and pulled her to the floor with him. He kissed her nose, her eyes, her forehead, then pulled her hands to his and kissed the palm of one, then the other.

"I love everything about you, especially your innocence, your giggles, your laughter, your eyes, your nose, your lips. I especially love your lips." He raised an eyebrow.

"Yes, you do seem to like my lips. It seems you have liked them far longer than even I have known."

He lifted her into the chair and picked up the ring and case from the floor where it had tumbled. He took a knee before her, holding the small box.

"I need to know something very important." His throat was dry and scratchy. He paused for a moment and surveyed her dusty riding habit, the smudges of dirt and straw stuck in her clothes and hair.

"You know this is nothing like what I had imagined. I had a heartfelt poem carefully learnt and pictured you in a lace-covered satin dress and..." he wiped a smudge of dirt from her chin, "and clean..."

"Sorry. I was riding, but you know that...",

She turned the back of her gloved hand to her chin attempting to remove the remaining traces of grime.

"Uh, yes, and playing with foals." He dropped the case and began tugging at her fingers one at a time, pulling the riding gloves loose and slipping them from her hands.

"Yes, that too, but can I say something?"

He placed two fingers over her lips and smiled, as he tossed the gloves to the side and retook his place with the box, taking her hand again.

"No…you can only say yes, you will be my wife." Olivia giggled and then laughed.

"Then, yes." She tossed her head to the ceiling laughing, then quickly returned a glowing face to his. "Yes, yes, a thousand times yes!"

She flung her arms around his neck and her body slid from the chair, toppling Jack backwards to the floor, her sprawled atop him. He was laughing, she was giggling with delight.

"You know the last time we were in this position; I could not do what I wanted so desperately to do."

"And what was that?" Olivia chortled, still lying across him, remembering that embarrassing day the year before.

He moved both hands to each side of her face and held them very still, grinning sheepishly into those crystal blue eyes, his dark blue ones burning into her.

"This." Jack pulled her face to his and devoured her soft lips. Olivia melted into his arms.

EPILOGUE

At the end of the following month, they were married. Lord Birkshire decided that his late friend, Lord James Sinclair, would never have settle for anything less than the reading of banns for his only daughter. Lady Birkshire was thrilled as she had time to arrange a proper wedding. She took Olivia to London for her favourite modiste to design and sew her gown. The two also procured all that was necessary to complete a proper bride's trousseau.

The wedding dress was designed and sewn of thin white silk, with a silver slip, covered in transparent silver lame, adorned with tiny pearls and small appliqued flowers. The sleeves were trimmed with Brussels lace, and the six-foot train was made of silver lame covered with tiny pearls.

The morning of the wedding found the countess and Olivia sitting in her bedchamber, crying, and holding one another's hands.

"I often thought of this day with regret. I was afraid of losing you to another family. You had become a daughter to me and yet, you were not, and I could not bear the thought…" she choked back tears. "The thought of letting you go, I could not. I know that is the reason I held on so very tight and kept you from London. But now, I shall never lose you, and my heart is full." She pulled Olivia to her chest and clutched her tightly. When she pulled back, the countess could see the mature young woman she held before her.

"I could never have left you. Jack told me once in London that I would be leaving here someday. I had truly never thought of it, and I never wanted to. I could never think of life without you and Uncle John. But most of all, I could never dream of life without Jack. I had no understanding of wifely duties, but it did not matter, I knew in my heart, I could face anything with him. He has always been my life, you know, for as long as I can remember. I could not live it without him."

They hugged one another one last time.

"It is time to go. I love you with all my heart, my child." Annabelle giggled and raised her hands, "Bless my very soul, you are really about to be my daughter." She pinched Olivia's cheek, turned, and left the room before her tears began again.

Olivia sat quietly for a moment, glancing around the bedchamber she had called her own since she was seven. She had been blessed. But on this special day, she could not help but think of her parents and how young she had been when they were taken from her. What little she remembered was of the laughter, her father tickling her and the loss of breath from the explosion of uncontrollable giggles and her mother's smile as she sat next to them filled with mirth. Olivia's life had been filled with love and happiness. They must have always been watching over her.

She was about to marry, her knight in shining armour, her fairytale prince, who had been a part of her every memory since the day she was born. She had dreamed of this moment her entire life.

***

Later that morning Jack and Olivia, before God, their family, and friends, were pronounced man and wife. The ceremony was perfect, although Jack did say a prayer as Olivia walked down the aisle, unsure of what his little chit might stumble across in the short walk to him.

The Marquess of Sheffield, standing at the altar next to him, noticed the crossed fingers of his friend and grinned. James envied his best friend but also knew this was right. He would have married Olivia if she would have had him, but she would never have loved him the way she loved Jack. It made him smile as he watched his only love walk down the aisle into the arms of another.

The breakfast was a feast, and the ball lasted until the wee hours of the morning. But the newlyweds had long exited the celebration to their set of apartments on the fourth floor. Their home was to be Eustace Hall, but the first few nights would be spent at the home that held all their memories.

Olivia nervously ran her fingers across the thin silk nightgown, as she dismissed Sarah for the evening. She thought of her conversation with her aunt; no, not aunt, she smiled, now her mama. She was thankful for the conversation, albeit embarrassing. But there was a sense of anxiety she could not dismiss. She consoled herself with trust in her new husband; there was never a doubt he would guide her with gentleness.

Heavy bare feet slowly padded across the Aubusson carpet, admiring his wife with every quiet step. She was silhouetted by the moonlight flooding the room, making her deshabille appear invisible. The sight of her small but voluptuous body heightened his need for her. He had longed for this moment for so long, his body shuddered. As he touched her shoulder, she turned and looked up at him. The purity in her face, blonde hair, blue eyes, made her appear angelic. He saw the apprehension and concerns. Standing in front of him, her arms hanging motionless by her side, not speaking, just looking into his eyes with wonder.

"Trust me?" He whispered.

She nodded but could not find her voice. She had no idea what she was supposed to do. "I don't know...." She murmured; Jack placed two fingers to her lips.

"Shh," he whispered, hoping to calm her. "I will show you."

"I am sorry, I truly am." Her voice was raspy, her entire body trembling. He pulled her to him and wrapped his arms around her. She buried her face in his chest, her heart pounding, his own convulsed at her touch. He had been taught by a master, and yet he felt like a schoolboy. He had to remember this was his wife, this was Olivia, the woman he vowed to love, to protect and to cherish. He alone would be responsible for his wife's enjoyment and desires in the marital bed. He had to be gentle and patient.

He pulled her arms from around his waist, stooped, and placed them around his neck. He slipped one arm under her knees, the other around her back, lifting her into his arms, hugging her tightly and kissing her lips, carried her to the bed, laying her down as if she was a fragile piece of crystal.

She held onto him. "Do not leave me." She cried.

"I am not going anywhere." He touched her lips, removed her arms from about his neck, and ran the back of his fingers down her face.

"You are so beautiful, Olivia. I need you more than I need to breathe."

His eyes were glistening from tears that formed in his eyes. Pure instinct and her love for him as her guide, she raised her hand to his face and cupped his cheek. His body quaking at her touch. Taking her hand, he gently turned her palm to his lips and started a trail of kisses, softly moving to her wrist, back to her palm. She groaned, and her back arched, and her breast heaved upward.

It felt like a lightning bolt hit her. She did not know what was happening, but she knew it was right. She felt her stomach quiver; her senses were aware of every touch. She was tingling in places she never knew could feel. He moved to her neck, nuzzling it, her head turning to the side, opening to him, shoulders curving up from the bed, she moaned.

He was kissing her neck down to the top of her shoulders. He slid the sheer gown down one arm and then the other but kept his eyes on hers. He grabbed the bodice with his teeth, lowering it until her breasts were exposed to him.

"Oh, God." He felt his entire body jerk. She could not respond; her body was burning. His screaming for more, forcing himself to remember, this time was for Olivia. Hearing her moans at his touch, took all his strength to hold back…for her.

His gentle suckle of her breast was divine; his soft lips and tender manipulation of them made her body ache with passion.

She arched from the bed with every touch. He raised himself from the side of the bed and stood over her, reached for her gown, and slipped it past her hips.

"I have dreamed of this moment, but you are more beautiful than any dream."

He softly ran his hands across her, taking in every inch, slowly moving his hands from her shoulders. Lips parting, he lovingly discovered the curves of her, stroking down to her ankles, feet, and toes. He wanted to know every inch of her. He had waited a lifetime to discover the woman beneath him. As he slowly moved up her tiny frame, he heard her gasp, her cheeks burning red as he watched her close her eyes.

"Open your eyes." His voice was stern but tender. She opened them focusing on his.

"Do not ever be embarrassed in my presence. We will soon be joined as one, my body belongs to you and yours to me."

"Please," she shuddered, her body begging for release as she sank into the soft mattress.

Jack raised himself from the bed one last time. Olivia watched as he removed the brocade velvet robe. Her breath caught in her throat. Oh, Lord, he was gorgeous, his skin darkened from the sun, and his muscles bulged everywhere - his shoulders, his arms, his chest, the ripples on his stomach made her tingle. As her eyes lowered, she was stricken with panic at the sight of his manhood. He was large, and instantly she could not see how… how he could possibly.

"Oh, my God!" she gulped.

He glanced quickly at her face and smiled. "It will be fine, I promise. You said you trusted me."

"I do, but where, how? I do not think…"

He shushed her as he crawled back onto their bed. He placed his hands on each side of her hips as he moved his body closer to hers. He felt the breath leave her as she exhaled.

"Relax, my love… breathe."

Olivia could hear his voice and willed her body to obey. "Oh, my God."

"Am I too heavy?"

"No…please." Her arms were stretched to her sides, fists grabbing the soft material of the linen bedsheet within her reach. Her body was throbbing, intimate places aching. She could feel him, and her body was responding to her own needs and desires.

"Breathe, Olivia." He reminded her.

She nodded her head. It was all she could do. Her body rose to meet his, demanding things she could not understand. Her breathing was fast and heavy, and she was uncertain how much more she could bear.

"Please, please," she cried.

Jack knew she was craving the release as much as his own. His body coercing him to press forward, but his mind forcing him to remain gentle. Short of breath and eyes closed, he was trying to control his own desires. Olivia slung her arms around his waist, trying to force him down and further inside her.

"This may hurt a little, but not for long." He whispered against the skin of her neck.

"I do not care," she screamed; her voice shuddered.

He felt fingernails digging into his back, trying to heave her body to him. It was more than his own body could stand.

"Oh, God!" She wailed.

He knew he had hurt her, but his body was now forcing him onward. Her pain quickly fading was replaced with the steady rhythm of lovemaking. Each thrust coming harder and faster. Jack tried to control the pace and think only of her, but her response to him was inciting him.

She suddenly screamed in pleasure, digging her nails into his back, then slammed her arms to the sheets, as she shattered into a million tiny pieces. He clutched her body tightly holding her as he spilled inside her, his body jerking with uncontrollable convulsions.

They collapsed into one another's arms, and stillness overtook them, totally exhausted, joined as one body, one soul, they slept.

Jack's eyes opened with a flutter, and he felt his body regaining strength. He smiled and placed a gentle kiss on her lips. He nuzzled her neck with his nose; she moaned as he moved his tongue from her neck to her ear. The moment his lips touched hers, she responded. Releasing her lips, he began to move away.

"No!" she demanded. "Not yet." She wanted him to remain.

"But I am too heavy." He protested.

"I do not care; I do not want…" She stuttered and blushed, "… to lose you yet."

She looked at him with those crystal blue eyes filled with tears. "I am not ready for you…" She struggled for words of which she had no knowledge.

But he understood. He reached under her bottom and pulled her to him, holding her tightly against him, he rolled to his side, squeezing her hips to him.

She glanced at the upward curve of his lips and knew he was holding back a laugh.

Arms sweeping upwards, placing them on his chest, she propped her chin on her crossed hands and eyed him suspiciously. "What?"

"Are you always going to be this demanding?" Lowering his eyes to the face gazing up at him.

"What do you mean?"

"I have never tried to do this before. It is not easy, after, after…" Now Jack was unable to articulate the difficulty of her request.

Her cheeks were pink; she had no clue what he meant. She only knew they were one and she wanted to prolong the euphoria of this impregnable moment.

He began kissing her neck and caressing her and without understanding she could feel their connection improving.

"Can we remain like this for…" she paused.

"For…?" He looked at her smiling.

"It is silly, but I was going to say forever."

"Music to my ears, Lady Andovir." He quipped.

She looked up at him and beamed. At that moment, Jack could see she was finally completely happy. In the depth of her eyes, he could see the little girl he cherished, the young lady he adored, and the woman he had always loved in so many different ways. He too discovered his own life was complete. God, he loved her so. He was a prisoner to her every want and need. She had always had that power over him.

The vows taken in the holy sanctuary of the chapel and the papers signed indicated by some antiquated English law, she belonged to him. But in his heart, he belonged to her. It had been so since the day his mother opened that swaddling and he saw her tiny pink face sucking her fist and declared, 'girls were no fun.'

He smiled and kissed her brow. "God, I love you, Olivia, with every fibre of my soul. You are finally mine, Olivia Catherine Norrys."

She placed a finger to his lips and softly whispered, "Oh, Jack, don't be silly, I've always belonged to you. Don't you know, haven't you always known?"

Olivia smiled with such contentment and love as she gazed into his eyes… "I was born for you!"

We hope you enjoyed "Born For Love"

The Born For series continues with Born For This, the story of Thomas Worthington.

A Match for the Marquess will be available in all formats soon. Follow Thomas, who, at the age of nine and twenty, learns he has been betrothed since childhood. He is determined to escape the contract until he meets the stubborn, free-spirited Mediterranean French beauty.

Until then, follow S.K. Snyder on Facebook, Instagram, and YouTube.

If you enjoyed Born For Love, please let us know by leaving a review on Amazon or Goodreads.

Made in the USA
Columbia, SC
13 October 2024